LAST DAY

LAST DAY

A novel

Domenica Ruta

SPIEGEL & GRAU · NEW YORK

Copyright © 2019 by Domenica Ruta

Published in the United States by Spiegel & Grau, an imprint of Random House, a division of Penguin Random House LLC, New York.

SPIEGEL & GRAU and colophon is a registered trademark of Penguin Random House LLC.

LIBRARY OF CONGRESS CATALOGING-IN-PUBLICATION DATA
Names: Ruta, Domenica, author.
Title: Last day: a novel / by Domenica Ruta.
Description: First edition. | New York: Spiegel & Grau, 2019.
Identifiers: LCCN 2018051202 | ISBN 9780525510819 (hardback) |
ISBN 9780525510826 (ebook) | ISBN 9781984855879 (international)
Subjects: | BISAC: FICTION / Literary. | FICTION / Coming of Age.
Classification: LCC PS3618.U776 L37 2019 | DDC 813/.6—dc23
LC record available at https://lccn.loc.gov/2018051202

Printed in the United States of America on acid-free paper

spiegelandgrau.com
randomhousebooks.com

9 8 7 6 5 4 3 2 1

First Edition

Book design by Jo Anne Metsch

For Will Stanton

Planet Earth is blue and there's nothing I can do

LAST DAY

"THERE SHE IS," he whispered to himself, as if a little surprised to still see her twinkling in the darkness.

It was universally agreed, Earth was always *she*. The astronauts needed to latch onto this umbilical pronoun, a reminder, while they were as far from home as one could be, that they were still human.

The form she took was different for everyone. Some astronauts saw an eye, others thought of her as a jewel. Just today Bear saw something new: the blue head of a baby, slathered in a caul made of clouds, crowning from out of a black womb. Bear remembered his own daughters being born, and the happy terror of that first, sickening glimpse.

It was the twenty-sixth of May. He had completed six months of his mission on the ISS and was already preparing for his exit, still six more months away. He was a three-hour ride from home, and though it was technically possible to make an early departure, no one in the short history of the International Space Station had ever deorbited before they were scheduled. What would it take, Bear wondered now, to justify an early exit? A medical emergency, or a family tragedy? What kind of calamity could he in good conscience withstand?

Bear stopped himself. This kind of future-tripping was dangerous. He knew that. He'd advised other astronauts at Johnson Space Center against the countdown mentality when preparing them for their missions. You can't stop the demons of isolation from knocking on your door, he'd say, but you can stop inviting them in for coffee.

He decided to take his own advice and redirect this morbid longing into something more productive: drafting notes for the things he would say about this mission after landing. There would be a barrage of interviews, both in-house and for publicity, and Bear put a lot of pressure on himself to say something no one had ever said before about the experience of space flight. This womb-birth analogy was quotable, with potential to go viral in the media, just the kind of thing he needed to preserve. He reached for the pad and pencil attached by cords to his sleeve, catching the pad but missing the pencil. He reached again and missed it, again and then again. Entwined with the floating pad, it eluded his grasp like a tiny pet playing tag.

"Got you," he said at last. He scribbled down his notes about the earth looking like a birth in progress, then immediately crossed them out. It was a stupid metaphor. He watched the sun rise over the earth for the eleventh time that day. The clouds unthreaded for a moment and he saw the staggering blue that could only be the shallow waters of the Caribbean.

No, he decided, taking one last look at the earth before heading back to work. What he saw through the windows of the Cupola was so much more than any single human birth, more than any man could pin down with words.

He pressed his hand against the thick glass. "There you are."

She was the biggest thing in the galaxy from this perspective, though really just a pebble. Less than a pebble. But a pretty one, Bear thought, prettier than any other; he wasn't afraid to admit this most basic chauvinism—to think of his home planet as better than all other bodies in space. She was his, after all. Or he was hers. He'd felt that on his first mission over a decade ago, and now on his second mission he felt it even more, a sense of humility so precious it dangled wildly on the edge of tragedy.

His watch vibrated with a reminder that his break in the Cupola was up. He'd spent as many minutes as he could possibly spare in this Earth-sick reverie. It was time to go.

SARAH MOSS HATED her name. It was a mistake, a fundamental one, with possibly catastrophic results for the rest of her life. Her last name, Moss, was okay, she guessed. Monosyllabic, rhizomatic, and green, *Moss* was actually pretty cool. *Sarah* was not and never would be.

But did she really *hate* her name? Hate had lust at its core, a dark quicksand of desire, which was a little dramatic, even for Sarah. And besides, how could she bring herself to hate something that was essentially a gift from her parents? The second gift they'd ever given her, life itself being the first. Even though her parents were the most annoying people she knew, they were eternally well intentioned, so it felt wrong to hate in any official way the name they had chosen for her. She was their first and only child. They must have been fumbling in a postnatal stupor when they'd picked out the name Sarah—she had to believe this. Something as boring as *Sarah* could not have been premeditated. They were probably tired. What could she expect of people in that state? They didn't even know her yet.

When Sarah was three and a half, she requested that her parents start calling her Buckle. Those two smiling syllables, like a drink of sweetened milk, never mind what they denoted. But her parents laughed at her—an eternally well-intentioned laugh—because it was funny, this tiny girl with big owl eyes and toy-sized glasses, asking to be called Buckle, and Sarah had burst into tears.

Science was a later pseudonym, the brainchild of her seven-year-old self. Science was her favorite subject at school, so adopting it as her name seemed like the next logical step. She confessed this wish only to her babysitter. Her parents had laughed at her once; she would not allow them to do it again.

"Human beings can't have names like *Science*," her babysitter snorted. She was an elderly next-door neighbor with black wiry hairs sprouting from her chin that she paid young Sarah a dime per hair to pluck out with rusty tweezers. "Especially not little girls," Mrs. Whiskers had said as a final judgment. Older now, Sarah knew this was a sexist and small-minded thing to say. It was pathological how much resentment she still harbored toward that lady and her chin hairs.

She asked her friends at school to call her Claudia when she was eleven. It sounded elegant and strong, as a girl approaching adolescence should be. But everyone kept forgetting, so Sarah let it go. Just last year, she'd made a case for elective name-changing at school, trying to piggy-back onto the burgeoning transgender rights movement. "It's transnominalism," she'd said to Dr. Vasquez-McQueen, her guidance counselor. It didn't go over well. Sarah was a freshman in high school by then. It wasn't cute to think like this anymore. She understood that completely. She'd actually understood it the same day she tried (and failed) to pull off the Claudia conversion. It had been embarrassing and lame four years earlier, and now even more so.

There were over 1.6 million Sarahs in the world (she'd looked it up), and eight of them were at her high school—eight!—out of a student body of only fifty-two students. Plus at least a dozen more Sarahs in the lower school, and probably close to a hundred in her town's overcrowded public school system.

Famous Sarahs throughout history failed to inspire her. Even supposedly cool historical Sarahs couldn't be trusted, because who knew what was real and what was fiction when it came to famous people.

Of the not-famous Sarahs that Sarah Moss knew personally, all of them were seriously lacking. Sarah Wilmington, for example, was a senior at the Phoenix School who collected pewter figurines of dragons and unicorns, wore a variety of hand-stitched velvet capes, and wrote sad, sensual poetry, especially discomfiting, Sarah Moss felt, because everyone knew that Sarah Wilmington was a virgin. Sarah W. often hijacked the weekly all-school meetings to read her poetry out loud in that lispy voice of hers. "Juicy mangoes" and "sweat-studded skin." It was enough to make you puke. No one at school could really look each other in the eye after a few couplets from Sarah Wilmington.

Sarah Burke was a sophomore like Sarah Moss. She'd come to the school in the middle of freshman year, a transplant from some suburb in Connecticut that sounded identical to Edgewater, Massachusetts, their home now, though Sarah Burke loved to insist it was *so* different there. This Sarah had a nose so large it cast a shadow across her face, a feature Sarah Moss would have completely overlooked if Sarah Burke had been at all nice, but, and perhaps because of her nose, Sarah Burke had a cruel hatred of the world. The opposite of Sarah Wilmington, Sarah Burke had lots of sex. Sarah B. bragged that she blew random guys she met on the commuter rail to Boston. It was obvious to everybody but Sarah Burke that sex was a weapon she wielded with zero mastery, only hurting herself. She was often found crying in the girls' bathroom as she texted novella-length screeds to her uncaring lovers. Poor Sarah Burke. Except—no, she'd once made fun of Sarah Moss's dirty sneakers, so screw her.

Sarah Curtis and Sarah Mitzenberg had been best friends since fifth grade. They had a secret sign language and were totally insufferable. Sarah Hunt was way too proud of all the antidepressants she was taking. Sarah Jones picked her nose in public, then examined whatever she'd excavated on her fingertips for a long time. Up close. She had Asperger's, or something like that, it was reported, which made her easier to forgive, but the sight of her, even when not engaged in her oblivious grotesqueries, made Sarah Moss cringe.

And then there was Sara-without-an-H Toomey. A junior, this stream-lined Sara wasn't so bad. But she wasn't so good, either. She represented a perfect mediocrity, equally as far from being cool as being awful. Five minutes alone in conversation with this Sara left one longing for any-thing that evoked deep feeling—even failure, cruelty, pain!

These were her closest namesakes, this pseudo-sorority of Sarahs. It was dispiriting, and maybe even a portent of the coming end. The signs were everywhere. Genetic diversity was in decline—not too long ago there were thousands of species of apples grown in North America alone. Now? A few dozen. There were too many people in the world, and not enough resources to sustain them, not even enough names to go around. This was what was really troubling, Sarah thought—the growing lack of creativity. How many movies were exactly like other movies? How many times could people tell the same story? The world was running out of ideas. If there was any death knell for humanity, it was not peak oil or global warming or beehive collapse but the superfluity of Sarahs.

And her parents' response to all this?

"Stressosaurus Rex! Lighten up!"

The kitchen was warm and filled with the scent of butter and sugar. Light streamed in from the east and north, easing any sharp edges in its glow. The radio was set as ever to the local public classical station, to which the Mosses contributed annually, amassing an absurd number of tote bags. The first low notes of a Wagnerian prelude lapped over each other like currents in a great river.

"You're just a kid, Sarah. You should be worrying about boys."

"Or girls? We don't care. We love you unconditionally, no matter what."

"Have a brownie, kiddo. They're perfectly undercooked, just like you like them."

Their abundant love was an unwavering beam of light in Sarah's adolescent universe of doubt and dread. And it hurt more than anything else in the world that this did nothing to comfort her.

CHRISTIAN FUNDAMENTALISTS EAGER for Armageddon were always relatively calm on Last Day. Their Lord and Savior Jesus Christ would never pick some heathen festival for His rapture. No way in hell.

And yet these faithful lovers of Christ's promised end times were mistakenly lumped in with another faction known as Doomsdayers. A loose confederacy of pagan fundamentalists, Doomsdayers subscribed wholesale to all apocalyptic prophecies, regardless of contradiction: the almanacs of Nostradamus, the Book of Revelations, the Mayan calendar, the underwhelming turn of the millennium, the coming of Bahá'u'lláh, the prophecy in the Book of Daniel, the Frashokereti, and many more humble, homely tales spun out of that comforting nightmare that everything comes to an end.

Like alcoholics passing for normal amid the debauchery of St. Patrick's Day, during Last Day these apocalyptic lovers found a yearly pass to come out of their gloomy, conspiratorial hovels and party. They would take to the streets, littering city parks with their encampments, scaring away tourists with their sloppy bivouacs and homemade signs. Their children were pulled out of school, all normalcy and basic hygiene jettisoned, so that they could band together in a public display and wait for the inevitable nothing.

What they did after, when the world did not end, was almost sweet in its resilience. It never actually mattered to these people that the prophecy failed to fulfill. Their love for the end was everlasting. And so as the month of May ended, the Doomsdayers would slowly dismantle their camps, pour sand on the fire pits, fold up the tarps, pack up their vans (they were a van-driving folk), and return to whatever temporary place — in the worldly sense — they called home. They went back to normal, to *their* normal, in which fear and righteousness attended the mundane business of living. Standing over a sink of dirty dishes, a battered mother of three could look with tenderness toward the coming end. All those unmade beds, the children with ringworm, the bills in arrears, would eventually be obliterated. The abuse and betrayals, the longings and resentments, all the little and big failures, would be irrelevant. They simply had to wait for the next sign, the next opportunity, to give it all up again.

It was a miracle that none of these sects had yet to absorb the likes of Karen Donovan. She certainly met the criteria for a militant Doomsdayer: her passions were scattered all over the occult; she held fast to wild misinterpretations of life's most basic systems; she was all too willing to believe any message whose messenger burned with intensity, stoking her own easily inflamed heart; and finally, as she'd been excluded from every social group in her life so far, including the most basic unit of family, she was so hungry just to belong.

But you had to be willing to rough it to be a member of a doomsday cult, carry your share of canned goods, weaponry, and bedding, and Karen hated walking almost as much as she hated carrying. She would rather wait forty-five minutes for the bus than walk the five blocks from her house to the local library. And though her mental landscape was scorched with traumas, both real and grotesquely imagined, the end of the world didn't register high on her litany of fears.

Karen belonged to a different caste of crazy. Heavily medicated and monitored by a slew of social workers her whole, well-documented life, she had a talent for causing trouble for herself even within narrow parameters, restricted to her job at the YMCA, the Boston public library system, the counseling center where her long-suffering psychiatrist, Nora, saw her pro bono, and a group home where she was currently on very thin ice. At twenty, Karen was too old to qualify for many of the social services that had sustained her as a child, and the current administration's refusal to fund what few programs were out there for people at strange intersections of lunacy and competency limited Karen's options to only four group homes in the state, three of which she'd already been booted from.

Her most recent infraction had occurred at the Copley branch of the Boston Public Library, where she'd frightened little children with her totally earnest though still elementary attempts at augury. Sitting in on the library's story hour, the only adult without a child, she noticed a little boy's aura glowing wan and misshapen around his head and shoulders. After the story was over, she informed the child that although she wasn't totally sure, there was a good chance he had been raped, or if not, would be soon.

"It's okay, you can tell me. I have signed a safety contract with Nora to be always vigilant and aware of inappropriate touching," she'd explained to the boy, who ran to ask his unsuspecting mother, "Mummy, what's rape?" Phone calls were made, though not many. The trail back to Karen was straightforward and short. Nora was able to pull some strings and arrange for yet another relocation to her current group home at Heart House, as well as stop the library system from completely banning Karen, if she promised to switch branches and never enter the children's section again. Nora tinkered with Karen's regimen of antipsychotics and mood stabilizers and begged her, please, absolutely no more caffeine.

"Even Diet Coke?" Karen cried.

"Diet Coke has caffeine," Nora sighed, tugging on the gauzy scarf knotted around her throat as if to strangle herself.

"Okay. But what about Diet Pepsi?"

Together Nora and Karen wrote another social contract, which Karen signed and dated. Karen was quickly sobered by bureaucracy. Paperwork elicited in her a solemn deference, a tool Nora utilized in their ongoing therapy. Karen promised in writing that she would no longer talk to strangers about death, monsters (even in an allegorical sense), rape, natural disasters, or anything that took place in a bathroom.

So there was no way she was going to tell anyone about the voices.

They were old, familiar. She almost welcomed their return after such a long silence. Whispers tangled into her hair, making a nest. Only at night. They sounded like lizards, and hummingbirds, and sometimes mice, speaking a heavily accented English, their patois fractured and inconsistent. No instructions so far, Karen noticed with relief. Just a pleasant hypnogogic phenomenon, they disappeared once she fell asleep.

But after a few weeks the voices began filtering into her morning, then gradually persisted throughout the day. Karen attempted to greet them cheerfully, as Nora instructed her to do with difficult people in the realm of the real, to let them pass before her without engaging in a fight.

Then, on the evening of May 26, Karen heard a ghastly scene taking place under her bed: a snake was suckling the udder of a cow. She was alone in her room, waiting for her sleeping meds to kick down the door of her consciousness and carry her fireman-style over the threshold of dreams. But the sucking and slurping! It was so loud her eyes, dry and open, scarcely blinked in their vigilance. She didn't want to report this to Nora, who would furrow her brow in such deep, empathic pain. The two of them sometimes got caught in a regressive loop of empathy, Nora tearing up at Karen's stories of abandonment and degradation, Karen weeping at the sight of Nora's tears, a dolorous, tissue-strewn stalemate from which there was no productive conclusion, only release when the clicking of Nora's clock at last signaled that Karen's fifty-minute session was over. Besides, Nora was on vacation in Mykonos for Last Day, and why should Karen be the one to ruin her trip?

She couldn't tell the counselors at Heart House. They'd make her go to the hospital, which was what had happened the last time she'd started hallucinating. Once she was gone, they'd give her room away to someone else on the miles-long wait list. Then where would she live? Where would she go?

And besides, maybe these voices weren't so bad. For a few years now, Karen had been trying to heighten the sensory acuity of her soul. She studied everything she could at the library: the zodiac, divination, reincarnation, Tibetan demonology, the hierarchy of Christian angels. The floor of her bedroom was stacked with spiral-bound notebooks filled with arcana. Deep inside her, Karen believed, extraordinary gifts were about to come flying out, if she could just cultivate the right conditions. It involved deeper perception, but so far, only blur and jumble led the way. Perhaps these voices were just part of the path.

Then, before the sun rose on the morning of May 27, the snake slurping ended abruptly, and in the silence that followed she heard a voice say, "Dennis."

She got out of bed and yawned loudly. The wood floor groaned beneath her feet. She'd gained so much weight on her new meds. She stomped loudly, hoping to scare the voice away.

"Dennis," the voice said again. The clarity of it rang like a high church bell on a cloudless day.

"Yeah, but why now?" she asked.

There was no answer. She called her friend Rosette, the only civilian outside of Karen's company of professional help whose phone number Karen knew.

"Rose," Karen said when her call went straight to voicemail, "does the God of your understanding concern him/her/itself with details, or just big-picture stuff? Examples off the top of my head: the exact size of a tumor, the eye color of your soulmate, the sequence of songs on a random shuffle. Because that seems like a lot, even for an omnipotent—"
She was cut off.

Fine.

Karen knelt before her closet and pulled out the only shoes that had laces, a pair of generic-brand sneakers bought from a discount store. She unthreaded the lace of the right shoe and slurped it down like a noodle. It burned her throat and esophagus, but a moment afterward she felt strangely peaceful: it was gone. Done.

And, Karen thought brightly, she now had an excuse to wear her good shoes today, her party shoes, those little strappy leather sandals with the kitten heels! This afforded another fun opportunity—to build a whole outfit from the bottom up! She chose her pistachio-green Easter dress, not that there were many other options that still fit her, and her tan purse, not her backpack.

More would be revealed. It always was.

Walking the two unrelenting, uphill blocks from the group home to the bus stop, her feet were already protesting. Karen had to stop midway to catch her breath. She bent down and inspected a bed of spring flowers. "Look at living things and imagine them already dead," was one of the dictums of her extrasensory training. She gazed at the tulips and daffodils, their petals splayed open, their anthers naked and stigmas caked with powdery residue.

"Sexuality is sacred!" she yelled at the tulips, whose petals had curled so wide open that the rounded edges now tapered blade-like to points. But, no. No. Try not to view these flowers moralistically, Karen thought a moment later, squeezing her thighs together as she sat down on the bench at the bus stop. After all, who was *she* to pass judgment on perennials? In the not-too-distant past, Karen had rented her mouth to a homeless man in exchange for a swig of cough syrup with codeine.

Karen was not crazy to notice the profligacy of plants that spring. Pollen counts for May had already broken records. At night the silent sex of angiosperms left a golden sheath of pollen so thick it choked the grass beneath it. People were scraping it off their windshields like ice in winter, Karen noticed as she trudged the last block of her trip from the bus stop to the YMCA. In the parking lot, someone had traced the word *asshole* into the yellow film on the back window of a minivan. Karen wiped it away with her hands. Negative thoughts were like twigs floating by in a tiny babbling brook, Nora had told her. Even less than twigs — like ripples in the water. You weren't supposed to get attached. Just let them pass, Karen reminded herself. But it was hard. She licked the yellow dust off her fingers, her eyes watered with the urge to vomit, then this, too, passed.

Karen was opening the YMCA by herself for the first time that morning. Her boss, Roberto, had given her a set of keys earlier in the week, entrusting *her*, Karen Donovan, to captain the ship in his absence. To be chosen, to be seen and selected as special enough to perform this job — it was a sign that things were moving in the right direction. The keys glittered in the morning light. Her hands shook a little with their eminence.

As soon as Karen unlocked the doors, she spotted two women waddling arm in arm from the parking lot up the front steps. Myra and Marlene. They lived at the luxury retirement condos down the street, Morning Pines, a name that made no sense at all, because the building was not even adjacent to a single conifer and what did morning have to do with it? If anything, Marlene and Myra were in the twilight of their lives. They were devoted to fitness, though in their eighties, their bodies were getting worse, not better. It was their cells, Karen wanted to explain to them. All the yoga and aquacise and squats in the world could not stop cellular decay. Keeping your muscles strong was pretty much useless. But there was no arguing with these two. Marlene was a Taurus and Myra a Scorpio, Karen had discerned from their account files, where their birthdays were listed. She smiled at them as they entered. They sang hello to Karen, grabbed their towels from the pyramid Karen had stacked so neatly on the front desk the night before, and waddled with impressive speed toward the women's locker room.

"You have to wait, I haven't booted up the computer yet. . . ."

Three more members glided past her as she hurried behind the reception desk. Where the hell was Rosette? Karen picked up the phone to call her, then remembered that Rosette had put her on restriction. She was only allowed to call her friend's cellphone once a day, excluding emergencies, which Rosette had defined as events that involved police, fire, or ambulance personnel. If Rosette did not call her back, Karen was supposed to pray for acceptance. Those were Rosette's rules. Karen had an eighty percent success rate in obeying them, which both women regarded as a real victory.

Karen wiped her fingers clean on the towel at the top of the pile and rearranged the remaining towels in a pyramid. A woman she'd never met before walked in. Strapped to her stomach was a large sack printed with little turtles. Karen tried to make conversation but the woman was no-nonsense, tapping some haiku of love or hate into her phone with one hand, her membership card at the ready in the other. She had brown curly hair graying at the roots, which gave her whole face a kind of silvery aura. She didn't look at Karen, nor at the perfect pyramid of towels. Instead she grabbed one recklessly, sending the whole structure tumbling to the floor. Karen knelt to rescue them, her knees aching. By the time Karen got up, the woman had disappeared inside.

An hour passed and no word from Rosette. Karen microwaved two French bread pizzas and read the classified ads in the newspaper. She remembered there being so much free stuff in the classifieds when she was a little girl. Hardly anyone gave stuff away for free anymore. Not even kittens. Something that comes in dozens and totally by accident now cost a truckload of money, and anyway, Nora told her she had to start saving. In "Lost and Found" someone in Arlington was looking for her wedding ring. The ad offered a five-hundred-dollar reward. It was a long shot, but Karen decided to check the lost-and-found box in the ladies' locker room. All kinds of stuff turned up there. Five hundred dollars would buy a really good kitten. Maybe a Persian or an Egyptian Mau.

Myra and Marlene were standing near the water fountain in the ladies' locker room, wearing nothing but flip-flops. Myra lifted her arm, exposing the prickly skin underneath where a surgical incision had healed into a long purple stripe. Marlene examined the scar coolly and nodded.

"How're your knees doing, Karen?" Myra asked. "Are you having that surgery? What did your ortho say?"

Before she had a chance to answer, the brisk, silvery woman walked in carrying a baby.

"Where did that baby come from?" Karen yelped.

"From my uterus," the woman sniffed.

"Oh," Karen said. The specificity of *uterus* threw a stick in her spokes. She sat on a bench and fished around her pockets until she found a paper clip; swiftly, furtively, she swallowed it like a pill.

Myra and Marlene exchanged looks. Did Karen-from-the-Y, as she was named by them, not know how babies were made? It was plausible that she didn't, given the other insane things they'd heard her say. Both women filed the conversation away, to be discussed later, over Chardonnay on the patio of their retirement condo. The more compassionate YMCA members learned how to steer around Karen, restoring the gym banter back to its rightful domain of injuries, fitness goals, and weather.

"How old is she?" Myra asked the new mother.

"Two and a half months," the mother answered.

"Oh! Brand-new!" Myra wrapped a towel beneath her wrinkly arms and tickled the baby's foot.

"Welcome to the world, little one," Marlene cooed.

The mother held the baby and twisted her hips from side to side. Karen stayed planted on her bench but leaned in for a closer look. The baby's face was hidden somewhere inside the soft yellow folds of blanket, behind the mother and the two elderly, half-naked women whispering gentle, knowledgeable things among themselves. Motherhood was a coven Karen had forfeited when a faith-based group home convinced her to get a hysterectomy at age eighteen. She had always been indifferent to her body's reproductive powers, and at the time had thought, *What the hell, at least now I can swim whenever I want and never worry about menstruation.* She did not regret this decision now.

When Myra and Marlene headed off to the showers, Karen was alone with the woman and her baby. This made her nervous. She didn't want to stay or leave, so she rummaged in the lost-and-found box and pulled out a comb. She raked it through her long, tangled hair.

"Would you mind doing me a quick favor?" the woman asked Karen. "Would you hold her for just a second?"

If you pick up a fallen hatchling and return him to his nest, his mother will smell your touch and be repulsed, Karen remembered learning. One whiff of you on its downy little feathers and the baby bird's mother will say, *You are not mine, not anymore.* She will shun the entire nest you'd tainted with your smelly hands, leaving her babies there to starve, and it would be all your fault.

"Oh God," Karen whispered, "oh God."

The mother stood on the scale while holding her baby, then stepped off and walked toward Karen. "I just want to see how much weight she's gained," she said, handing the bundle over like an offering. Karen took the baby confidently in her arms. *How did I know how to do that?* she wondered. Then she remembered that one of her foster families had had a baby—the redheaded family in Somerville. They were all so covered in freckles it looked as if they needed to wash their faces even when they were clean, and when Karen had pointed that out, the father pulled down her pants in the middle of the kitchen and spanked her with a spatula.

Karen looked at the baby, at her small, flushed face, her short almost translucent fringe of eyelashes. Babies knew everything. Their eyes quivered with the opaque knowledge of the world. That's why they cried so much. They were trying to tell us, and no one believed them.

"You might have come just in time for the end," Karen whispered to her.

The mother weighed herself and frowned.

"Well, I'm not losing any weight but my baby has gained one pound."

"We grow imperceptibly every minute of every day."

"That's a nice thought," the mother said, taking her baby back from Karen.

Rosette stormed into the locker room. She'd had her hair done that morning, Karen could tell right away, the mystery of her lateness explained. Rosette was a pious Christian, but vanity was her weakness. Her hair was a gleaming auburn color with a few purple and magenta feathers tightly woven in. Her bangs cut a crisp line across her brow. Karen could see that Rosette had also hit the tanning salon recently, as the pale outline of eye goggles betrayed.

"Stay, Mr. Cox," Rosette shouted through the open door. "Sit there, I tell you, and don't you move."

"Rose, did you read that article I sent you? About the pod of dolphins who killed themselves all together on that beach in England?"

Rosette looked at herself in the mirror, squared her shoulders, and turned her head from side to side. "Too terrible! I was shocked. Even the animals now are sinning against God who made them."

"Rosie, my stomach hurts. Can I have one of Mr. Cox's pills?"

"Hush your mouth," Rosette scolded. She was wearing cosmetic contact lenses that made her dark brown eyes appear a shattered, reptilian blue. She nodded at the woman with the baby and rolled her eyes, the YMCA's universal code for *You know crazy Karen. Can't believe a word she says. . . .* Rosette laid her hands on Karen's shoulders and gave them a deep, penetrating squeeze. "You're too fat, babygirl. That's the problem. You're not doing your exercises."

"I am. Sometimes. Sometimes I forget."

"You have to do them every day. That's how you change yourself."

"A guy in India grew his muscles just by thinking about lifting weights."

"Lord, help us all today. She's making up stories again," Rosette said to the mother, who packed her gym bag silently, avoiding eye contact. The woman, tired from the demands of new motherhood, felt entitled to withdraw from polite civilization. She was in no mood to connect with the human periphery, the Rosettes and Karens of the world. Not even on hallowed Last Day.

"It's true," Karen cried. But as usual she couldn't prove it, the source of the story long lost in the unmapped city of her mind. The part about the guy being from India she'd made up. But it was probably true. India was one of those places where elemental shape-shifting was still possible. Karen attributed this to all the wild animals roaming the streets. She had never been there, but she'd seen pictures. What mattered most was intention. Sometimes, things are true simply because they are supposed to be.

A CREW OF megalomaniacs would not survive very long in the cramped white tunnels of a space station, and so, while astronauts cannot be classified among mere mortals—their expertise in so many areas is too extraordinary—they are distinguished less by their talents as by a level of humility unusual among the rest of us who live and work our entire lives on Earth.

So there are mortals, and there are astronauts, and then there are astronauts selected to go to space, and an even smaller pool of astronauts called back for a second mission; and even among this elite group, Thomas "Bear" Clark was known as the human avatar of humility. According to a biography of him slated for release in the next year, his ex-wife attributed Bear's humility to the fact of his growing up as the middle child of two sisters, one taller than him (he'd inherited their mother's good looks as well as her small frame) and one born with Down syndrome.

"No, that's not quite it," his mother had reported to the biographer, not long before she died. "They are how they are from their very first day," she'd said, insisting to the author that Bear had been a cooperative, mild-mannered soul from his infancy, long before he was aware of the compensations he would have to make as a brother or a son. His deep sense of humility was simply part and parcel with all his other gifts.

If function followed form, Bear should have been a quarterback, with his square jaw and steep cheekbones. He was so good-looking as a child, old women in the grocery store used to give him money just because. Bear would save these quarters and dimes in a piggy bank, then buy presents for his younger sister, his mother had told the biographer.

He'd grown up in San Diego, in a ranch house identical in size and shape to all the other ranch houses in their neighborhood, in a WASP family that could trace its roots back to the crew of the *Mayflower*. As a boy, Bear aspired to become one of the sandy-haired surfers who eked by on hobo jobs. There was a purity to that kind of life, lived in obeisance to the ocean, that Bear admired. He loved surfing and all it encompassed: studying the waves, asking permission to walk on their backs, waiting with sublime patience for their consent. He could have made those vows and been just as happy as a beach bum as he was now on the International Space Station. But when his father was killed by a drunk driver, the most sensible response to that stunning pain was for Bear to distract himself, his grieving mother, and his sisters with his achievements. He turned his attention away from the sea and toward his studies, where he excelled in math and science, and was encouraged rather glibly by a high school physics teacher to pursue a career in astronautics.

"Sounds neat," young Bear had said.

He was the blue-eyed only son of a nice family in Southern California, a place where the climate and culture are suffused by an optimism that stands in utter defiance to geological reality, as though dangling on the edge of a chthonic fault line could be made A-OK if you believe in goodness, in your ability to manufacture safety and hope, and in that erratic human covenant that promises anything is possible if you only put your mind to it.

Which is exactly what Bear did, and like a curse in reverse, everything he touched turned to gold. He joined the Air Force, studied at Stanford, was accepted into the NASA training program, and flew his first mission while still in his thirties, on the now-retired Space Shuttle. His crew then was rescuing a wayward satellite that had failed to reach its optimal orbital height, offering Bear the opportunity for an Extravehicular Activity, the golden ring of all astronauts. Floating outside the shuttle, he had seen asteroids streak the black sky beneath his feet. "If this is the only chance I get, if I never get called up for another mission, I will still die the happiest man on Earth," he told his wife then.

With the same combination of humility and hard work that had gotten him into space, he devoted himself to a grounded life mentoring other astronauts, working in Mission Control for other flights, being the best team player he could be. When this current mission came up—one year on the ISS, the opportunity of a lifetime—his dominant feeling was not pride but gratitude.

From a distance his whole life glittered with the charm of the elect. Which is why his dark mood, and the accompanying dark thoughts of calamity, were so alarming to him.

He made the mistake of confessing this in an email to his ex-wife. *The only thing worse than being with your family on the holidays is not being with your family on the holidays,* she replied. *But that has always been your MO—to make yourself busy when there's something you want to avoid, hiding behind "work." I tried to explain to the girls that that is just your love-language—you're a provider, so you feel the need to work hard to provide. But they could use less providing and more of your time.*

He hated that she talked to him like this now. She took the familiarity between them too far, exploiting their post-divorce friendship as license to casually criticize him. But in that same castigating email, she had also included very helpful links to the things their daughters wanted for their Last Day presents, a considerate gesture that would make shopping from space easier.

Thanks was all he wrote back to her.

Bear worked with his customary efficiency that day, despite a persistent headache, and was able to recoup eleven minutes of R&R before dinner. He used the time to do a three-minute meditation exercise in the privacy of his crew quarters, part of a thirty-day challenge he was partaking in alongside a group of high school kids on Earth, and then tackle his holiday shopping. His younger daughter, Kayley, both needed and wanted a new phone. For Elyse he got a little silver dove for her charm bracelet. For his ex-wife's birthday, which fell on Last Day, he found a specially designed foam roller—she had been complaining about leg cramps during her marathon training. He placed all the items into his virtual cart at the mega online retailer Jungle.com and clicked "Purchase."

A minutes-long delay was followed by an automatic return to the Jungle home page. His shopping attempt had failed. He would have to search and select the items all over again. These precious minutes had been wasted. Bear punched the quilted walls of his CQ.

Immediately he blamed Donna: it was her gift that had crashed the order. It was irrational, he knew, but he resented that he felt guilty if he didn't buy her a birthday gift. Being the amicable ex-husband was Who He Was. It was part of the reason he had been selected for this second mission in space. Lots of astronauts were permanently grounded after a divorce. It was an unspoken practice of NASA, with roots in the military component of the program—if you couldn't keep the peace in your own household, how could they trust you on board the $2.9 billion operation in space? But not Bear. He was agreeable. He was good. He followed the rules even when he broke his marriage vows.

His daughters hated Jungle.com anyway. It was a corporate overlord, or some such fulmination they'd picked up in college. They always made smart comments about it. And Last Day was not really a gift-giving holiday. This shopping was a gesture reaching out of Bear's guilt for being away from them for so long.

Was it even possible, Bear thought, for a good man to do the right thing anymore?

Perhaps it was the excess CO_2 in the station that was making him so sloppy and morose. The second CDRA was broken—again—leaving just one operating air scrubber for the six people on board. But that was changing tonight. Three of the six members were leaving first thing in the morning. Even if Mission Control would not grant Bear permission to try and fix the CDRA, halving the population of the station would lighten the load of the one that still worked, and the air would be a little cleaner.

Bear floated into the Russian module, where the mission captain, Mikhail Mikhailovich Svec, was cementing a crown in his own molar.

"I could have done that for you, comrade," Bear offered.

Svec snorted. "Hyouston never allow extra time for you Americans in schedule. I can do myself. No problem."

Svec was something of a legend in the international space community. Among many more obvious triumphs of physicality (mountaineering, dead-lifting) he had inured his mucus membranes to withstand pepper spray. It was a trick that got a lot of applause at bars across the globe. He never soiled his space diaper, not even during launch. "Well-trained dog can hold bowels for twelve hours. So can I," Svec declared. His record for holding his breath underwater was six minutes and three seconds, and he was a skilled practitioner of tantric sex.

He also claimed to have willed the color of his eyes to change from brown to blue. As there were no color photographs of a young Svec extant, this claim could only have been substantiated by his now long-deceased mother, an infamous alcoholic in a city where binge drinking was hardly noteworthy.

The mythology Svec perpetuated was that on his thirteenth birthday his mother had confessed to him the identity of his father. Before that day, the only thing Svec knew about this man was his shoe size—forty-three—the worn number on the sole of the boots his father had left behind one night when Svec was still a baby. These boots remained by the back door of their apartment for years, an eerie, truncated effigy to the man who'd left and never come back. His mother would sob whenever Svec asked her about them—the disembodied *them*, never *him*, never the man the boots represented. Svec knew his patronymic was a sham, that it was derived from his maternal grandfather, and that these things—

his name, those boots—were a source of deep pain he must not aggravate if he wanted his mother to sleep at night.

But on his thirteenth birthday Mama Svec sat him down at their kitchen table, sliced some sour pickles and pumpernickel bread, poured a shot of vodka for each of them, and told him the whole story. It was a short story in the end, a disappointingly common one at odds with young Svec's already burgeoning notion of himself as a heroic figure with mythic origins. His dad was a high-ranking Roscosmos administrator who had another family, a legitimate one, that prevented him from acknowledging the alcoholic waitress he had impregnated, other than the occasional envelopes of cash he left her, usually enough to buy a week's worth of groceries but never more than that.

From that day on, Svec despised his father. He was obviously a coward. So close to the ships that could reach the skies yet he chose to become an administrator? He cursed this man and the short limbs and brown eyes he had passed down to Svec. He and his mother took turns refilling the glasses of vodka until the bottle was empty, and moments before throwing up, Svec vowed to grow taller than six feet, to change the color of his eyes from his father's cow-dung brown to his mother's forget-me-not blue, and to become one of the few men to touch the void of outer space. He failed at only one of these, and could not entirely forgive himself.

It was Svec's honor and duty as captain to give the goodbye speech and toast to the departing astronauts, an American whom Bear knew from the Air Force, a Swiss particle physicist, and a Canadian industrial engineer. It could not be a real toast, Svec felt, without alcohol, but the Westerners were strict about the ban on alcohol in space and so he did his best to incant the drinking spirit into their sad little pouches of reconstituted apple juice.

". . . and so I say to you, our comrades Linda, Deitiker, and Sanjay, fly straight home. No wandering. Do not go like arrogant bird of our Russian fairy tale and fly directly into sun. . . ."

The other astronauts, including Bear and a billionaire Japanese space tourist, Yui, listened patiently while microwaving their individual dinners as quietly as they could. Svec did not let their eating stop him.

"... *Budem zdorovy*—to our health. *Na pososhok*—safe travels ..."

The crew hovered awkwardly around the table bolted into the wall. Bear wolfed down his barbecue beef and used his leftover tortilla to hold a polite sample of the caviar Svec offered each crew member to commemorate the occasion. The smell of it, mixed with Yui's crabmeat and the odor of Deitiker's irradiated sausage, was making Bear's stomach turn.

He gulped his nausea stoically and told the group, "I also want to say a little farewell, but I'm not as good at toasts as our Commander Svec. So if you don't mind, I've been practicing this for weeks. . . ."

Svec watched with a bemused smile as the American pulled a harmonica out of his zippered pocket. It was the captain's job to oversee special functions, and Bear was second seat.

"I hope I'm not overstepping," Bear said.

"*Nekogda*," Svec said, nodding.

Bear played a jazzy rendition of "Mercy Mercy Mercy" that he had been practicing for this night's farewell. He chose it because it was a bit more upbeat than the standard blues and gospel tunes in his songbook. As he played, one by one the other astronauts drifted away to their CQs to watch TV on their personal laptops.

Only Svec remained, and Bear was touched by this show of solidarity. The Russian commander was almost stereotypically macho, and came off to Bear as downright cold at times, but like many other Russians Bear had known, Svec was a sentimental man with a tenderness for ritual, tradition, and symbolic gesture. Bear took Svec's quiet attention as a cue to keep playing, so he tried a more modern pop song he was just beginning to learn. He fumbled a bit through the chord transitions, but Svec was a respectful and sympathetic audience, listening in perfect silence. Bear had begun the second verse when he heard the rattle, then the rasp, followed by a snore.

Those legendary eyes that could withstand pepper spray and allegedly change pigmentation could also remain open during sleep, it appeared now, as Svec snored. Drool gathered on Svec's slack lower lip and remained there, weightless, shining like a pearl. Bear dabbed Svec's face with a tissue—stray particles of water, even tiny ones, were dangerous for the ship—and woke him. Svec snorted again, and floated off without so much as a goodbye.

LAST DAY WAS an oddity on the calendar. Slightly more than one day, but not quite two, it began at some point on May 27 and ended on May 28. Whether encircled by sunrise, sunset, midnight, or quitting time, the parameters of the day were entirely personal. This lack of clear boundary was just one of the many reasons Sarah Moss hated the holiday. As a child she would cry and cry for the duration of Last Day, refusing to fall asleep all night, making May 28 cranky and miserable for both her and her parents. Everyone assured her she would grow out of it. When that didn't happen, she affected a teenage air of disavowal. The perfect mask for her shuddering fear.

The fear was totally irrational, she knew. Despite what felt like a never-ending fountain of oil spills, carbon emissions, and toxic waste, the planet had yet to smolder into one big ashtray. Life marched on. It always did. It probably always would, at least in her lifetime and for many thousands of lifetimes after hers. No big deal. It was a dramatic holiday of self-inflicted upheaval drawn out into a public performance. Collective catharsis and all that. Right?

Sarah had researched the many apocryphal histories of Last Day for various school projects. The earliest antecedent supposedly took place during the Babylonian era, on the last full moon of the vernal equinox of 2807 BCE, when a meteor struck the Indian Ocean during a total lunar eclipse. Terrified, the Babylonians scurried to propitiate whichever god they had offended, slaughtering prized animals, building pyres, bathing in sacred waters, giving gifts to loved ones and strangers alike, and this crisis narrowly averted gave rise to a tradition of yearly reckoning.

Later, astrologers of the Ayyubid empire predicted the end of the world for May 28, 1186. The sultan Saladin, in flagrant mockery of his superstitious advisers and his primitive father-in-law they still loyally served, held an open-air candlelit party for all the nonbelievers the night before. They danced and ate and drank themselves into an orgy that would make a Dionysian blush. The lines between man and woman, ruler and servant, pain and pleasure shattered.

In illuminated manuscripts of the fourteenth century, later proven to be forgeries made by Romany peddlers of the seventeenth century, was the story of a Florentine village that had lost more than half of its citizens to the plague. The story went that a Franciscan monk took a vow of silence after the last of his brothers had died. Alone in his monastery, he meditated day and night, hoping to understand the wisdom in his God's seemingly sadistic plan. He spent weeks in this trance, sipping only water steeped weakly with nettles, fasting in solitude. Then, in a very Italian mix of Christian and pagan devotion, he emerged from his monastery naked as a baby, trundling a small cart full of linens. He built a fire in the town's piazza and urged passersby to add their garments, their bedclothes, the shirts on their backs, right then and there, into the fire. At last the whole village stood naked in the chill spring air, their bodies warmed by the enormous fire, and on that day ever after, not another soul was touched by the Black Death.

All of these stories could not be more obvious bullshit, Sarah thought, and yet the broader her knowledge of Last Day mythology grew, the deeper her fear took root. Sometimes people will things into being, so what possible good could a couple thousand years of end-time fetishizing bring?

For her school's chapter of Mock Trial, from which she had defected earlier that year (high levels of theater-kid solipsism and disenfranchised-nerd neediness—an insufferable combo), she could wax philosophical on the mythopoetic function of Last Day, its vitality and necessity in today's techno-dependent, isolating world. But every word she'd uttered in those debates had been insincere, a homily delivered for a teacher's approval. And she was ultimately annoyed that she'd brought her team to victory in the debate. The opposing team should have won. Their argument was much better—that Last Day was a perpetuation of an intensely self-centered lie: the world could not go on without us.

"A product," her best friend Terrence pronounced, "of our pattern-making brains, that so crave completion they cannot hear *tick tick* without the inevitable *tock.*"

Now, that was a good point. But when being judged by a committee, especially of high school teachers, sentimentality was going to take the prize over bleak truth.

Almost sixteen now, Sarah realized for the first time that Last Day was completely racist. Its seeming ubiquity was actually, like so much else, a consequence of Western hegemony. "And! It ignores, like, the whole *continent* of Africa, which is made of, like, so many different ethnic groups that don't know or care about it. And Native Americans— they have totally different creation and apocalypse myths. It's a stupid, largely Western, *white* invention."

"Oh, you're such a Scrooge," her mother said, which made Sarah wither. For one, as a literary allusion it didn't even make sense. Sarah had read Dickens, and that novel was about a character suffering from a general spiritual bankruptcy that transcended culture and calendar, thank you very much, and besides that, Sarah really liked Christmas. Christmas was about a little baby and farm animals and hope. Her dad's Judaism was pretty much phoned in. He'd taught her to light candles on

Chanukah but he didn't know any prayers, so the blessing he recited was a gibberish they pretended was Hebrew. On Yom Kippur they flushed a crust of rye toast down the toilet, a tradition she'd always looked forward to. She liked the renewal of New Year's, and at least it made sense on the calendar. Halloween was always fun. The Mexican Día de los Muertos was even better. Easter was the coolest, a mash-up of seasonal changes and diluted paganism and Christianity and zombies. Easter was about surrealism and chocolate. What was not to love there?

Maybe she just needed to ignore the holiday and focus on school-work. She had a paper to write that weekend on *Lear*. She was toying with a thesis about impotence, but broader, like the ultimate human impotence in the face of Nature. Or Time. Or something like that. She regretted not having written a draft by now. Deadlines scraped away at her already fragile nervous system, and she hated herself a little for letting this one creep up on her.

It was hard to make plans for a day that you secretly considered to be your last. How could anyone enjoy herself under that kind of pressure? It made every idea feel holy and totally wrong at the same time. She knew some kids from school were dropping acid on Crane Beach, and while it was fun to watch her friends' pupils dilate and to listen to their mad prose-poems of insight, eventually Sarah, as always the only sober person there, would get bored and want a coherent dialogue, which she realized made her a total loser.

Her parents were having their annual pizza party but they said she could skip it this year if she wanted. Last year she'd met the love of her life at her parents' party. It was, she realized now, the one-year anniversary of their *whatever*.

He was her mother's colleague's plus-one, the unwitting boyfriend dragged to a lame work party where he knew no one else. Sarah's mother taught women's history at a small, private Christian college. She invited only the select few faculty members who shared her liberal politics, and last year she'd used the holiday to win over some more support for her personal campaign to repaint a dated, early-seventies-era Eve-shaming mural of the Book of Genesis in the student union. (In the mural, Adam looked like a hapless dork, shrugging his shoulders in a sitcom pose of "Take my wife . . . please!" Eve was narrow-eyed and ugly, with a darker complexion than Adam, a blatantly racist choice. The mural had to go, Dr. Moss insisted.) One of the invitees to the Mosses' Last Day pizza party was Emily, a young creative-writing adjunct, a newly minted MFA with two minor publications to her name. She'd been particularly vocal in support of repainting the mural at a faculty meeting. Dr. Moss was eager to get to know her better.

The man Emily brought as her date to the Mosses' Last Day pizza party was hungover and gray. He was tattooed everywhere you could see, his arms sleeved in ghouls and skeletons, a storm amassing above his collar shooting lightning up his throat.

"Kurt is a visual artist," Emily announced several times after her boy-friend mumbled his hellos and nice-to-meet-yous to the other guests.

"I'm a tattooer," Kurt said to Sarah, who discovered the nauseous-looking man skulking in her most favorite place to skulk, down the hill from her house. They'd both found themselves sitting on the stones that encircled the Last Day fire pit, watching silently as the flames fizzled down to black and white embers. "This artist shit is about her, not me. She keeps telling people I'm working on a graphic novel. I mentioned to her once that I had half an idea for a comic book, but she knows as well as I do that I work and drink too much to ever get it started, let alone finished."

"Women will say absolutely anything to justify their sexual selections," Sarah replied in a matter-of-fact tone. She felt equipped to judge because her paper on *Madame Bovary* had gotten an A. "It would be so cool if people could just say, 'His pheromones smell like safety' or 'She successfully distracts me from thoughts of death.' And then we could all nod and be like, 'Yeah, mazel tov,' and move on to more important stuff."

"Huh." Kurt inhaled his cigarette and held the smoke for a long time in his mouth, like an actor in a movie. "Yeah, I guess you're right."

"Self-deception is the greatest crime," Sarah said, then wondered if she believed this was true or was just saying it to sound cool. Surely there were worse crimes. Like rape, and anything involving children. Her companion looked at her with his squinted, bloodshot eyes and nodded in agreement, which made her feel, in the dumbest possible way, so good.

Up the hill, Emily teetered across the yard, continually sinking then extracting the heels of her muddy sandals out of the soft, moist lawn. A hard rain had fallen the night before and relented suddenly, as though bidden to do so, just before dawn. Sarah had listened to every drop fall with an impatient, hopeful heart. She was panicked as usual, waiting for the end, or not the end, and had refused to take even one tiny milligram of the Valium her mother saved for long airplane flights and Sarah's Last Day panic attacks. Though she changed her mind about everything every single day, exasperating her parents with her constantly relapsing vegetarianism, she knew one thing for sure—if the end was coming, she wanted to be fully awake to see it.

"I'm still here," she had wept silently in her bed once the rain had stopped and the sun rose. "We must be okay."

This long, anxious night had made for a groggy, exhausting day, but sitting next to this man now, she felt she was falling into a deep, transformative sleep and waking up from it at the same time.

"She shouldn't have worn heels," Sarah observed of Emily.

"Are you a student at the college?" Kurt asked.

"Yes," Sarah said. The pistons of her heart quickened, fueling the audacity she needed to lie. "My name's . . . Sarah."

"I'm Kurt," the man said.

"One question." Sarah touched his shoulder, an action that surprised her. She was not a hugger. This was often remarked upon at her very emotive private school. "If you did write a graphic novel, what would it be? I don't care if you ever do it or not. I'm just curious."

"It's from a dream I had once a long time ago. About a little boy who swallows a butterfly, then one day coughs up an egg that hatches into a lizard who becomes his best friend. Their adventures and stuff. I don't really like writing. So it would be mostly pictures."

"Like a fable."

"Yeah, but not a fairy tale. Not for kids. They would get into real danger. Ghosts and hurricanes and serial killers would come after them. Did you ever see M by Fritz Lang?"

She had not. She had seen the movie poster for *Metropolis*. Her friend Terrence's parents had a large vintage print framed in their upstairs hallway.

"Totally," she answered. "That would look awesome. Like, as your aesthetic."

"Here's the prototype." Kurt pulled up his T-shirt. His torso was largely untouched by ink, which made the few images tattooed there even more vivid. He twisted to show her a tattoo on the left side of his rib cage. A blue-and-yellow lizard munched on a turquoise butterfly. The attention to detail was remarkable. The butterfly's tiny face was etched with infinitesimal agony. Crumbs of its iridescent wings fell from the lizard's smiling mouth. There was a quality of light to the tattoo that Sarah thought miraculous. Even flat against Kurt's pale, dry skin, the lizard and its prey seemed to glitter.

Again she reached over and touched him, this time letting her fingers run over his skin for what felt like a long time, as though deciphering a code written in the rise and fall of his ribs. She looked at the tattoo on the other side of his ribs, the happy lizard's evil twin—a scorpion that was inked too dark and was now fading, looking more like a badly healed scar than a picture of anything. She looked at Kurt's thick waist, his softly protruding beer belly, the way the hair sprouted erratically over his abdomen, then gathered darkly, with purpose, at a central point below his navel. She imagined where his spleen was hidden. She thought about his kidneys, the ruffled scarf of his intestines, how fragile and alive he was, all the secrets he was keeping beneath his skin.

What?

This was something new. Sarah was a sworn asexual. It was a well-explored part of her identity. Ninth grade at the Phoenix School meant completing Dr. Heather Vasquez-McQueen's practicum in human sexuality. Dr. Heather made her class read selections from the Kinsey report and Freud and the newest edition of *Our Bodies, Ourselves*, which the boys in the practicum protested. What about *their* bodies, *themselves*, hmmm? Dr. Heather was a lesbian married to a transgender man and she had no time for parity, what with eons of subjugation to counterattack in one semester, one abbreviated semester, as the practicum was supposed to be finished before Thanksgiving break. In just ten weeks they had to cover STDs, rape culture, masturbation, gender identity, the whole sexuality-is-a-continuum-not-a-fixed-point thing, and still drive home all the practicalities of how to put on and properly dispose of condoms as well as other safe-sex options and watch at least one documentary on *Roe v. Wade.*

Their final project was to "map your sexuality" in a four- to five-thousand-word essay. It was optional to read this essay out loud, though highly encouraged by Dr. Heather, who said it was a critical strike in the war against repression. The Sarahs Wilmington and Burke naturally jumped at the chance, but that year a surprising number of other kids did, too. Even Terrence. He wrote about the time his mother walked in on him jerking off and the shame that followed, which got a lot of sympathetic head nodding from Dr. Heather. Sean Fusco talked about knowing he was gay when he was a little boy watching soap operas with his grandmother, how he'd wished the men would kiss each other. Lindsey LaSalle wrote an essay on pansexuality that had Dr. Heather practically weeping with pride.

Sarah Moss wrote her essay about the parallels between the energetic attraction of subatomic particles in the first microseconds following the Big Bang and the attraction of humans, and how attraction plus collision makes new matter, whether that matter is a universe or a baby. The connection was flimsy and kind of sentimental, she knew, but the story of baryons was rife with meaning, worthy of a B+ at least, though she'd hoped for more.

"The energy of creation is attractive but it is not sexual. It's narcissistic projection to label it as sexual when these forces of attraction and creation began before there was carbon-based life," Sarah read.

Dr. Vasquez-McQueen smiled a smile that made her face look like a rag being wrung out to dry. After class Lindsey told Sarah that she should get tested for autism.

"Don't worry, kiddo. They think everyone is autistic these days," Sarah's father consoled her later. "The noise of the world is deafening. People shut down."

"And besides, you're not autistic, pumpkin," her mother added. "You're just a late bloomer."

Or maybe she was not made to bloom at all. Never in her life had Sarah been sexually attracted to another person, male or female. She'd never had a boyfriend or a girlfriend, and had never wanted one. It was rumored that Terrence had a crush on her, but he was shy and waiting for her to make the first move, which was perfect—it meant she could stall him forever, or at least until graduation, without losing his friendship.

That fall Sarah had kissed a freshman named Marcus Stroman at the school Halloween dance. He'd pushed himself on her but she was able to shove him away. He was drunk and arrogant and smoked unfiltered Camels. Sarah could taste the cigarettes on his teeth, and the acrid residue of his spit lingered on her tongue for a while after they stopped kissing, like the gentle pain of a tiny animal's bite. She'd kissed Lindsey LaSalle one day two summers earlier. Lindsey had talked a lot about consent beforehand, so much so that Sarah finally blurted, "Yeah, fine, let's kiss or whatever," just to shut her up. Lindsey's mouth was soft and a little sandy because they were on the beach. Both times, Sarah had opened her mouth, and there the experience had lived and died. Besides a tiny splash of fear that had quickly turned to tedium, clock-watching, when-will-this-be-over, she felt nothing anywhere in her body. Not even a tingle. But she couldn't write an essay about that. It was the most shameful thing anyone could possibly admit in Dr. Heather's class, that she was fifteen and asexual. It was worse than getting aroused by mascot animal costumes or period-staining your skirt or getting caught jerking off in the living room. Sarah was the biggest freak of them all.

A phase, her parents said calmly, a rebellion in reverse. They'd raised her in such a loving, accepting, shame-free milieu that she was forced to reject basic biology to be different.

"You're just afraid of getting hurt," Terrence suggested.

But what if they were all wrong? What if she was born this way, part of a growing number of genetically unproductive people, evolved because the world had reached its limit and humanity was coming to its end?

In her sunny backyard with Kurt that day almost precisely one year ago, Sarah had been able to forget all about the end of time. They had talked for two hours in a breathless, exhilarating way about music and movies and forgivably embarrassing things they had once done. Full disclosure was still out of reach; both had wanted to impress even as they'd pretended to disarm. For example, Sarah did not tell the story of the time she'd pissed her pants during a cross-country track race. Kurt did not reveal how much debt he was still in ten years after opening his tattoo studio. They'd told innocent tales of pratfalls and mistaken identity instead, pretending to be more mortified than they actually were.

They'd discovered that they both loved a graphic novelist named Val Corwin, a reclusive artist and writer whose controversial work was published sporadically, always to mixed reviews, and about whom not much was known personally, not even the gender of the author. The biggest commercial and critical hit was Corwin's fully illustrated version of Kafka's *Metamorphosis*. While many other graphic novelists had taken a stab at this story, Corwin's edition centered on Gregor Samsa's sister, casting the ordinarily tragic beetle as an ugly antagonist. The book was hailed as a feminist masterpiece, but the graphic novel that followed it, about a lecherous Hollywood screenwriter and his chronic impotence, was both lauded and reviled for its grotesque precision. An entire chapter was devoted to the protagonist's botched penis-enlargement surgery, one that many readers, even devoted fans, found hard to take. Like most of Corwin's work, it was an uncomfortable mixture of the sacred and the profane that left readers uneasy.

Corwin's work, in different ways, had carried both Sarah and Kurt in their darkest hours. The newest book, release date unknown, was rumored to be an illustrated anthropology of the Last Day holiday. Sarah had gushed that it was her greatest fantasy to meet Corwin in person. Kurt confessed that when he was a teenager he had staked out an address in Boston he had heard belonged to the artist. He'd stood outside in the rain like a creep until the owner of the house invited him inside for a cup of tea. She was an elderly woman adorned head to toe with silver and turquoise jewelry and a caftan, under which she wore no bra. The woman claimed she didn't know who Val Corwin was, though she had the charcoal-stained fingertips of an artist at work.

"All Corwin's work is black-and-white!" Sarah swooned.

"I know. I can never prove it, but I swear it was her."

"I always hoped Corwin was a woman."

"Me, too."

Sarah and Kurt sat on the low stones around the fire pit, close enough to feel the discrete energy of each other's bodies without touching. The heavy rain had prevented a proper fire, but Sarah's father had stayed up all night like the good patriarch that he was, and once the storm had subsided, around four in the morning, he'd built a small, sputtering flame in the pit. Now the ashes had turned smoldering and white but were still radiating heat. The sun shone on the glittering grass.

Up the hill, Kurt's girlfriend, Emily, had finally extracted herself from an awkward conversation with a theology professor. She was beckoning Kurt with a wave. It was time for him to go.

Kurt got up and gave Sarah a long hug.

"Keep in touch," Kurt said, and handed her his business card.

Sarah opened a new email account, pretending to be the fictional college student Kurt thought she was, and wrote to him the very next day. *We made it. The end is not for us, not this time,* she said.

Over the course of the past year, Sarah had revealed herself in a way she had never done before with another human being, all the while remaining perfectly hidden behind a screen and the false identity of a Christian college student. Sarah was good about spacing out her correspondences—she didn't want to appear needy or deranged—and Kurt responded, when he responded, either with long, stream-of-consciousness tracts or incomplete sentences that made him sound drunk. For the most part his messages were funny, cryptic, and a little sad. He refused to use first-person pronouns, giving his voice a foreign, disembodied timber.

crazy busy indulging artless drunks their shamrocks and roses and yin yangs. possibly ruining lives. wicked cool. you??

Later that fall when Sarah had planted a strategic line about Emily in her email, Kurt reported that they had broken up.

disappointed her to death, he wrote. *only way to get her to leave. otherwise you stay stuck forever. she doesn't even realize it wasnt me who disappointed her—her imagination of me did.*

Bummer, Sarah wrote back, a word she would never use in real life. Cool, slightly archaic, self-consciously retro, totally blasé. She took this opportunity to copy and paste the final draft of her essay for Dr. Vasquez-McQueen's sexuality practicum (peppered with strategic spelling and grammar mistakes, to make it appear like her own spontaneous, stream-of-consciousness rant). It was a test—to see if he would get weird and/or dismiss her. Also, he'd once told her, apropos of nothing, that the TVs he'd grown up with, when disconnected from their antennae, had produced a flurry of black and white dots (a snowstorm effect Sarah had only ever seen replicated on the digital screens of her lifetime) and that this static contained one percent of the big bang. He had not clarified what that meant—*contained 1% of the Big Bang*—but he had honored the birth of the universe with a rare use of capitalization, which made Sarah's heart thump so loudly she could hear it.

Kurt did not respond for three months, almost four. In that time Sarah sustained a mood of bridled alarm; his response times usually ranged between two days to two months. Not that she was measuring. She didn't need to. She had looked at his emails so often and for so long that they were burned into her memory. All she had to do was close her eyes and the beaming white screens appeared on the backs of her lids, where she could see with perfect clarity the always blank subject lines and the dates of his pithy, precious missives.

So she panicked, waited another day, and then another, until she couldn't stand it any longer and wrote to him in late March, just two months ago now, deploying a calculated terseness, a deliberate absence of capitalization, so he would know just how cool and fine she was, what a not-big deal it was, this silence, his silence.

how's tricks, stranger?

She considered, even wrote a draft, without punctuation, but couldn't bear to send it.

The next day he responded. *sara my dear you are too good for this world.*

Who said things like that? No one, Sarah was sure. Kurt was the most fascinating creature she'd ever met. He'd spelled her name wrong but she didn't care. Reading this one sentence over and over, she'd never been so sure that she was doomed, that everyone, the whole world, was inescapably, officially doomed, and coming from Kurt, this eulogy was glorious.

ᴀFTER THE DAILY inspection, Bear microwaved some coffee for Svec and himself and prepared Yui's pouch of matcha so that all three beverages would be hot and ready to drink by the time they gathered in the galley for their debriefing with Mission Control. His strange mood of the last few weeks was now infecting his dreams, a fact he would have ordinarily ignored if he had not been assigned the task of recording his dreams for a NASA psychologist who was doing heavens-knew-what with the information. Just before waking, he'd had a nightmare that was following him through his morning now. In the dream, he was at summer camp, on a bunk bed thousands of miles above the earth. Trapped in a cycle of paralytic analysis, he wondered, *Am I an adult or a child? Should I climb down or stay here and radio for help?* He ran through a series of disaster inventories and decision trees — his dreams could not relieve him of this responsibility to rational thought; he was an astronaut even while unconscious. He determined, at last, in the credulity of dreams, that he was suspended in a middle-gravity zone where the rules shifted often and without warning and that everything he knew, everything he'd studied, was no longer relevant.

Bear thought the dream was psychologically significant, illuminating his fears about what *might* happen with the subtle power dynamic that had emerged, leaving Svec, Yui, and him alone. But Svec had put a moratorium on the discussion of dreams.

"*Nekogda*. We will die of boredom."

"I had a dream," Yui announced as he floated over to them later that morning. "I rented the special observatory deck in the Tokyo Tower," he went on, ignoring Svec's thick brows pinching toward the center of his forehead. "The floor is covered by people. All naked. Lying like tatami mats. Covering the entire floor. I do not have to yell at them because they know they are under my command. I go down on my hands and knees and do a somersault. Then another and another until I cross the whole floor like this. When I get up, I bow, wave my hands, and say, 'Thank you very much. I am finished now.' The people say nothing. They will not move until I leave. I know this because it is my dream."

Svec gazed out of a porthole, watching the sun being snuffed out behind the earth like the ember of a cigar. "Dreams are garbage of human mind," he pronounced.

"I am not telling you another part of the dream. I cannot."

"Good," said Svec, wiping his mouth and hands.

"It is too dangerous for me to tell you. You would not be able to sleep or eat or think or work if I told you."

"Today's agenda is ridiculously packed," Bear said. "We'd better get to it."

"Our countries could go to war." Yui chewed thoughtfully on strips of dehydrated salmon. "If I told you."

"He reminds me of my son," Svec said, not without a tinge of affection. "Relentless."

"No, I will not tell you. I must not. I care about peace," Yui declared, and somersaulted the whole way to the exercise station.

Bear saw on his schedule that he had finally gotten the okay from Mission Control to fix what they referred to as the "extra" CDRA. Both CDRAs were necessary at all times; excess CO_2 in the air affected mood as well as mental acuity, Bear had argued, but NASA contended that the effects were "negligible" and that the levels were acceptable.

Technically, this was a victory for Bear, who'd been lobbying for permission to service the machine for over two months, but the feeling of triumph was short-lived and he quickly slipped into a state of quiet resentment. He worked alone for hours, dismantling the large machine one piece at a time, taking care to seal each tiny part in a series of ziplock bags tethered nearby or affix them to a large magnetic board. The station had a habit of swallowing small objects, and once lost, there was no sensible way to search for them in the floating chaos of microgravity. The sounds of the ISS, grating and constant, were somewhere between a factory and a hospital in terms of ambience. The idea struck Bear that some music would be soothing while he worked, then a moment later he forgot about the music and kept working in silence, only for the thought to resurface after another hour.

Again he counted the weeks he had left in this mission, breaking them into days, hours, and then individual tasks he had left to complete. How many more urine samples would he collect from now until departure? How many more hours would he log on the treadmill? It was a depressing arithmetic.

Another hour passed like this, in a silence scraped by groaning filters and fans. When he reached a benchmark in the repair process nine minutes earlier than planned, Bear felt a surge of dopey joy. He did some quadriceps stretches and tried again to do the three-minute breathing exercise he had learned in his meditation challenge that was supposedly so therapeutic. But the good feeling evaporated as quickly as it arrived, and Bear felt worse than ever.

Bear liked to describe himself as easygoing, rarely angry. He believed he was among a minority of humans organically hardwired toward contentment, and that the unhappiness of others was a maladaptive trait inherited from primitive ancestors—to hold on to bad memories at the expense of the good ones. And yet he had woken up this morning—at that artificially contrived moment they called morning—with such rage at his surroundings it felt like a fever, an angry longing for Earth consuming him with a quality of light, aching, and burning, both particle and wave.

At last Bear discovered the faulty valve in the CDRA and was pleased it was something simple enough that he could make a new one in the 3D printer right away. He sent his design for the part to the printer, then again found himself imagining a catastrophe that would require him to deorbit immediately. A medicine-resistant bacteria, one that significantly impacted his ability to function—that would do the trick. What symptoms would he be willing to endure for this to happen? Hyperemesis? He hated puking so much. Maybe an upper respiratory infection would be enough, if accompanied by severe chest pain. Ideally it would be quick, acute, and a manageable amount of pain soldiered by him alone. He didn't want anything to happen to the station—no fires or breakdowns of essential systems. The success of the ISS was too important to mankind, this was one of his core beliefs. The only other option besides personal illness was the death of an immediate family member on Earth. . . .

"Your face," Svec remarked, sounding a little unnerved at the sour expression on the ever-smiling American. "Your health? No good today?"

"Perhaps our Bear-o might be constipated," Yui suggested. He was upside down from the position Svec and now Bear had chosen to orient themselves, a thick hardcover comic book in his hands. "Perhaps our friendo might need to reach inside anus to—"

"Nope. Regular as always, Yui."

Svec was making what felt like an endless series of tiny plastic coils on the 3D printer. "You almost done with that, comrade?" Bear asked him. Bear felt that because his work today on the CDRA would improve the CO_2 levels for the whole ship, benefiting them all, his job should have priority on the printer. "I only have one small part to print. How many do you have left, Svec?"

"Thirty, maybe thirty-five more."

"I am concerned about our American friendo," Yui said. He closed his book and held it against his heart. "I look at you and I wonder, *Why he is so sad?*"

"I think we'll all feel a lot better once I get this second CDRA up and running, friendo. And I only need to print this one part to finish up. . . ."

Bear stifled a yawn while waiting for Yui to search his vast, largely libidinous vocabulary bank for the right words. Yui's fluency in English, while advanced by any metric, still lagged behind the lightning field of his mind. He refused to make a mistake or be misunderstood when he spoke, so sentences issued from his mouth with impeccable care, the delivery painstakingly slow.

"No, I don't think that is it," Yui replied. A series of lewd hypotheses cycled rapidly through Yui's brain. When at last he spoke, he looked at Svec, not Bear: "Commander, perhaps you did not remember to brush your teeth before you kissed your little Bear good night?"

"*Nyet.*" Svec shook his head. "Am thoughtful lover. Is known across globe."

Svec sipped kvas from a plastic pouch and waited patiently as the printer issued coil after coil. He looked to Bear like a coffee shop folk singer, with his thinning gray hair plaited in a French braid that floated off his neck.

"Not now, boys," Bear said, his voice wilting. He was in no mood for the locker room antics that Yui spewed so automatically it seemed a reflex, and that Svec, as commander, did nothing but indulge. Svec derived no pleasure from policing grown men, and so saw no benefit to censuring Yui, who was not an astronaut. This trip on the ISS was an expensive research vacation for the crude savant, one he had paid forty million dollars and trained for six months to attend.

An almost perfectly circular break in the white clouds opened over the coast of New England. Bear spotted the battered, imbecile forehead of Maine and, a click below, the palsied arm of Massachusetts.

"You guys ever been to Boston?" Bear asked.

"Ah, yes, Boston," Svec said, a memory returning suddenly. "I go once. Very pretty city. Spoke at conference at Garvard. Big lobsters, big as my arm. Ate three for dinner. Met beautiful woman. She own dry-cleaning business. She and I had fun for night. All pubs have televisions. This I did not like."

"Harvard is in Cambridge, not Boston."

"True," Svec said.

"Cambridge isn't so bad. The way the necrotic tissue surrounding a tumor is not as bad as the tumor."

"Very interesting," Svec said. "The sunshine American astronaut has dark spot after all?"

He did. If there was a nucleus for all of Bear's pain as an adult, it was in Boston. His older sister had moved there after college, gotten married, had two daughters, then drank herself into near psychosis after her younger daughter died. Once their mother died, this same elder sister moved their disabled younger sister from their childhood ranch house in San Diego to a group home nearby in Boston, ostensibly so she could visit more easily. Bear had disagreed with this move, and he doubted very much that his older sister ever made good on her intention to visit their younger sister, but he could not bring himself to confront her. They'd been through too much already. It was better to swallow his opinions and anxieties and quietly foot the bill for it all.

"It's too cold there," Bear said.

Svec sneered. "You cannot say to native Russian."

Yui said, "Boston is the home city of my favorite writer and illustrator. Val Corwin."

"Never heard of him," Bear said.

"Here." Yui thrust his book into Bear's hands. It was a galley copy, bound in a plain white cover free of ornamentation. Yui's assistant had secured an advance copy just before the launch. The type was in Japanese, but Yui explained that it had been translated from the original English edition. "I cannot believe you do not know who he is. He is one of the most popular in Japan."

Bear and Svec looked at the pictures. A pregnant woman watched in horror as the lower half of her body liquefied. Each panel moved closer to her agony as her body and that of her fetus became a dangling tendril of mucus. It was, Bear thought, unnecessarily grotesque.

"Ha-ha," Svec laughed. "This comic book? For children? Can't be. Picture very—how do we say? Corrupt and bizarre?"

"No, definitely not for children," Yui said.

"Well, I'm heading back to the CDRA. I'll print this missing part later, I guess. Hopefully we will all be feeling a lot better soon."

"Have not been feeling bad, comrade." Russians were loath to complain, as Roscosmos docked them pay for ingratitude. So maybe he was lying. It couldn't be Bear alone who was feeling off. Bear looked to Yui for the truth.

"How about you, friendo? You been experiencing any headaches lately?"

"I feel . . ." Yui thought a long time. "Extraordinary. Ten years younger. We are weightless, friendos. Nothing can keep us down. Now I will go and play with the two-headed mouse."

"Don't be crass. Please," Bear said. Without some reining in, Yui could quickly become a hazard on the station. If Svec wouldn't take this duty seriously as commander and nip his behavior in the bud, Bear was not afraid to step up and be the adult.

"I promise that I am not joking, Bear-u."

"Yes. True," Svec said. "Mutation. Born this morning. Your NASA very excited. You don't know?"

"I've been busy," Bear said.

"Perhaps you should work a little less, friendo," Yui said, bowing to him. "You would see more."

Through the porthole Bear saw clouds swirling over North America, their long white skeins pointing like the thin spectral fingers of a ghost casting spells.

HISTORICALLY, LAST DAY was celebrated with a community pyre. It is legend that in Egypt stray dogs were corralled for the sacrifice, and in parts of southeastern Europe, a stillborn baby was included in the pyre to prevent dark spirits from repopulating the newly evacuated earth. On top of these embers townsfolk would toss their most beloved article of clothing, a perfectly useful, well-conditioned saddle, a warm, clean quilt. The offering was not a bargain to forestall death but rather a tiptoe-ing into the greater sacrifice possibly awaiting, to prepare the living for the coming of the end.

Now, for most Americans, throwing some hot dogs on the grill was considered an adequate homage to the pyres of antiquity, and piñatas stood in for live animal sacrifice. What was once a communal cele-bration, Last Day became more personal and private, confined to one's own backyard. But some cities were making a return to large public ob-servances, such as the Brooklyn Do or Dye. On May 27 volunteers built a series of stations throughout Prospect Park in which New Yorkers could screenprint a T-shirt with a confession to be worn all day on May 28:

I pray that my good friends fail
Hey, Bill: EAT SHIT AND DIE
The condom broke
He hits me
I told my best friend I had an abortion to get her sympathy
It doesn't get better
Will you please hug me please

A macabre swap meet was held annually at the Drake Hotel in Chicago, where people brought a cherished object—"the one thing you would take to the grave," the invitation commanded—and left it on a table for a perfect stranger to claim. Someone's childhood teddy bear might be traded randomly and anonymously for another's illicit love letter. The wait list to be included in this somber gala event was over two years long, and the price of admission was five hundred dollars and a quart of blood donated at a designated blood bank one week prior to the event.

Minneapolis had an annual Zombie Parade, a ritual adhering to the discomfiting fiction that, somehow, some people would survive the end of the world (never a tenet in any culture's interpretation of the day) and that those survivors, for inexplicable reasons, would be transmogrified into movie monsters. The parade ended with a twelve-hour dance-off-cum-fundraiser for the homeless, which had raised over three million dollars to date.

In Boston, a city subject to wild vicissitudes of weather well into the month of May, a city where joy not earned by a measure of pain was not to be trusted, there existed a singular Last Day celebration. Each year for more or less twenty-four hours, from whatever time they felt like opening on May 27 to whatever time they closed on May 28, the staff at Redemption Tattoo inked free of charge anyone willing to wait in line. The catch was that you could not choose your tattoo. You were at another man's mercy, and the men who worked at Redemption were notorious drunkards even on non-holidays.

Kurt, Tom, Jake, and Ringo. That was the Redemption crew. Kurt was the owner of Redemption. He was in his forties, short and muscular with a growing beer belly, often mistaken as languid, even serene, until he rolled up his shirtsleeves and revealed the black and gray ghosts screaming in violent despair down his arms. He had made a living saying yes to whatever asinine idea his customers proposed, tailoring his at times ingenious craft to meet their vulgar needs. He created this Last Day tradition simply so that for twenty-four hours he got to do whatever he wanted at work.

"Is it hopeless?"

The customer who first sat in Kurt's chair had a jolly face. His hair was strawberry blond and curly, his eyes a bright, easy blue. "I started it this morning," he said, sipping beer from a red plastic cup. "But, fuck, man, I can't finish it."

Kurt probed the man's bloody sternum with his gloved hand. "You do time, man?"

"Old Colony Correctional. You?"

"South Middlesex. That's where you learned to tattoo?" Kurt asked him.

"Yeah. And I give myself a new one every year on Last Day since I got out. But this time, I don't know, this time it *hurts*. I couldn't finish."

"What's it supposed to be?" There was a mess of sloppy tattoos on the man's chest. Celtic knots, mostly.

"It's the letters *CEC*. For *Cecilia*."

Kurt took the man's plastic cup and handed it to Ringo. "Refill this, man, will ya?" He looked at the brick wall and was quiet. Ringo passed the fresh beer back to Kurt, who handed it to the man.

"Okay," he said. "I'm not fixing what you've done and I'm not finishing it, either. Instead I want to do a hanged man whose foot is just barely touching the petal of a huge fucking flower. A daisy, but a nuclear mutation of a daisy. Enormous. Bigger than the man. Meaning that the petals are firm enough to stand on, to support some but not all of the hanged man's weight."

"Where you going to put it?"

"Your left arm. The hanged man takes up the whole outer biceps. The spot where the dangling foot makes contact with the petal will be here, inside your elbow. The daisy or whatever will go down the underside of your forearm."

The man's face softened. He had never, in his entire life, felt so seen. He drained the beer and crushed the empty cup in his fist. "Okay," he finally said. His eyes welled up in a slippery, wobbling membrane he would not allow to break.

On the morning of May 27 the line outside Redemption stretched a mile down Commonwealth Avenue. The next person to appear before Kurt was a woman in an artfully ripped-up T-shirt, attended by a coterie of less attractive girlfriends. A woman, Kurt could tell just by looking at her, who vacationed in the realm of darkness but had never actually lived there.

Kurt bent over his notebook so that she couldn't see what he was drawing. "Okay, check this out." He handed her his notebook, then sat back and sipped his beer.

She and her attendants peered at the drawing.

"What is it?"

"Are those twigs?"

"It just looks like a bunch of lines."

"I don't get it," the pretty woman finally declared.

"It spells *wrong number*. I'll do it vertically down your spine. Gotta warn you—people say the spine hurts a lot. It's my personal experience that that's horseshit. It all fuckin' hurts. But this is what people, mostly girls, tell me. So I'm telling you. You've been warned."

"Can you do it around my ankle instead?"

"No."

"Can you do it in a prettier font?"

"If you make one more demand, you have to get out of my studio," Kurt said, his tone so gentle it sounded like a concession. He took another slug of his beer. He'd been nursing this cup slowly for the last hour.

It was warm and delicious. A line of bubbles collected on his upper lip and he made no move to wipe them off.

"I don't know . . . ," the lady whined. She was not a regular, no one Kurt recognized anyway. Many first-timers like her waited in line on Last Day, then chickened out at the last minute.

"You can go back to the end of the line, try again with another artist," he said.

"Nope," Jake shouted over the din of the crowd. "She'll never get another chance." He was delighted by this prospect. Jake had red hair and small, beady eyes that also appeared red. Exclusivity jazzed the hell out of him.

The woman bit her lip. She squinted, closed her eyes, took a deep breath, paused, then took another. It was a pantomime, this deliberation; she was riding a three-mimosa buzz and not in the mood to give much thought to anything today.

"Okay," she exhaled. "I'll do it!"

Her gaggle of friends woo-hooed and high-fived. They'd brought with them a shopping bag full of holiday-themed party favors and started handing out strands of purple and gold beads, fake engagement rings, and novelty condoms to all the people in line behind them.

She was lucky she hadn't gotten stuck with Jake. By that point in the morning he was so swirly, woozy, rope-a-dope drunk that every single tattoo he gave for the rest of the day and night was the single word: RE-DEMPTION.

"It's an exercise in formalism, eh, man?" said a hipster with a goatee and a Mao Zedong T-shirt.

"Shut your whore mouth," Jake drooled as he needled REDEMP-TION in sloppy cursive across the man's left calf.

It was like this every year, and yet people still waited for their turn. They waited for hours in all kinds of weather, happy to sign the waiver releasing all rights to any expanse of skin claimed by the artist as his canvas. People brought beach chairs and blankets and picnic baskets to the line. Outside the studio, strangers were sharing sandwiches and beers. This year it was seventy-nine degrees out, the smog-blue sky covered in a gauzy heat. Magnolia, forsythia, and cherry blossoms were past bloom, carpeting the sidewalk with a confetti of browning petals.

"Nothing like last year," someone said far down the line, slurping the dregs of her iced coffee.

"Our basement flooded," a fellow line-waiter chimed in. "And our insurance had lapsed. We got black mold. I'm still paying for that storm."

"What a nightmare that storm was," another man said, spitting brown tobacco juice into an empty seltzer can.

"You kids don't even know. Before you were even born we had the Last Day nor'easter. The bums in Public Works were all shitfaced. Good for nothing. I had to drive around with a chainsaw to break up the fallen trees blocking the roads."

"Yeah, 1985. I remember. We lost power for two friggin' weeks."

"Remember the year that asshole set off fireworks inside North Station?"

"To be honest, I thought that was kind of awesome."

"A lady got burned. Like, bad. Her ear was maimed for life."

"It's just an ear. It could be worse."

Back at Redemption, Tom was inking those exact words, *it could be worse*, onto a customer's rib cage. Tom was the looker of this quartet. The women always gravitated toward him. The other guys joked that Tom laced the ink with aphrodisiacs, though it was the much simpler combination of good looks, confidence, and implicit willingness. He had large brown eyes and a handsome face you knew without any picture of proof was the mirror image of a very pretty mother. He kept his dark hair combed back in a neat pompadour and wore T-shirts and jeans that showed off his muscular body without appearing to try too hard. When dressed in long sleeves and a tie, Tom could pass for a respectable family man with a white-collar job, but in reality it was a miracle that he had maintained employment at Redemption for as long as he had. Color was not Tom's strong suit—Kurt was the master of color—but his black and gray shading was impeccable, the best in New England.

Tom had started celebrating the night before and had woken up that morning already feeling tired. He wanted to call it quits, but one look of disappointment from Kurt would set off a slew of latent emotions he did not have time to drink away today. So he'd decided to forgo his typical Gothic images, and taking a page from drunk Jake's playbook, he began tattooing simple words. Lettering was easy—all you had to worry about was proportion. It was like taking a break without taking a break, if only the man on his table now would stop squirming. The man was probably in his late thirties but had the scrawny build of a twelve-year-old who happened to hit the gym and hit it hard. His rib cage was delicate and narrow, like the hull of a toy canoe. The man mentioned that he was a lawyer. Tom pulled the gun away.

"You signed the waiver, right? It's airtight. You can't sue me later."

"It is absolutely not airtight but, no, I'm not going to sue you. Jesus."

"I have nothing," Tom replied. "I live in the back room of my friends' apartment. We call it a room but it's actually a porch. Beautiful this time of year but fucking freezing in the winter, and you know what? I will stay there until those guys kick me out, because I spend all my money as soon as I make it on bars and restaurants and grass and girls. Sometimes coke, but mostly I let people buy coke for me, which is easy, because cokeheads never want to get high alone. I own nothing and have zero dollars in savings. If I ever get sick, with, like, cancer or something, I will invite that shit to multiply all it wants because I will never, ever be able to afford treatment. See these boots?" Tom lifted his foot up so that the man lying prone and shirtless in his chair could see it. "These boots were three hundred dollars and I will wear them until they fall off my fuckin' feet. The boots I had before these ones I wore for eight years and not until I started feeling the pavement through the soles did I buy these replacements. If you sued me, these steel-toed bad boys would be the best thing you would get."

"The legal system doesn't work like that, asshole. And don't worry. I don't want your boots."

"I don't want the headache of showing up at court, either. I'd rather be flogged than sit around and wait. Hit me in the face with a brick. Pry out my toenails. I'd take that any day over waiting for the judge to call me."

"Just finish my tattoo, all right? I got a party to go to later tonight."

"I know all about you lawyers," Tom said.

"You're right, okay? Lawyers are bastards. I'm a bastard. She fucking left me because I was a coldhearted bastard. . . ."

RINGO WAS BOTH the youngest and the newest artist at Redemption. His real name was Patrick. The other guys had christened him Ringo as a joke, and after a while it stuck. Ringo was a good sport about things, and he had a long, beak-like nose, so the name seemed to suit him. He was twenty-three and wide-eyed, a tall skinny boy whose specialty was flowers. Ringo had been raised by his widowed grandmother, a gardener who'd taught him the name of everything green that grew. As a young boy he liked to draw pictures of flowers, filled whole notebooks with them; then, with a twist of pride and shame, he hid the notebooks under his pillow, knowing that his grandmother made his bed every morning after he left for school. The old woman would look at his drawings, then place the notebook in the same position as she'd found it under the pillow, never saying a word.

Ringo's first customer on Last Day was a man with broken yellow teeth who asked for a derringer pointing down his calf. Ringo gave him a lilac cluster shaped like a gun. This man was followed by a college kid who asked for Jesus on his back. Ringo gave him a skull blooming daisies out of the eye sockets. One lady asked for the dates of her daughter's birth and death inscribed inside a heart. The kid was not even three years old when she died. Ringo thought long and hard about that one. He gave her a piñata burro exploding with every kind of flower he could fit on her shoulder.

Kurt had taken a break to check his text messages, coming to terms with yet another promise he had made in a drunken state that he was now regretting. Staring at his phone, he overheard the young mother crying softly to Ringo, who made an effort to touch her body with care, even as he made permanent scars in her skin.

"You are too good for this world," Kurt said, shaking his head.

"Who is?" Ringo asked. He had just been thinking the opposite— that he had such an easy life and he'd done nothing to deserve it, while other people, like the grieving mother in his chair, had to live with a reality that was unbearable. It felt cruel and unfair, even if such things were beyond fairness. "Not me," Ringo said, dabbing at the red trickle bleeding from the rose he'd just finished.

"We all are," Kurt said, already looking exhausted.

B y popular vote, the local classical station was piped into the weight room at the YMCA. That day the entire fifteen hours of Wagner's *Ring* cycle was being broadcast without interruption in honor of the holiday. At that point in the morning, mortals and gods were still wrestling for control, as if they had a chance.

"Rosette, do you ever feel like your shoes might hurt just as much as your feet do?"

"My shoes take me where I need to go," Rosette answered, "and that's all they need to do."

Rosette was watching with great admiration her own body as she did squats in front of the giant mirror. Her charge, Mr. Cox, sat on the floor snoozing against a stack of yoga blankets. He was sixty-three, physically healthy enough to live another twenty active years, except for the plaque in his brain, gumming up the pathway of his thoughts, even simple thoughts like *Red means stop, Don't drink the Windex, My name is George Dean Cox.* For twenty bucks an hour under the table, Rosette picked him up at Morning Pines and took him with her to do whatever she wanted to do that day. "A program of enrichment," she billed it to his adult daughters, who were happy to pay any price not to worry about him.

"How do you know when you, specifically, are doing what your God wants you to do? I mean, anything can be an augury of anything. Like, a leaf on the sidewalk shiny side down could mean yes as well as no, depending on your interpretation."

"No leaves, Karen baby. God trying to tell you to follow Him and you looking at the ground."

"Yeah but follow *where*?"

"If what you want is so hard to get, if you have to stop all the time and red lights are everywhere, and no no no is all you hear, and you still do it, and then you feel terrible after, that was because you not on God's path. If God is making a way for you, it's always easy."

"But bad things are so easy."

"Because sometimes what we think meant evil for us meant good for God's plan. Sometimes God uses us to make pain because then that can make others do good. Jesus would never have died if Judas didn't betray him."

"Oh." It hadn't occurred to Karen, in all her studies, that she could use her powers for evil. Or that she ought to. She picked a corner off a pockmarked old yoga block. Rolling the purple foam between her fingers, she heard a twitter. *Do it.* Karen plopped the bit of foam into her mouth and swallowed it.

"Mr. Cox!" Rosette slapped her hands together, trying to wake the old man. He had slid off the pile of blankets and was lying awkwardly on the floor. "Help me get him up, Karen. Now. Before he gets stuck like this."

"I want some candy. Can I borrow some money for the vending machine?"

"No. You can eat lunch when it is lunchtime."

"I didn't bring a lunch," Karen said. A lie. She'd eaten both of her frozen pizzas in the first hour of her shift.

"I always bring extra for you, my friend," Rosette said. She had made fried pork chops, a fact she kept to herself for now, or the girl would be begging like a stray dog until it was time to eat.

Karen both was and was not a girl, Rosette felt. Bulk collected around her hips like a mother of ten, but her voice fluttered and shrieked like a toddler's. Her breasts were enormous and scored by the lines of an ill-fitting bra. Her blond hair curled in girlish ringlets and her big blue eyes protruded with the never-ending alacrity of a curious, slightly stunned child. Rosette didn't know Karen's whole story, but she could tell the girl had been raped at least once, probably more. Karen bore the unmistakable stain of sexual trauma. There was the way she walked, a broken, yelping gait, not quite mannish but definitely not feminine. And she was obviously protecting herself from fleshly danger through many extra pounds of fat. That much was obvious. Rosette didn't need to ask, nor did she want to. The fountain of Karen's crazy was hard to shut off once it started, she'd learned regretfully after giving Karen her phone number.

All Rosette knew for sure was that Karen had no family, no one to teach her right from wrong. Such a pity, though unsurprising in this godforsaken country. Rosette had been in the U.S. for twenty years, long enough to know it was a beautiful land tilled for doom. Her island in the Azores had its problems, yes, but was superior to her new home in most ways. Though of course superiority did not guarantee admittance to the afterlife. You had to work because it was good to work, to sacrifice and be glad about it. In time Rosette knew she could make Karen understand. As insufferable as the girl could be, she had a good heart, and Rosette wanted to prepare her for the possibility of deliverance. Why else had God put this annoying woman into her life?

First Karen would need to lose weight. She was big as a hippo. It would be rude to arrive in Paradise with all that fat, like showing up as a guest in someone's house carrying more luggage than could fit in your room. Also, Karen's mind jumped around like a grasshopper. She needed the focus of the one true God. More than once Rosette had had to reprimand Karen for reading YMCA members' palms. "The Devil's sideshow!" Rosette had screamed, and had given a reproving tug, short but sharp, on Karen's bouncy ponytail. But even these palm readings she did with good intentions, Rosette had to admit. Karen just wanted to be liked, and she was willing to learn, especially when Rosette offered to feed her.

Rosette was no angel, she was the first to admit. But all had been forgiven when she'd turned her life over to the Jehovah's Witnesses. The main reason Rosette had joined was because she liked the idea that the unfaithful would be destroyed in a violent cosmic comeuppance, as this surely included her ex-husband, the most unfaithful human being to walk this rotting earth.

For a time she'd wondered if she had brought this misery on herself, if her ex-husband had been sent by God to punish her for the wanton-ness of her youth. But this theory didn't hold up to scrutiny. All Rosette's childhood friends had been rapacious sluts — it was something about the plaid jumpers of their Catholic school, so ugly and itchy. It wasn't enough to take them off after a long day; you wanted to rip such a skirt off your body in a violent passion and throw it in the face of a man pant-ing with lust. And all of these Catholic school friends were in blessedly boring marriages now.

When she was only thirteen, Rosette had seduced a seventeen-year-old neighbor, a boy who later flung himself off a fishing boat in a storm when he learned that Rosette had also taken his cousin as her lover. There were plenty of other boys to follow. São Miguel had become too small for her by the age of twenty. She decided to hunt for bigger game in the States. Once she had saved enough money for airfare and tuition, she'd enrolled in a nurse's aide program in Boston, where there were enough other Azoreans to ensure that she could still find her native food and music and laughter. She told her friends and family she would come back as a millionaire's wife.

She knew her life was unfolding according to plan when she met Joey Mazzone in the Italian restaurant he claimed to own. He bought her gold necklaces, silver bracelets, and emerald earrings. He gave her the keys to his car and his golden American Express and said, "Don't come home, sweetheart, until you've spent at least a grand."

After they'd exchanged vows at City Hall, she learned that Joey was in staggering debt to multiple credit card accounts. And he was the manager, not the owner, of Enoteca. He didn't own anything, in fact, not even his car, a Lincoln Continental that belonged to his mother, who let him drive it whenever he wanted as she had become legally blind.

They'd been married two years when, one miserable Saturday night, Joey was "out" again, and Rosette, quaking with rage at her kitchen table, couldn't stop imagining a violent collision. And while Joey was out riding the Vespa he had bought with Rosette's paycheck, impressing some harlot—which harlot Rosette no longer cared, there were too many to count—he hit a pothole and their two bodies went flying. Joey smashed into the overarching beam of a streetlamp, snapping his neck instantly. The harlot skidded across the pavement, crushed and skinned like a rabbit.

Rosette believed she had made this happen with her mind. Guilt and pride swirled in a sour mixture in her mouth. If Rosette had given it a little more thought, she would have tempered the violence. Have Joey choke to death in his sleep, or develop spontaneous nut allergies and die of anaphylaxis. Yes, a good old-fashioned poisoning by natural causes, that would have been a peaceful end to him and his passions. But in her grief and rage that night, she'd had no control over her imagination.

As a widow, Rosette was angrier than ever. She'd remained sitting at her kitchen table for days after the funeral, her thick black hair growing into a dark shroud around her face, her eyes swollen with powerlessness and mania. All day she nursed a coffee mug full of rum, occasionally, in the middle of her sobs, stopping to blow on the rim of her cup, as if there were really hot coffee in there that needed cooling. She didn't want God to see her carrying on. She'd feared Him all her life, even when she'd blocked Him out.

So it seemed like a message from the Divine when two teenage boys in short-sleeve shirts and skinny black ties knocked on her door, bearing the good news.

"He float, he float, he float. This woman, that woman. But he always float back to me. I ask the Lord let me never ask him where he goes. And one day I did. Joey say it was because he was Italian. It was his nature, his God-given duty, to please as many women as he could. But it was my fault he ran off with harlots," Rosette wept. She catalogued her flaws for the two boys—big feet, sagging breasts, excessive pride, and a very promiscuous past. "My mother tell me when I was a little girl, 'Men love a wild woman for fun, but they only marry a boring one.' I wanted to get married. So I pretended to be boring. Now look at me!"

Her head collapsed onto the table and she sobbed into a pool of rum spilled from her overturned mug. One boy got up and found a rag to wipe it up with; the other began sorting through her mail, stacking neatly all her unread newspapers and magazines, throwing out the coupon circulars that were now out-of-date. They did her dishes and made her some toast. After she had nibbled a little of the crust, she said, "So, what do I do now?"

The two young men were immigrants like Rosette. Their parents had brought them from Haiti to give them a better life in the States, even as they sought to protect them from so much of that new life. As Jehovahs they were not allowed to go to college, making this door-to-door ministry an important outlet for their youthful energy and ingenuity. They made sweet attempts to connect their ultimate message to Rosette's story of betrayal and grief. It was Satan's rule on Earth, they explained. It really wasn't anybody's fault. Lots of innocent people and nearly all politicians were under Satan's spell and couldn't help it. They told her about the End of Days, which she welcomed. The Catholics of her childhood had preached that all would be one in heaven. Hell no, Rosette thought now. Heaven on Earth, as the Jehovahs promised, was much more selective. It was a place that definitely excluded her dead husband, meaning she would never have to see that man's bloated, stubbly face again. All that was required was her belief.

Karen had shown some interest in Rosette's church, but to her it was more like a cabinet of wonders. She was fascinated by their arcana, their chosen symbols and songs. She'd read that the Jehovah's Witnesses were not allowed to participate in any war, that they hated flags and were terrified of blood. Even if Rosette was dying, she was not allowed to accept a transfusion.

"What if you were unconscious and the doctor went ahead and gave you a transfusion anyway, then what?" Karen asked.

"Your mind jump on all the wrong things," Rosette responded.

Karen's head was resting on Rosette's thigh. Rosette pulled one of her blond curls straight, then released it. Karen had traded Rosette a couple of her tranquilizers for one of Mr. Cox's painkillers. The three of them lay beneath the lifeguard's chair in a listless calm, watching diamonds of sunlight rupture the surface of the pool.

TERRENCE HAD CALLED the night before to say that someone had dropped out of the Habitat for Humanity Club's camping trip and there was an open spot. Did Sarah want to come? Sarah had no gear, but Terrence assured her he had plenty for the two of them. Sarah allowed an awkward pause to speak for her.

"B-besides," Terrence stuttered, "these guys know how to build houses. They can make a shelter out of wet leaves and a shoelace. If there's anyone you want to be with at the end of the world, it's the Habitat for Humanity Club."

She said she'd let him know after her morning run.

"Meet us at the train depot. We have a charter bus. Leaves at 11 A.M."

Sarah double-knotted her sneakers and hit the road. Even Terrence was so goddamn glib about the world ending. She was furious at him. He of all people should know better: this whole stupid holiday was nothing more than a political distraction from the real destruction and cruelty happening worldwide; everyone was celebrating an imaginary apocalypse while schools filled with children were bombed by dictators and pipelines leaked millions of tons of crude oil into the sea. It was so obvious it was stupid, and Sarah hated herself for being sucked into the myth, for being so afraid.

She ran until her legs seemed to disappear. She stopped finally at the Edgewater causeway to catch her breath, a good eight miles from home, not remembering the preceding hour of her life. Two egrets stood on either side of the channel, their legs so lissome and still as to appear invisible at that distance, making their round white rumps seem to levitate above the marsh. The water was mute and silver, flowing eastward into the sea. Sarah listened to the wind, her soft panting breath, and the sound of the water. One of the egrets took three steps on its spindly legs, then stopped, plunged its nose into the tall grass, nibbled on something brackish and small, then stood erect and still once more. The other egret did not move at all.

"I know the world is shit, but I still don't want to lose it," she said, gazing now at the birds. She felt tears welling up. A hollowness in her chest rose to her throat and pushed hard on the walls of her soul. The membrane between her mind and the atmosphere was burning away. She felt like she was being lifted out of her sneakers, off the pavement, about to be hurtled into the endless sky.

This is it, she thought, *this is what the end is.*

Then the feeling passed, her feet were on the ground, it was still morning. She began to run again, hitting a 7:30 mile on the way home, a personal best.

Her parents were in the kitchen still, twirling globs of dough into pizza crusts for their party. Sarah breezed past them, took the quickest shower of her life, then stuffed a backpack with clothes, her journal, and a sleeping bag.

"Where are you going?" her mother asked her. She was wearing a frilly pink-and-red apron that Sarah's father had bought as a joke for Valentine's Day. They'd been married nineteen years and were the two happiest people she had ever met in her life.

"I'm going camping," Sarah answered.

"Where? With whom?" Her father taught in the physics department at the college, on the floor above her mom.

"Don't say 'whom,' Ari. You sound like a pedant."

"Which friends, Saralita?"

"The Habitat for Humanity Club."

"Oh, good. You'll be in good hands."

"Do you need any money?"

"No," Sarah answered. "I mean, yes."

Her parents exchanged looks. Her dad wiped his hands on his wife's apron and looked around the kitchen for his wallet. Sarah inspected the toppings. Eggplant and mango.

"Purple and gold," her mother explained. Sarah's pulse fluttered in a bitter, stringy rhythm. "You've got to try this marinated chicken. We used pineapple juice! Your dad and I are geniuses. We're going to quit academia and sell this stuff full-time at farmers' markets. You won't mind going to a state college, right, honey?"

"Very funny, Mom. I'm in a hurry. I've got a bus to catch."

"Here you go, kiddo." Her dad handed her two damp twenty-dollar bills. "We'll save you a couple slices for when you get back, okay?"

"I'm not eating meat, remember?"

"That's right," her mother said. "Oh, that's too bad. These are going to be so good."

"We can just make one without chicken," her dad suggested.

"Of course! That's what we'll do. Sorry, I'm frazzled. You know how I get on the holiday."

"You guys, I really have to go."

Did she kiss them goodbye? she would wonder later. Did they say they loved her? It was an utterance so common in their happy house that the sounds of those words had lost all resonance over the years. It had become a reflex of the mouth, a hum as constant and forgettable as the refrigerator's motor, audible but seldom heard.

ANOTHER OF BEAR'S directives was to maintain a social media presence for the ISS, curating images and short videos that people on Earth would find interesting, in the hope that it would stoke an electorate with a dispiriting apathy toward science to vote for more government-funded space projects. This doubled as an excuse for Bear to hang out in the Cupola, as it provided the best optics, where he liked to take what he'd come to think of as a nice cool drink of Earth.

Just looking at her made Bear's mouth water, as though at a cellular level his body was aware of the artificial environment he was in, where the only water existed in plastic sacks. He attached his camera to the end of a selfie stick and positioned himself so that a glimpse of Earth was behind him in the shot. He was recording a laymen's guide to the weather research NASA was conducting at the moment, but his spiel, which he'd written out beforehand on index cards, kept losing focus when he tried to go off script. He could see in the camera's screen that they were flying over Africa now. The Nile River appeared as a crack in a thin shard of clay.

"Look," Bear heard someone say, and he turned his head away from the camera and past his feet where he saw Yui floating toward him, his hands cupped against his chest.

"They are so cute. Too cute. I cannot believe how cute," Yui said. As he got closer he showed Bear what he was holding so delicately in his hands. It was the infamous newborn mouse pup, about the size of a cashew nut, scrawny and gray with one white belly, four tiny paws, and two heads curled into each other as though taking refuge.

"No way," Bear said. He quickly hit "Pause" on the recording and swatted at Yui like an errant child. "Get that thing back to the lab before it—"

"Too late."

A string of gold liquid issued from the mouse pair and re-formed into a ball. Yui let go of the mouse, whose legs paddled against the air as its ball of urine floated aimlessly away from its body.

"Awww, even their urine is so cute," Yui said. He cupped his hands around the wriggly animal again and gave a gentle kiss to each of its heads. Bear wrapped his hand in his T-shirt to catch the floating globule of piss before it hit the sides of the ship.

"You absolutely cannot do this, Yui."

"I may not, but I can. A surprise for you. To cheer you up. You looked so lonely this morning. You are very welcome, friendo," Yui said.

Yui was a man who had never been asked to grow up. He and his twin brother, Tadeshi, were born into oceans of family money, wealth so vast and deep and regenerative it strained the imagination to picture a future when it would be depleted. Their father had inherited a fortune from his own father, a Tokyo real estate mogul, and increased this fortune exponentially by starting what became the largest, most successful video game company in the world. Their mother was a child model-actress who had married their father at nineteen and committed suicide eight years later. Yui and his brother did not mourn her for very long; they were raised by a staff of doting, indulgent nannies who insulated the twins from every blunt strike the world might fling in their direction. Their father was distant and impossible to impress, and their mother, while alive, had been a very pretty ghost, striking a vision in the hallways as she glided in and out of rooms in her bright silk dresses that, lacking the creativity to do anything else, she changed several times a day. A creature of alien and alienating beauty, she was less like a parent than a tropical bird whose clipped wings prevented her from going anywhere beyond their lavish compound in Roppongi.

Yui began sketching ideas for his company's newest virtual reality game, a strangulating dreamscape of outer space in which the first-person player-protagonist is confronted by the myriad buttons, dials, and instruments of a space station without any knowledge of what function each instrument performs. He was populating the game with monsters, real and unreal: vanishing air pressure, missiles from warring nations, mendacious aliens, synthesizing the horror of banality—*I can't breathe! I'm trapped!*—with the elaborate terrors of the mind. It was to be his magnum opus.

And as he drew and dreamed on this thesis now, his mother stole out of his unconscious for the first time in years, appearing on his tablet as a sketch of a bird of paradise flitting improbably across the black velvet void of space.

Yui had awakened to the alarm at 6 A.M. Greenwich Mean Time along with his other two crewmates, then retreated back to his sleeping pod to masturbate, reread his favorite graphic novel, and nap. Napping was an essential step in his creative process. He believed it re-created the bleary color splash between sleep and consciousness that fueled his imagination. As he hammered away at his game now, another vision emerged—that one day he and his brother would open the first brothel in space. He smiled to himself, already proud. Yui was the idea man; Tadeshi made things happen. Because of this, there was perfect harmony in the world.

Yui closed his eyes and swallowed three times, a fraternal ritual encoded in childhood for sending thoughts back and forth between the twins without speaking. It worked at least half the time. Yui would call his brother later to ask him if he'd received the transmission. He hurried to scribble down the last few notes about the game before he forgot them: the protagonist of the game would have to decide whether or not to follow this bird of paradise, to determine as one of his many possible obstacles if she was real or not, trustworthy or not, as the player swam in his unwieldy spacesuit between the unblinking stars in search of help.

Along with his work on the VR game, Yui was supposed to be aiding the other astronauts with their ongoing scientific experiments and representing the nation of Japan in the spirit of cooperation and brotherly love. So far he had used his time perfecting the art of peeing upside down.

"Not so perfect," Bear pointed out as he flew out of the bathroom with a wad of paper towels and slammed them into the trash receptacle. Yui did manage to take many of his duties on this mission seriously, but cleaning up after himself as diligently as was required in these cramped quarters was not one of them.

"To be fair, he's probably not used to cleaning up after himself," Bear said to Svec, after reporting the mouse incident to him. Much had been written about Yui and Tadeshi, the CEO counterpart of their video-gaming dynasty. In his attempt to be more empathetic to his annoying crewmate, Bear had taken the time to read a ridiculous, panegyric eight-thousand-word *New Yorker* profile of him that only succeeded in deepening the mystery. Both Yui and his twin were married to women, both fathers now, yet the two brothers maintained a shared apartment separate from their wives, and this flat, small even by Tokyo standards, had only one bedroom. The article painted them as post-modern Castor and Pollux. *Strange ducks indeed*, Bear thought.

He had to be politic, to convince Svec of the severity of the situation without seeming to be culturally insensitive. The problem, he argued with Svec, was not that Yui was careless or willfully destructive, but that he simply didn't see the messes he left behind, let alone the ramifications for the station, because living with servants had meant that such messes, for all intents and purposes, had erased themselves from his vision.

"I'm trying to think of it as a kind of handicap, really," Bear said.

He and Svec had both ended up in the American lab at the same time, a rare occurrence on this ship where daily work was carried out in the seclusion of each national's module. Yui, they assumed, was still in the Kibo laboratory, drawing in staggering detail portraits of the monotony that surrounded them—the white tunnels they'd come to think of as rooms, the arrows and instructions in various languages printed everywhere like cheerless, obsessive graffiti.

Bear pricked his finger with a lancet and watched the blood bubble onto his skin. He flicked it gently, allowing the orb to float like a tiny red gem in the air before catching it on the plastic slide he inserted into the cholesterol meter. "Developmental delays as a symptom of ultra-wealth."

"Bullshit," Svec answered. He scratched his thick beard, his fingers disappearing inside a wiry bib of black hair. This was his third six-month term on the ISS. He could not have gotten to this stage in his career if he had not known how to play well with others, but he brooked no tolerance for Bear's particularly American tendency to wrap piss-poor excuses in a ribbon of unflagging cheer.

"Serfs played tricks like this. They pretended to be stupid, to be lazy. But really this was their way to say 'fuck you' to masters."

"You might want to speak to him about it, Captain. Before it gets out of hand." Bear sealed his blood smear in a plastic container, reset the meter, and handed it to Svec.

"You can be his master if you want. I don't want."

"Perhaps a report to JAXA could do the work for us. Coming from his home space agency, a reproval might inspire more respect in him. Keep him in line. "

Svec lanced his own finger and squeezed blood to the surface. His face creased in what might have been a smile. Bear could never decipher Svec's moods from his facial expressions. The smirk he saw now could just as easily be derision or affection. "He is only here for six more weeks."

"You will cry when I am gone," Yui said, floating noiselessly into the module. He waited while the two men squirmed in their mutual embarrassment. After a long silence, Yui bowed to them.

"This is the day that could be our last," he said when he lifted his head. "I give you my deepest forgiveness."

"You mean apologies."

"No, friendo. *Mou ii yo. Kin is shinade*. All is forgiven."

KAREN KNELT ON the floor and pulled the trigger on a bottle of glass cleaner. The liquid looked like fireworks smashing against the window. She had thrown up from Mr. Cox's painkillers, as she usually did, just a little. Rosette had, too. But now they were better. She watched the blasts of liquid start to run, their wild rays dripping into tentacles.

"There's no point in cleaning," Karen mumbled. She let the blue cleaner stream down the window in pale streaks and walked hunchbacked to the front desk.

"Hmmm," Rosette replied, simultaneously texting and peeling the black reptilian skin of an avocado.

Cleaning was the stupidest thing about life. First, with the pollen outside, she could clean and clean all day and the windows would still look dirty. The world was golden and hopeless out there. Second, Karen was not a good cleaner. She got demerits all the time at Heart House because her room was such a disaster. The staff said it was a fire hazard with all her library books and journals and newspapers stacked up everywhere, but the house was run by Lutherans, or used to be once upon a time, so there might have been a strain of puritanism in all the insistence on cleanliness.

"And third, it's Last Day. These are possibly the last moments on Earth. I mean, I don't really believe this year is the year. Plus there are so many other astral conflicts with today's position in the zodiac. It's a day for planting, not reaping, technically. But who even cares?"

Rosette shot her a stern look. She dragged a spoon across the soft green flesh of the avocado and fed it to Mr. Cox. "This attitude is poor. You need to be grateful. We gonna make a list. This will help."

Rosette gave the spoon to Mr. Cox to hold. He was very tall with broad stooped shoulders. His hair was thin and gray, pasted by sweat against his brown-spotted scalp. It was getting a little too long in the back. Rosette charged his daughters extra to bring him to a barber, then cut it herself and pocketed the cash. Mr. Cox stood up, clenched the spoon in his fist, and examined it. "Princeton," he said.

"That's right, Mr. Cox. Now sit down like a good boy."

"Princeton!" he said again, the veins on his forehead swelling blue.

Rosette waved her hand in his face as though shooing a mosquito, and Mr. Cox sat down. She rummaged through her purse and slapped a pad of paper down on the front desk. "The lady on TV say this is the key to happiness. They studied the brain. People who do this every day don't get depressed. Write down a list of everything you grateful for. I'll make one, too. You'll see. No matter what happens, you can't do nothing to change it. But you can face it all with a grateful heart."

"How many things should I list?" Karen asked.

"As many—" Rosette began, then thought better of it. "Five."

The two women bent over their papers and wrote their lists.

"So fun! Now let's exchange," Karen suggested. She took Rosette's paper and read:

Lord, I am so grateful to You for all that You have blessed me with,
but today most of all for—
Your kingdom, in Heaven and on Earth
Pastor Alfred
Freedom from lust

Not being born Italian
My mother's cozido

"Your handwriting is so straight and tall. Like you," Karen exclaimed. "Mine is so loopy."

"Ha-ha! Like you!" She read from Karen's list:

Things Karen (me) is grateful for:
Candy
Tigers
Kittens
Swimming
Rosette

"That's sweet of you, baby. I am grateful for you, too. Sometimes."

"Rose, do you think, when the end comes, that we will melt or explode or crumble or what? What does your new church think will happen to those of us who aren't saved?"

"I think every bad thing will happen all at once. Fires and floods, earthquakes and volcanoes, freezing nights and boiling days. But I am ready, so I don't worry about it no more."

"Yeah, me, too," Karen said. Her stomach twisted hard around the remaining objects she had swallowed but not thrown up that day. She knew in this case, as many times before, that more was not better. She called upon the voice of Nora in her head and Nora agreed. She looked at Rosette roughly wiping the avocado off Mr. Cox's face and knew that if she asked her counsel, Rosette would say the same thing: *No more.* But there was another voice, hungry and hoarse and whining like a baby. *One more. One more and you'll be done. Just one more.* Karen broke the eraser off Rosette's pencil and swallowed it. Again it burned and then she felt nothing at all.

THE CHARTER BUS grumbled in the parking lot of the Edgewater train station. Terrence stood outside it tapping on his phone. In her pocket Sarah felt her phone vibrating with his message.

U coming? We're waiting 4 u

Sarah hid behind the pillars that supported the depot platform. The ground beneath her feet began to rattle. In the distance she heard the train's approaching horn.

I can't. Sorry, she texted back. She watched as he received the message, slid his phone into his front jeans pocket, and knocked on the door of the bus. With a great gaseous sigh, the door opened and Terrence disappeared inside.

What was wrong with her? Why couldn't she just fall in love with Terrence and climb into a sleeping bag with him under the stars? That was romantic, normal, and probably fun. Sarah Burke would have killed for Terrence's attention. Sarah Burke had even tried to seduce him over spring break, but Terrence had refused. He was saving himself for love, for Sarah. And what was she doing? Obsessing over a strange man she'd met only once, a grandiose imaginary friend.

"Train to Boston. Train to Boston. Last Day, no fare. All aboard. Train to Boston," the conductor sang.

Maybe she didn't have to know the answer. Maybe she just had to show up and see what happened. That was the Last Day spirit, wasn't it? Sarah hopped onto the train just as it began to depart from the platform. It was already so full that she had to take a seat among a group of teenage boys, all of them wearing dirty white baseball caps. They were passing around a pint bottle of liquor wrapped in a brown paper bag. They laughed and jostled each other in a way Sarah found cute, sociologically speaking.

One of the boys noticed her watching them and offered her a sip from his bottle.

"No thank you," Sarah said.

"You're beautiful. You know that?" the boy slurred. He was a bit older than she was. His cheeks were rosy in a way that suggested skin disease. "Sweetheart," the boy said, leaning so close to Sarah she could smell the cheapness of the booze on his breath. "You gotta boyfriend?"

"I do." Sarah smiled. *Sort of.*

"Lucky man," the boy replied. "You tell him I said so."

He turned back to face his friends, who were covering their faces, laughing into their shirts, so ashamed for and of him.

"Don't laugh," the rosacea-faced guy told his buddies. "At least I take risks. That's what today is all about." He lit the wrong end of his cigarette, then flipped it around and burned his lips with the ember.

"Relax, dude. She's a seven."

"Not even. She's a six, max."

"A blond six is a seven, bro."

"Guys, it's *Last Day*," Sarah's former suitor insisted. "We should strive for eights. Eights or higher."

"Good call."

"Even O'Keefe can score a drunk-enough eight tonight."

"I don't care. We're on the road. A two is a ten on the road."

As the boys evaluated her worth and laughed, Sarah looked for an escape route. So many more people had gotten on at the succeeding stops that there was not even room to stand in the aisle anymore. She was stuck with these boys, who were so much easier to confront in the abstract, in her journal or in her opinion essays at school. In real life, boys like this made her feel nervous and depressed. She looked out the window of the train as it glided over a marsh—thick green grass studded by pools of water that reflected the broken blue of the sky. She didn't want any of this to end. It was too beautiful. Even if it meant sharing the world with snot-nosed sexists in Patriots hats.

Maybe, Sarah thought, she could create a cosmic reversal. Maybe, if she made the day *memorable*, it would beget a future from which she could stand and look back and remember. There would be another new day, and then another and another. For a few seconds this possibility felt real.

But.

What if today, with its too-nice weather and too-pretty sky, was too ordinary to be anything but profoundly, ironically doomed?

Maybe her parents were right. Maybe she should try going on medication.

When she got off the train, she marched into a convenience store and asked the cashier for cigarettes. "Pack of Reds," she blurted, not entirely sure that was a thing people actually said. She could feel her entire body shaking under her clothes. "And this." She slapped an issue of that week's *The Economist* on the counter. The cover was an illustration of a dead dove, belly-up, a stock market ticker tape streaming from its beak. Outside, Sarah inhaled three drags of her first ever cigarette and promptly threw up.

"What am I going to do?" she said.

Sarah's psyche was in its chrysalis, a place where all the inventions of her childhood, her desires and opinions and perceived truths, were being dismantled, then liquefied into a putrid ooze out of which her adult character would eventually take shape. But before she could emerge from that glorious unfiltered roux of teenage narcissism, she would have to spend hours that added up to days of very sincere, very insane, unattractive but psychologically necessary navel-gazing. All sorts of thoughts sprang delightfully from this moody introspection. Some of them — for example, that algebra was pointless for all but computer programmers and should be cut from the school curriculum — she had believed passionately, then dismissed later. Others cycled more quickly through the inchoate intellectual mill in less than a day, such as *I will never be the kind of girl who gets pedicures*. (Until she did, and loved it.) There were ideas she cherished and would have nurtured for the rest of her life, like the realization that she was wanted into existence by two people in love, wanted even before she was born. And then there were overzealous opinions that would later embarrass her: that Kerouac was the Blake of the twentieth century. The unifying thread in all her meditations was the seriousness she applied to them.

So when a reckless mix of fables, myths, movies, and self-importance presented her with one particular idea at around noon of Last Day, Sarah felt deeply and instantaneously that this was right and true: *if I have sex with Kurt tonight, the world will not end.*

It made a comforting kind of sense — how about supplanting a fear of the apocalypse with a new set of more tangible anxieties? Like, would he even want to have sex with her? How would she broach the subject? What was she expected to do? Were there prescriptive movements and sounds she should perform? Would it hurt? Would she hemorrhage like courtly maidens on their wedding nights? Was she pretty enough to pull this off? What if Kurt wasn't there? What if he had made other plans? What if she got pregnant, or herpes, or both? Wasn't it tradition not to use a condom on Last Day? What if at this very moment he was in Buenos Aires? What would she do then?

She closed her eyes and saw a vision of Kurt beside her on the beach, a pink sun emerging from the ocean. Watching the sunrise was cheesy, she knew. There were so many nauseating movies and TV shows and commercials about Last Day set against the backdrop of a shy but indefatigable rising sun. It was the universal symbol of the holiday, representing the hope that life would go on. (Duh.) It wasn't the sun's fault that sunrises had become a cliché. Natural phenomena were always getting co-opted as symbols for causes that had nothing to do with them. It happened to rainbows and lightning and shooting stars. So why not, Sarah reasoned, do the thing that everyone else said was so special and watch the sun rise on May 28? Maybe doing this was so trite that it actually doubled back to being cool. And Sarah had never watched the sun rise over Last Day, and never having done something before seemed as good a reason as any to do it.

Y UI GRABBED THE cholesterol meter from Svec and took his own reading. "Who will be master of all men now?" he said, his eyebrows arched.

Yui had inaugurated an ersatz Olympics with a game of space darts the moment the previous crew had departed. With a woman on board, the atmosphere had been less competitive. Bear had known and respected Linda for many years, but he had to admit that she wafted a relentlessly feminine air of consensus-building and kinship throughout the ship. As soon as she and the other two astronauts were gone, Yui burst out of what little shell was restraining him and the games began.

It was hard to prove one's prowess with nothing weighted to lift. There could be none of the push-up contests both Bear and Svec had grown to love in the military. So the three men relied on vision tests, space darts, chess matches, and even cholesterol readings in their not-quite-kidding quest to assert personal and national dominance over each other.

Yui frowned at his daily cholesterol reading. "Typically, Japanese people have very low cholesterol," Yui said. He rubbed his soft, protruding belly. "I am not typical Japanese."

"You are not typical nothing," Svec replied.

Bear wrote down their results in the notebook where all their competitions were recorded. Instead of their names, Yui had drawn penises in the colors of each man's flags (the white and red penis of Japan was pornographically large and erect while those of the U.S. and Russia were flaccid and small). Svec was in the lead almost across the board, though Yui was a formidable threat in chess; cholesterol was the one category where Bear had the other two squarely beat. He stuck the notebook back to the Velcro strip on the wall.

"Sixty-nine HDL, Yui. Not too bad," he said, trying not to gloat.

Svec and Yui were already absorbed in a game of speed chess they played with Velcro chess pieces on the galley table.

"Got to go do that video conference," Bear said to them as he exited.

"Check." Svec slapped the timer, and Yui let out a belch before replying with his own move and subsequent slap.

"Check, friendo."

Bear rigged up his laptop in the Cupola and set up the connection with the high school in Pasadena. There was an annoying delay, more than the usual one- to two-second pauses that punctuated conversations with Earth. Bear tried to explain this to the teacher, a young woman in a bright green cardigan with whom he'd been corresponding for over a month now. She had convinced him to do the meditation challenge alongside her class and then discuss the results, her goal being to bridge the gap between science and spirituality.

"Happy Last Day from the International Space Station, kids!" Bear said brightly. "I have to say I am impressed that a bunch of teenagers would come into school on a Saturday, a holiday no less, to talk to me."

"Oh, we don't recognize that holiday at Pasadena Christian Academy," said the teacher. Bear was embarrassed. He could have sworn that the teacher, who had reached out to him over social media, and whom he'd found attractive, had been very flirtatious in her emails with him, and never once did she mention her school's religious affiliation.

"Well, any day that I can connect with people on Earth is a good one for me, and I am happy to talk about what I have learned from this meditation, but I'm more interested in hearing from you guys."

In varying degrees of elegance, bravado, and embarrassment, the teenagers spoke about finding clearer focus after meditation, about the way time seemed to expand, the short sessions of sitting and breath somehow generating even more space inside the day. What had begun as an assignment, all of them reported, became something they greatly looked forward to.

"Since I started meditating, I can hear, like, literally *hear* the fear in my dad's voice when he criticizes us. He's, like, just a man, a person. And he's afraid."

"I wasn't feeling anything. But I kept doing it, at least when I had to in class. Then one day I was sitting at home and closed my eyes—not to meditate but to rest—when I felt a big *whoosh* and I saw a white light. It turned out to be a lightning bug, but how did only one lightning bug get into my bedroom in the middle of the day when all the doors and windows are shut in my house?"

"This is so dumb," one girl said, her voice lisping through the heavy-duty mouth guard holding back her wayward teeth. "I had this thought, listening to all of us breathing, and shifting in our seats, and, like, sniffling and stuff, that we are actually just different parts of one body, and that one body is trying to get comfortable, which is hard with all us different parts thinking we're in charge of it."

The kids laughed nervously at that last one, and their laughter, after a second's delay, made Bear laugh. He was slightly jealous—he had not experienced any of what they described; most of his meditations were consumed by a chastising inner monologue about not being better at meditation—but he was also moved to see these kids, with their plump faces and muddy pores, engaging with the world on a level so beyond him.

His eyes moistened a little as he listened to one boy say, "It's like I found another room hidden inside my own house, where I've been living my whole life, a room I never knew was here."

"I see so much destruction up here," Bear replied. "From my vantage point, I can see the visual evidence of pollution, global warming, deforestation, like a doctor sees disease in a microscope, and it gets very depressing," he confessed. "Sorry, not depressing. Discouraging. But listening to you, I have so much faith in your generation, in the good you are capable of—"

"Who is the master of all men now?" Yui cried, thrusting the scorebook in Bear's face.

"Ha-ha, sorry, folks, that is just another of our crew members here on the station, Yui Yamamoto, of the famous Yamamoto brand, doing some research for—"

"Sir?" The teacher looked into the camera. Her face was disconcertingly close, her hands shielding the rest of the space in the frame. With a sting of shame, Bear realized that the screen image he was projecting back to the classroom on Earth had frozen on Yui's graphic depiction of Japanese, Russian, and American flag penises in their record of contests.

Bear heard his last faltering attempt at diplomacy finally reaching the class, a disconcerting echo repeating every syllable of his apology. He saw his own blinking eyes freeze, then release in the small square at the bottom of his screen. Then, after what felt like the longest delay yet, he watched with a feeling of suffocation as the video feed to the kids on Earth disconnected.

Records of last Day good deeds and acts of chivalry dated back to medieval Europe. In the seventeenth century a tradition of the settling of all debts arose, evolving at last to the present custom, borrowed from the self-help movement of the twentieth century: that of making amends to all those you have harmed before the sun sets on May 28.

There were as many different practices as there were people practicing this secular sacrament. Some were very public apologies on television, radio, and social networking sites. For $200,000 you could buy a whole page in *The New York Times* to print such cryptic poems of contrition as:

Evan, I'm so sorry I stole from you. I've made a donation in your name to Save the Pandas. Sincerely, Nick

There was a retainer wall in Cleveland Heights, Ohio, where someone once spray-painted a florid apology, and decades later the trend exploded until it became the Wailing Wall of the Buckeye State. The city eventually started whitewashing it every April in preparation for the yearly onslaught of apologetic graffiti.

Some folks chose one person every year to seek out and apologize to; others made long, exhaustive lists of people and tried to contact each one in twenty-four hours, going "on tour," sometimes traveling great distances over the holiday just to make face-to-face apologies. It was considered good form to make appointments ahead of time, many etiquette columnists wrote, so that the former victims of whatever moral crime you had committed could be prepared for the inevitably awkward conversation.

Karen's plan was backward. She started with a list of things she had stolen: underwear; a cheese grater; an expensive pair of scissors; Pop-Tarts; a very pretty spoon—tiny, as for a baby, with a soft white rubber coating the lip and a snail embossed on the handle; countless hairbrushes; a box of oranges—the whole box.

"This is what is holding me back—my past," Karen said to herself. She wondered, At what age did one's past transgressions start requiring Last Day amends? At eighteen? Twenty-one? Everyone's conscience emerged at a different moment. How were such things measured by the people of this world?

Rosette was gone now, so Karen would have to look up the answer herself. Except she was forbidden to use the internet at work. She'd gotten into trouble twice already and nearly fired both times, close calls, as consistent employment was one of the conditions of her stay at Heart House. The first infraction was when Karen tried to play matchmaker. Looking up members' confidential information, finding out who was not married, assembling romantic profiles according to astrological sign and address, she would try to bait unsuspecting parties with the details she'd unearthed from her research. People were understandably creeped out, and Karen got a month of custodial work as her punishment. The second infraction concerned a more sinister element. She'd become obsessed with registered sex offenders. There were over thirty in the same zip code as the Huntington branch of the YMCA, a fact she was happy to publicize while people did their circuit training, accosting members in the middle of their lat-pulls to report the names and addresses and descriptions of these local pedophiles.

"In case they were lurking in the parking lot," Karen later defended herself. Karen's abstention from the office internet was on the honor system—her boss, Roberto, never monitored her usage; he didn't even know how to. Since her second strike, Karen had only caved in one time, after listening to some members describe a video of a kitten that had gone viral. She simply could not wait until the end of the day to watch the video at the library. With heart pounding, Karen logged on to the front desk computer to find it. Two kittens crawled around the inside of a grand piano. Their legs kept slipping between the strings and they cried a lot. It was supposed to be cute, but Karen was disgusted. Their paws were too delicate for this! Then someone offscreen started playing chords, and the kittens tumbled over headfirst, their faces the very portrait of terror.

After watching the video eight times, Karen burned with the desire to discuss each and every layer of her outrage. For her there was only now; waiting until tomorrow, when she could pretend to have seen the video at the library on her own time, was simply impossible. It was just the punishment she needed—to have something so important to talk about, and for it to be verboten because of her own treachery. This was her definition of torture. She vowed never to go on the internet at work again.

But now it was Last Day. Surely these were extenuating circumstances. Rosette's gratitude list had inspired her, and after she and Mr. Cox had left, Karen made an exhaustive inventory of everyone she had ever harmed. It was, like so many millions of other Last Day inventories, a dishonest and manipulative tactic, a way to reach the collection of people she just wanted to touch again, to feel the static spark of drama, even if only over the phone.

Karen broke up her inventory into three columns: foster families she'd stayed with for under six months (they could wait, as she hadn't been with them long enough to cause any real harm); then families who'd fostered her for a year or more; and a third category labeled *Before*. It had only one name listed under it: *Dennis*. She was saving him for last.

She opened up a search site and started plugging in names. This meant, of course, that now she would need to add her boss, Roberto, to this very list, for this very infraction. But that could wait until next year.

Memories flew at her in clusters, the younger memories dark and globed while the older ones were translucent and pointy. So many families, so many houses, each one she remembered by its bathroom. Though the first few she totally forgot. That was in the very beginning, when the apartment was raided by the FBI, and their real parents went to jail. Dennis was still with her then. After that was the lady with the black hair. That lady straightened it out with the same iron she used on their clothes, which Karen, nearly eight years old, thought was novel. She had filthy wall-to-wall carpeting throughout the apartment, even in the bathroom. It was gray with a low loop pile. Karen remembered getting out of the shower and making wet footprints on the already soggy fibers.

Her list grew, first names, fewer last names, towns, and the occasional zip code—all of it ejected from her memory bank with a vile, emetic force. Like the Colsons. Where were they? Karen remembered at least six of them in the real family, all with the same carrot-colored hair. They were so proud of this fact that they found a way to work it into every conversation. "Do you know," Mrs. Colson liked to say, "that only one percent of the human population has true red hair?" Long, curly strands of their hair were always sticking to the porcelain of the bathtub, writing secret notes in a loose, lazy cursive only redheads could decipher. Karen was so angry when they said they were not adopting her that she broke a coffee cup on Mrs. Colson's gingery head. She wasn't sorry at first, and then she was never not sorry, because they had an in-ground swimming pool in their backyard. She'd slept with Mrs. Colson's hairbrush in her arms like a baby doll for months after she'd left them.

Karen wrote down *The Colsons* on the YMCA stationery pad. Then there was that woman who called herself Auntie. Auntie what? What was her real name? Her boyfriend was named Roger and he had inappropriate boundaries, Nora helped her to learn later. There was no column for such people, Karen decided. Let the stars in their pitiless wisdom handle Auntie and her pervert paramour.

The Giraud family was fun for a while. They fostered lots of kids, it was a career for them, their house a kind of outsourced orphanage. Mrs. Giraud made pancakes every single morning on a big griddle that covered half of her stovetop. Other kids got sick of pancakes and complained after a while, but not Karen. For her, there was no upper threshold when it came to breakfast sweets. She simply wasn't born that way. It was sad when she had to leave the Giraud house. Mr. Giraud was adventurous and he was usually hanging around the house, unlike most foster fathers. He worked from home, he used to say, but didn't say what work he did.

One day a huge cardboard box appeared at their house full of scratch tickets, and Mr. Giraud put all the foster kids to work scratching them. Karen wanted to be in charge of collecting the winners and tallying the earnings, but Mr. Giraud said only Barry could do that. It was because Barry was a boy, Karen thought then, and it wasn't fair. She complained about this to her social worker, who launched an investigation and later busted up the whole house.

After that Karen went to live with the old spinster in Dorchester who made her wear braids to school every single day. Karen was in high school by then. It was embarrassing. The old lady's name was Miss Catherine May and she had a short, thick tuft of gray hair. Miss May hung framed pictures of herself in her youth all over her apartment. There were never any friends or family in the pictures—just Miss May on the deck of a boat, Miss May on a horse, Miss May drinking from a coconut. At breakfast she would push Karen down into a chair and brush her blond curls until they were straight and frizzy, then braid her hair so tightly that Karen felt her eyes squinting. If she squirmed, Miss May would whack her several times with the brush. If Karen was more than three minutes late for curfew at 7 P.M., Miss May would lock all the doors and make Karen sleep on the wicker couch on the screened-in porch. Karen spent a lot of nights on that porch. Like cleanliness, punctuality had never been her strong suit.

What would Karen say if she got ahold of these people? *I'm sorry, I love you, Happy Last Day, goodbye?* She didn't know which of those things she actually meant, only that the need to say them was dire.

The internet was not the magical portal of solutions she had hoped for. It was as fickle and confused as any other augury. After searching all the names she could remember, the only phone number Karen was able to track down was for Deborah Giraud, the Girauds' one real daughter. Karen imagined this girl was still seventeen, beautiful, and glamorous, wearing high heels and ankle socks even when it was snowing.

"Did you guys end up winning a lot of money off those scratch tickets?" Karen asked her on the phone now.

"I don't remember much after the stroke, honey," Deborah replied. It sounded nothing like Deborah. Not that Karen remembered. But the woman on the other end of the phone did not sound pretty at all. Pretty was something you could hear, and this woman didn't have it.

"How's your mom's cat? Tabitha was her name. I remember her fondly."

"Tabs? Tabs was a trooper. Tabs will outlive us all." Deborah pulled her face away from the phone and coughed a very liquid, tumultuous cough.

"Did your parents ever talk about me?" Karen asked. "Did they miss me after I left?"

"They missed the checks, that's for sure. Mom had to get a job as a nurse's aide. She hated it. But then some rich old fuck left her a bunch of money, so she and Pop moved to Florida. They sell hot dogs and Popsicles out of a truck at the beaches down there. Happy as pigs in shit, those two."

"Can I have their number?" Karen asked.

"I don't even have their number. Couldn't come up with a lousy five grand for my wedding? Come on! I'm through with cheap people. Life's too short."

"Okay," Karen said, her eyes welling up. "Happy Last Day! I love you!"

"Good night, honey," Deborah said. She cleared her throat loudly before hanging up. It was quarter past noon.

S PRING WAS SHY that year, emerging slowly, raw, soggy, and pale like a newly healed limb coming out of a cast. There'd been a feeling of apprehension lingering in the air, a feeling of being run aground. Then the end of May brought a flamboyant display of sunshine. Overnight, flowering plants exploded, their pollen and petals scattering everywhere. By the twenty-seventh of May people were peeling off layers of clothing, letting the sun touch their skin for the first time. Sitting on the sidewalk of Commonwealth Avenue, waiting for their free tattoos, their skin began to burn. No one cared. The sky was nothing to them but a fresh swell of blue.

They sat and stood, flitted and danced, eating each other's snacks and drinking each other's booze on the sidewalk in front of Redemption. Suddenly a dog darted into the street and a car came to a screeching stop from hitting it. The dog, a stocky pit bull the color of baked yams, bounced off the front fender. The driver leaned on the horn. The dog shook his head, then his back, then his rump until the near-death experience had wriggled out of him; he bounded across the street and into the line of people waiting on the sidewalk for their tattoos. He smelled chicken somewhere and nothing could stop him, not even his owner, who was pounding her fist on the hood of the stopped car.

The dog at last plunged his nose into the purse of a woman sitting in line and chomped down on her half-eaten burrito.

"Hey," the woman said, laughing. "Let me peel the foil off for you first, boy."

Sarah had arrived just in time to see all this. The dog ate the burrito in three bites, then swallowed it foil and all. Laughter erupted among the few people who had looked up from their phone screens to see it. A couple tried to pat the dog, who sniffed their reaching hands and licked them profusely. When the dog trotted into the tattoo studio through the open door, Sarah saw an opportunity, and followed quickly behind.

"What the fuck?" A redheaded lady with thin penciled eyebrows stood up on her chair. "Jake, help me!"

"I'm busy, Janine," Jake yelled across the fray.

"For Chrissakes! We're being attacked by a wild dog."

"Kurt's paying you to handle this shit today. So handle it."

Janine was bossy and feckless and always hanging around Redemption, keeping a codependent eye on her boyfriend, so Jake had suggested to Kurt that she work a shift that day, helping sort out the holiday chaos, hopefully keeping busy and saving Jake from death by nagging. Kurt was happy to oblige. He loved Jake like a war buddy; theirs was a steadfast friendship free from scrutiny of any kind. For Kurt it was platonic love at first sight. He'd poached Jake from a rival studio after the two men had met at a tattoo convention in Providence over a decade earlier. Jake was the drunkest, meanest guy in the bar. Short and barrel-chested, he'd been trying to bait everyone, including Kurt, into a fistfight. He had a long wiry red beard forever studded with food crumbs and glistening beer foam, and his shaved head was branched with scars. The kid was a mess, and Kurt, who was a bit older and already softened by life's many defeats, saw Jake instantly as just that—a messy kid searching for direction. Kurt had met a lot of guys like Jake in prison, and it felt like a calling to take him under his wing.

That first night in Providence, Jake had flung every taunt and trap he could at Kurt, who blasted back with unconditional respect and affection. If Jake made a surly claim that the song playing on the stereo was shit, Kurt twisted a lyric of the song into a dirty joke Jake couldn't help laughing at. When Jake tried to punch the ironic mustache off a scrawny hipster's face, Kurt convinced him that the same guy had been talking about what amazing work Jake had demonstrated during the convention. And finally, in a last surge of primitive, almost comical jungle dominance, as Kurt helped a stumbling Jake into a cab, Jake accused him of potential faggotry, to which Kurt responded, "Nah, man. I had cancer of the prick a couple years back."

It was a response that made no logical sense at all, except to the Jakes of the world, drunken Irish pugilists who were eternally chastened by male confessions of cancer. "My uncle had that," Jake said, his face suddenly lamb-like in the glow of the streetlight. "Great fuckin' guy, though. Athletic, the whole thing."

"Good for him," Kurt said, and Jake slammed his fist into the roof of the cab twice like a judge's gavel.

Kurt had just signed a lease on the space on Commonwealth Avenue and saw in Jake skills of both muscle and artistry. (He was right; in addition to inking tattoos, Jake had experience in construction, light plumbing and electric, and bar security.) He knew that if he just let Jake be exactly who he was without trying to change him, he would have a friend for life. And as drunk as Jake got every single night, as fucked up on whatever cocktail of chemicals he packed into his bloodstream, the man was never late for work at Redemption. He puked outside in the bushes like a dog, he tortured the other artists, many of whom quit after a couple of months because of Jake's truculence, he raged about the customers as soon as they had paid and gone, but he never said no to Kurt, who in turn never needed to ask for anything, because Jake always volunteered.

He was thirty-five years old and ate acid, mushrooms, or mescaline almost every weekend. His ears were loaded with metal studs and bolts, and his lobes wrapped around black wooden discs the size of Communion wafers. He wanted to get horns implanted in his skull but his girlfriend, Janine, wouldn't let him. They were always on the verge of a breakup over this shit; Jake was always threatening to dump her, once and for all, but Janine was so damn shrill and Jake was just too high to argue.

Sarah grabbed the drooling pit bull by his collar as Janine continued to whine from her perch. The dog's fur was so thin in places that Sarah could see his pink skin scabbing already with sunburn. The muscles beneath his fur stretched and bundled as he prepared to leap over the desk and lick the screaming woman standing on a chair. He wanted her! Her breath had a whiff of bacon and eggs left over from breakfast! He wanted the stapler on the desk! He wanted the red plastic cups sweet with beer! He wanted everything in this new fascinating place! His owner finally made it into the studio and punched the dog's skull with a closed fist.

"Sit, Marshall. Sit! I said sit, goddammit!" She latched his leash back onto his collar, and Marshall jumped up, placed his paws on her shoulders, and licked her angry face.

"Get that thing out of here," Janine cried, still standing on her chair.

"My pleasure, you Visigoth slag," the dog owner yelled. She yanked her happy pup by the throat back onto the street and slammed the door behind her.

"Janine! Are you handling this or what?"

"Jesus," moaned Janine. "Who's next?"

"I am," Sarah said.

"Sign this." She handed Sarah a waiver. "Whatever the artist wants. No exceptions. Not invalidated by intoxication. Et cetera, et cetera."

Sarah signed quickly without looking. "I'm only here for Kurt," Sarah said.

"You get who you get," Janine snapped back. "Jake, who's next?" she screamed over the fray.

"How the hell do I know?" Jake answered.

Jake leaned over the body squirming in his chair and continued working. On the back of Jake's shaved skull was a tattoo of a hand flipping the middle finger. A terrifying man, Sarah thought. In the next stall a man who looked like a movie star Sarah couldn't remember was inking the chest of another man lying supine on the table, the two of them locked in a state of silent concentration. Sitting in the chair beyond them was a tiny woman with soft, almond-shaped eyes. She watched eagerly as the young tattooer in her stall washed his hands in the sink. He had a nose like an eagle and a goofy smile that seemed kind. Why hadn't Kurt ever written to her about the characters who worked for him? These were the people he saw every day, with whom he spent the majority of his time. There was so much more she needed to know about him.

"Okay, your wish is being granted today. Kurt's next," Janine said, pointing. "All the way in the back." She placed Sarah's waiver on the top of a messy stack of papers. "What are you standing there for?" Her skin was very white in the places not covered by tattoos. Sarah saw a vein throbbing minutely at the woman's temple.

"Don't worry, honey," Janine said. "It only hurts like hell."

T HE GENTLE OPIATE high of Mr. Cox's pills was waning in direct proportion to Karen's waxing spiritual angst. She held her fingertips to her collarbone and closed her eyes, trying to manifest an early dismissal from her work shift. Not long after, her wish was granted when a surly, self-absorbed member refused to return Karen's "Happy Last Day" wishes, and she snapped and called the man a cunt. She did this in full view of her manager, Roberto, who had recently arrived. Roberto gaped at her from a stool behind the entrance desk, a glistening slice of pizza resting on his lap.

"Did you just call that guy a cunt?" he cried.

"It was a term of distinction and honor in the Middle Ages," she said, trying to cover.

Roberto took a big, joyless bite of his pizza. "You're fired. I mean *done. Finito.* Life's too short for me to deal with this crap."

Karen began to sob. After the library debacle, she had been given one more chance at Heart House. She had tried to bargain for three strikes, but Nora had had to explain, "Not in this economy."

Karen gathered her meager belongings from her locker and headed to the door. She cried big shuddering sobs all the way to the bus stop.

The bus was crowded, and Karen, with her tears, expected someone to give up a seat for her, but no one budged. Last Day was supposed to be a holiday of grand and selfless gestures, but her fellow bus riders refused to acknowledge her, their mouths sealed in acceptance of this grim world. It was what made cities so lonely. So many people to talk to and not a word, not even a *hi* exchanged with the person who sat so close that her arm skin was sticking to yours.

Karen's stomach hurt badly. She'd been down this road before. There was a lot of tearing inside her viscera. She did visualization exercises every night to mend them, but it wasn't enough. The last time she was in the hospital, the doctors had warned her.

"You could die," one had said, a gastroenterologist. "Do you understand what that means?"

It means a lot of things, she wanted to say to him, *depending on your spiritual belief system,* but her mind was frothy with all the meds she was on. "Yeah," was what came out of her mouth.

"I saved your life!" the gastroenterologist cried. He was shorter than she was and had very cold, silky hands.

Another doctor had started her on a new antipsychotic that made her brain feel like it was blistering under her scalp. She had trouble reading. It was hell. These side effects subsided eventually but she was not willing to go through another adjustment of her meds. Her stomach hurt a lot now, but she was sure she would pass everything and prayed to be relieved of her worst compulsions.

HEART HOUSE WAS a large gray Victorian set back from the main road on top of a high hill. It offered a striking view of the city—the Prudential Building was visible from the window of the third-floor bathroom—though few of the residents had the faculties to appreciate it. A lovely building with ugly, utilitarian modifications for its new purpose as a group home, Heart House was surrounded by a neat, uncultivated yard where awkwardly placed benches green with mold slowly rotted in the damp air. The residents of Heart House were hopeless cases—schizophrenics and mentally disabled adults, unemployable men and women who watched reruns of game shows on a continuous loop all day in the common room. Narrative programming put the residents to sleep, which made them stay up all night, a hassle for the staff. Music triggered all kinds of agitation, fists flying, inconsolable tears, the occasional masturbatory spree. So the staff had compiled a library of game shows. Low stakes and solvable puzzles: it put the residents' minds at ease.

Karen never watched TV. The light gave her headaches, which she self-diagnosed as an allergy to gamma rays. She had a library card and stacks of books teetering on the sill of her bay window. She loved best thick, hard-covered romance novels with gold lettering embossed on their jackets. All those stories of damaged men and women in love. She had several slim volumes of Rudolf Steiner's sorcery that she saved for nights when she ran out of sleeping pills. And she had collected most of an incomplete set of outdated children's encyclopedias culled from the free box at the library. As the only high-functioning resident of Heart House, Karen had certain privileges. The library card and the biggest room with the bay window were two of them, she liked to believe, though the staff said the room was the luck of the lottery, nothing more. But she was certainly the only resident who was allowed a mini-fridge in her room. If she had had family, she would have been allowed to go visit them on her own, without asking for permission, for an entire day if she liked, as long as she was back by 8 P.M. She was not allowed to have a phone, none of the residents were, but she was confident that in time she would find a crack in that prohibitory wall and erode it with her insistent carping.

Buddy and Jon-Jon were hanging streamers in the front lobby when Karen got home from the YMCA. Lexi was frosting a vanilla sheet cake very slowly, her tongue pushed out of the corner of her mouth in deep concentration. Same as last year, Karen thought, almost exactly, this tableau. Lauren, the counselor on duty, sat at the front desk, her face resting on her fist, while the other hand punched out perforated cardboard crowns from a Last Day activity booklet published for institutionalized adults. Lauren was a pretty girl around Karen's age with a partially shaved head and a tongue ring. She liked to read Christian romance novels, which piqued Karen's interest: she was curious what nuances Lauren's savior allowed when it came to things like blowjobs. Karen's secular romance novels were teeming with them, and she was honestly curious how Christians handled it. For that query Karen had lost library privileges for a week, and Lauren never really forgave her.

"Why is the icing blue?" Karen asked her now. "It's not appropriate."

"Didn't stop you from digging your grimy fingers into the jar. Jeesh." Lauren took the tub of frosting away from her.

"Purple is the traditional Last Day color. This might very well be the last time we ever make a celebratory sheet cake. It might be the last sheet cake on Earth. We should try to get it right."

"There wasn't any purple frosting left at the store. I looked."

"We could make our own," Karen suggested, "by mixing blue and red."

"I don't get paid enough for that," was Lauren's reply. Karen frowned. She liked to think of the Heart House staff as distant cousins whose presence in the house was inspired by love or, in the case of curmudgeons like Lauren, familial loyalty. The fact that they got paid, and were unhappy with their pay, made the whole operation feel mercenary and gross.

Karen picked up the communal phone and ordered herself a large cheese pizza, her voice low so that Lauren couldn't hear her. She was supposed to get permission before ordering delivery, but Lauren loved to say no without reason. A vice principal in disguise, she always shushed the Heart House residents when they talked in the hallways, as though there were a religious ceremony or standardized test taking place somewhere else in the building. "Come to the back door," Karen whispered into the phone. The man taking her order said to expect at least a two-hour wait.

Karen went to her room and retrieved her safe from where she hid it under her laundry bag. Inside she discovered there was not enough money for even one slice of pizza. She'd saved over a hundred dollars since Christmas, but she'd forgotten that she'd spent it all on her donation to Save the Tigers. She had been promised a plush toy Bengal as a thank-you gift, but it turned out to be one of those cheap carnival versions, stuffed with Styrofoam beads that spilled out from rips in the stitching when she hugged it too hard.

How long would it take before Heart House found out she'd been fired and made her leave? At least a week, she figured. What would happen then? Nora's sphere of influence had been maxed out, and she had many times explained to Karen the boundary between therapist and client, that she would not be able to adopt her or even house her for one night.

That's okay, Karen thought. That was not her destiny.

"I have choices!" Karen said to the stuffed animals resting beneath the covers of her unmade bed. She packed a plastic grocery bag with essentials, filled her pockets with all the loose change she could find strewn about the floor, and left this lovely bedroom for the last time.

In the foyer of Heart House was a thick, leather-bound logbook where residents and their nonexistent guests were supposed to sign in and out. It sat regally on a podium, lit by an imitation Tiffany lamp, giving the whole Heart House operation the impression of a quaint New England bed-and-breakfast. Karen's name was the only one listed in the logbook. Line after line, page after page, her loopy script detailed every trip she had taken to work and the library for the calendar year so far. The constancy of her own life struck her as both gratifying and pointless. Surely she must have been other places, Karen thought as she flipped through the pages. She could only remember an apple-picking excursion with Nora, but that was last fall, recorded in last year's logbook.

Today she wrote out in her fat, bubbly cursive:

May 27 — Karen Donovan — 3:20 P.M. — Library
(Allston Branch) — Home by 8 P.M.

In the TV lounge the cheers of a once-live studio audience intensified and the voice of a game-show host strained amiably to rise above it. Sadie sat on the pillows of the bay window seat, pressing her hand up against the glass, then removing it. "Hello, brother bear," she said to the sky.

One story up was Karen's room, empty of her. Sometimes, when she entered her room after a prolonged absence, like when she'd had a long workday followed by a therapy session, she heard a sudden hush before entering, as though her clothes and stuffed animals and library books were leading a fantastic life that all jolted to a collective halt as soon as she unlocked the door.

What would happen to them, to all her things?

Lauren was scolding Gregory in the kitchen for eating an extra pudding cup. They were *his* pudding cups, Karen wanted to argue; Gregory's social worker bought them for him as a special treat. If he wanted to eat an extra one, who was Lauren to tell him no? But if she didn't leave right now, Karen knew, she never would, and with uncharacteristic quiet, she slipped out the door.

THE MORE KURT thought about the day ahead, the more he felt trapped. This feeling—even if it was an illusion, a recognizable haunting from his months in prison—was now worse than any possible outcome. But understanding things and believing they were true were not the work of the same organ, and so every attempt Kurt made to console himself only impounded him more.

He needed to stop mixing prescription sleeping pills with beer. That had for the last twelve years been both the solution and the source of pretty much all his problems. He loved the feeling—as if someone had pulled the plug on his consciousness—but he would wake up just refreshed enough to puzzle over what the hell he might have done during the previous night's blackout. In the past he had ordered and paid for an antique trumpet as well as four different books on falconry, made reservations at a bed-and-breakfast in Spain (impressive, he admitted to himself, as Kurt did not speak a word of Spanish), and, more than once, eaten a whole pizza and possibly some of its box. He drank every night, so if he didn't take pills when he was drinking, he couldn't take them at all. Maybe he should hide his computer earlier in the evening to prevent these fugue-state sprees. Or just disable his email account. If he could commit to that last option alone, it would cut his usual trouble down by about a third. But how many times before had he come to this precise realization and continued to do the same thing?

He drank one beer very quickly and another slowly. The idea for his next tattoo swam to him as if in a dream—an image of classical octopus *hentai*. When Kurt's next customer said he was a stripper, it seemed an example of what Kurt's old Irish grandma used to call *providence*. An encouraging step away from the ghosts of dread and guilt taking jabs at his peace of mind. Kurt rerouted his nervousness about the afternoon into the stripper's tattoo, the curves of the tentacles, the detailed suckers each with a tiny hook inside it. The squid's human lover arched her back; her long hair spilled down the calf of the man in Kurt's tattoo chair. Kurt was pleased with the finished product, and the customer loved it. For a moment Kurt relaxed.

He was washing his hands when a girl with long legs and dull blond hair hopped onto his empty chair. Dressed in magenta athletic shorts and a baggy blue T-shirt, she was obviously very young, though he couldn't tell how young. Her forehead bore deep age lines of wonder or distress, but her mouth, her cheeks, the delicate skin around her eyes were baby smooth. A neon-pink Band-Aid protected a nick on her shin, and a tiny spot of blood seeped through the plastic. Her sneakers were filthy. The most disgusting sneakers he'd ever seen. They smelled awful.

"Hello, I'm Kurt." He offered her a handshake.

Sarah Moss stared into his eyes. "It's me," she said. "Sarah." She sank her straight, slightly gapped top teeth into her lip.

He remembered the name but the face not at all. That girl from the barbecue? When was that? Fourth of July? Did he sleep with her? He was ninety-nine percent sure he hadn't. Yes, it was coming back to him, slowly: it had all been completely chaste, so chaste, in fact, he'd only jerked off to her twice, and one of those times by accident—in the pantheon of angels his subconscious had presented to him one night, these same long legs so pale and pure had randomly appeared in the fray. Kurt was relieved. As long as he hadn't slept with her, he didn't owe her anything.

"Kidding. How could I forget you?" Kurt said, and shuffled through the memories of so many mornings waking up with his laptop next to him on the bed, the screen wide open against the pillow like a lover with her mouth agape. Most likely he'd emailed this girl Sarah in a blackout, as was his wont. But he could have sworn she was in college. Young, but not *this* young. Though that was a piece of fiction he had told himself about many other girls many times before, with his faculties relatively awake and alert.

"You're a sight for sore eyes, Sarah. What can I do for you?"

"Oh, good," she said, recovering. "Okay. I've been thinking about this for a while actually. Since I met you." She searched his face for the light of love and thought she saw it, a tiny glimmer, in the gold flecks of his brown eyes. "I know I can't choose my tattoo, and I'm totally okay with whatever you give me. I trust you completely. Like, totally. But I want you to know what I would choose, so it can be, like, our common vocabulary for the moment. Right?"

"Go on."

"So, I've been obsessively watching birds my whole life. For as long as I can remember. My first memory is not of my mom or my dad but this time at the park when a swan bit my hand as I was trying to feed it my French fries. When I was little, as soon as I could walk, I was chasing birds across our lawn. I wanted more than anything to see them up close. As up close as possible. And obviously they never let me. Birds fly away. It's what they do. I love that about birds. Admire, love, and envy—like, there should be a word for those three things mixed into one."

"You want those words."

"Oh, no. No no no. I don't want any words on my body. I read too much as it is. I don't want to read my own skin."

"Good," Kurt said.

"Right? You get it. I knew you would."

Sarah was thunderstruck with self-consciousness. It was weird how you could totally forget you had a body, then suddenly remember and think of nothing else. She pawed anxiously at her bangs. It was an awkward fringe of hair she was trying to train into a swoop across her forehead. So far unsuccessfully. The rest of her hair was limp. It just hung there, as though it grew only as much as it wanted to and then gave up. She pulled it into a messy ponytail and prayed her armpits were not visibly damp.

"It was frustrating," she went on. "There's only so much you can learn from books. Field research is key. My dad bought me these amazing binoculars. Made by NASA. But I hate using them. I get seasick easily, and tracking a bird from tree to tree at such a close magnification makes me really dizzy."

Sarah could hear herself prattling on. I sound like such a *girl*, she thought, but felt powerless to stop herself. She talked even faster now.

"Then one day, I figured out that if I scattered birdseed on my windowsill, the birds would come and perch there, and hang out for a while, and let me watch them through the glass. Instead of chasing them, I could invite them closer to me. Which is, like, a metaphor. Right? I started scattering seeds on my lawn and other places in town. And as long as I sat still, and was patient, they would always come. Not quite close enough, but closer than before. And I know, it's obvious. But it was kind of a big breakthrough for me."

She lifted the fabric of her T-shirt off her belly in a weird flutter that horrified her as she was doing it. *Stop it,* she told herself. *Be normal. Just BE. NORMAL.*

"So for a tattoo," she said slowly, deliberately, until her voice did not sound real, "if I could choose, and I know I can't—you have your tradition and everything, which I think is amazing—but just for an exercise, this is what I'd want: a hand reaching out, palm open, all the lines and stuff, a real hand. And seeds falling in a light spray, and some collecting on the ground, though I don't want an actual line to demarcate *ground.*

And some birds eating away at those seeds. But cool, realistic birds. Nothing cartoonish."

"Like what?"

"Maybe a lark. Or is that cheesy?"

"The heart wants what it wants."

"You're right." Sarah smiled. "Thank you for saying that. I really like larks."

"Nothing wrong with that."

"So?"

"Yeah." Kurt scratched his neck. "I would love to do that tattoo."

"You would?"

"When you turn eighteen."

"I am."

"What year were you born?"

Quick arithmetic was not one of Sarah's gifts.

"Exactly," Kurt said.

"Come on!"

"I don't have many rules here. Especially today, as you can see. It's drunken pandemonium. But that is one rule I must abide by."

"Your ads promise free tattoos for everyone. Everyone is everyone. Including me."

"Drunks. Pregnant women. The criminally insane. Anything goes today, as long as you are the age of consent."

"I promise I will never sue you."

"Your parents might."

"You've met my parents. They would never do that. Not in a million years."

"I've heard that before."

"But I'm telling you the truth."

"And I've heard *that* before, too."

"You won't even consider it?"

Kurt ran his hands over his face like he was washing it. "I did consider it. I would be honored to do that tattoo. And I promise I will, free of charge, but next year. You'll be eighteen next year, right?"

Fat tears sprang from Sarah's eyes.

"Take a deep breath. You're way too emotional about this. You on your period?"

"Excuse me?"

"It's okay. I have sisters."

Sarah couldn't believe that the man she had decided to love could say such a thing. It was sexist and reductive and uncreative and *untrue*! If anything, she was closest to the ovulation phase of her cycle, a time of peak anxiety, she theorized, because of her asexuality. It was as if a part of her primitive biology despaired all those lost little eggs going to waste. The time of her period, on the other hand, was usually relaxing and productive.

She jumped off the chair and heaved her backpack over her shoulder. "Don't you get it? In the calendar of the cosmos, we're living—right now—at December 31, 11:59 P.M. It's the end. Every decision matters. I thought you—you of all people in the whole doomed world—would understand. . . ."

It was fascinating, disorienting, and unspeakably sad, Kurt thought, how still her face remained as she sobbed. It was like watching an animal cry. And yet, the sight of an attractive female in tears had always given him an erection—a phenomenon too shameful for him to explore. It was Kurt's sexual kryptonite and it had caused him nothing but pain.

As if to cement this point, another crying woman flung open the door of Redemption and scanned the studio with bleary, blackened eyes.

It was Megan Brown, aspiring model-actress and onetime fling Kurt had quickly regretted when she'd claimed a week later that he had gotten her pregnant. "I don't think that's possible," Kurt had said to her then, and her tears at that point turned to rage. "Don't worry—I had it *taken care of!*" she screamed loud enough for the whole tattoo studio to hear. A year later Megan returned on Last Day to drop another grenade: "I just wanted you to know that I am a lesbian and I am moving to New

York. You'll never hear from me again!" Kurt could not hide his relief, which enraged her all the more, so she swept her hand across his tray of inks and sent them clattering to the floor. A year after that she came to Redemption again on Last Day, this time to make amends. "I'm sorry. I made that whole story up. I was never pregnant. I never had an abortion. I was just—I don't know—I guess I wanted your attention." She offered Kurt a wad of twenty-dollar bills for the spilled ink but he refused to accept it. "It's all good," he assured her then, believing this was the last he would ever see of Megan Brown.

"Oh Christ. Not again . . . ," Janine growled. "Kurt!"

"I'm sorry, Sarah. Please forgive me. I'm just—really hungry. I don't know about you, but I start talking some nonsense when I'm hungry. You hungry? Let's get burritos. On me." Kurt wrapped his arm around Sarah's shoulders and ushered her toward the back door.

"I'm starving," Sarah admitted, her pulse bolting at his touch.

WHILE KURT WAITED at the counter for their food, he reviewed their correspondence on his phone. He'd gotten pretty intimate with this girl, telling her things he hadn't admitted to anyone else, not even to himself in the sober light of day. In her emails she went on and on, as most women did, but she seemed to really pay attention to him, and pick up on things intuitively. She might be young, but she knew what she was talking about.

"You're smart," Kurt said, taking a seat across from her. He placed the tray between them and started in on the nachos.

"That's so misogynistic," Sarah shot back.

"What? Why?"

"You say it like it's a surprise."

"I—I . . ."

"I'm choosing to take it as a compliment, because men are only surprised by intelligence in women they also find pretty. So, thank you. But also, you're welcome."

"Ok. Whoa. That's not at all where I was going."

"Then where were you going?"

"I was going to say, for someone as smart as you, did it ever occur to you that the calendar of the cosmos is just getting ready to turn another page? Everything looks like the end when you're moving forward."

"I wish it were that simple." She folded her paper napkin into a tight square that she squeezed in the palm of her hand.

"I know how you feel. And it's okay. It's normal. The end of the world is the scariest thing when you're young. Then you grow old and realize that dealing with a world of shit that never ends is even scarier."

"I saw a bumper sticker on the way here. It said, *Cat-titude*. That's it. Fucking *cat-titude*, with a picture of a cat apparently copping an attitude. And I was like, yup, we're done. Our reign here is over."

Kurt laughed a big expulsive laugh, with bits of rice flying out of his mouth, culminating in a choking cough; Sarah swore she could feel the serotonin surge in her own brain.

"And I know you're probably right. But I still can't get rid of the feeling that this year is different. This year is really the end. But then again, I feel like this every year. I don't know. My generation or whatever, which includes you, too, by the way—I mean epochal generation, not what-TV-shows-did-you-grow-up-with generation. We're all so—*derivative*."

She paused to scan his face for evidence that she was using the word correctly. He was handsome at the edges but not at the core, she noted with some disappointment, a diffused beauty that scattered and fled. His jaw was sharp and the shadow of his thick, short beard cast the lines of his cheeks and nose in a shifty light. His eyes were too small, too far apart, too determined. His nose looked like it had been broken and roughly slapped back together several times. His forehead was waxy with huge pores.

"Yeah," he said.

"Like, when was the last time someone thought of something new? I mean really new. Not an improvement on something that already exists.

And don't get me started on pollution. . . . This planet wants to scratch us off like fleas."

Kurt took two wolfish bites of his burrito. "What's the matter?" he asked her. "I mean really. The thing that scares you is never the thing that gets you. It's the thing hiding behind the thing. So the end of the world means, what? Your parents are getting divorced?"

"My parents are the most happily married people in the world. They're soulmates."

"That's cool. That's rare. My parents had an Irish divorce," Kurt said.

"What does that mean?"

"Sometime, when I was nine or ten years old, my dad started sleeping on the couch. Every morning he'd fold up his sheets and blankets and pillows and stuff them in the space between the couch and the front window. Like it didn't happen. Except we all knew it did. He did this every night until my little sister finally moved out. Then he repainted her room and moved in there. He died a couple years ago. They were still married, he and my mother, forty-two years. Still in the same house, they just never spoke to each other."

Women were always pressing Kurt for personal information, their blatant attempt to force some kind of emotional dependency. The longer he kept silent, the easier it was to stall. But with Sarah he kept blurting out these dark little tales. There was something about her that elicited his trust. It was more than the Ambien, more than the safety of near-anonymous email. It had to be, because he was doing it again here, sitting across from her.

"You going to any bonfires today?"

"I hate today," she said. "Everyone acts like it's a big joke. Or a big party. No one thinks about what it really means. What if we really lost the whole world? The whole world!" Her eyes started to well up again and she wiped them with the backs of her hands, smearing a bit of guacamole on her forehead. "And don't get me started on our lame-ass rituals. Beer and bonfires? What about a blood rite?" she said, composed again.

Kurt reached across the table and wiped the green off her brow. "My whole business is a blood rite."

"Yeah," Sarah said. "That's why I wanted to get a tattoo."

"You're still pissed about that, huh?"

"I'm ninety percent over it." Sarah sighed. "Fatigue makes everyone more forgiving."

"That's a good one. Who said that?"

It was the one gem of wisdom bestowed by her former therapist. "Free-floating anxiety is so bourgeois," Sarah had said to the old woman her parents' insurance policy had assigned to treat her. This practitioner, who was neither a PhD nor a shaman—which irked Sarah; she'd been hoping for a little of both, but Jungians, her parents explained, seldom accepted COBRA—had only the blandest anodynes, the saltines of psychiatric advice. "You judge yourself too harshly," this silver-haired woman would say. "The future is a mystery, so focus on the present." The moment their work together ventured into Sarah's fear of Last Day, she quit going and refused to return.

"I said it," Sarah lied, for what felt like the millionth time that day. It was getting too easy.

Kurt thought he was long past the age when teenagers would find him attractive. On occasion, a very drunk twenty-something would present herself as an option, if he hung around the bar late enough. Boston's blue laws were the biggest impediment, or lifesaver, depending on the night, the girl. Those drunk twenty-somethings had been offering diminishing returns lately. They fell into two categories: the ones who woke up, looked at Kurt and his pale naked body sliding off his tired bones like loose meat, and cringed with regret, tiptoeing out of his house while he pretended to sleep, the only remnant of the previous night a makeup-smeared pillow on his bed like a hideous Shroud of Turin; or the crazy-as-shithouse-rats girls with serious daddy issues who refused to leave the next morning. The former were ego-crushing, the latter ballbusting, which is why, in his forties, Kurt was wont to go home early and abstain from both. Sometimes things worked out all right. Another satisfied customer. Other times—*Jesus*. He didn't like to think about it too much.

"So you really have nothing planned for today?"

"Nothing," she blurted. "I mean, I have a bunch of parties I could go to, but I'm not committed to any of them."

"Right," he laughed. "We always have our parties. But how about we do something different?"

I N MOROCCO GRANDMOTHERS make a spicy root vegetable stew on Last Day, and the greater the number of mouths they can feed that one night, the longer it will take for the end of the world to come. There are conflicting algorithms in this calculus: some believe each mouth fed is equivalent to one hundred years, others one thousand years. Throughout Morocco and parts of Algeria it is considered impolite to refuse the food of any married woman on the night of May 27, a tradition expanded over time so that it has become standard to say yes to any offer made by a married Morrocan woman on Last Day.

In Laos and some parts of Vietnam, people don't speak after the stroke of midnight on May 27. Except for those necessary to sustain life, all noise-making machines are shut down. No televisions, no radios. The night is a pool of inky silence. The following day no one speaks except to assist children, and even these directions are whispered. Doors are shut with such softness, footfalls are slow and gentle. As a prank, children will try to startle their relatives into shouting by jumping out of a dark corner or placing a sharp pin on their chair. If you are caught in such a trap, you have to pay the cunning child a small amount of money. It is very bad luck to be born on Last Day unless your mother can claim she birthed you without screaming and that you took your first breaths without a cry.

Western Europe, like North America, has its bonfires. Italians burn their old bed linens. During the Great Wars, when nothing could be wasted, they used Last Day to cut up their old linens into bandages. Nowadays most Italians burn a sacrificial dishrag. The holiday is marked by special sales in the home-goods sections of department stores. Italians believe that sleeping in a bed whose sheets have not been changed over Last Day will result in a year of impotence.

Hungarians burn broomsticks. The Dutch burn all the candles in their houses down to the nubs on May 27 and walk through their neighborhoods on May 28 gifting brand-new candles to their neighbors. Women in Iceland throw one piece of jewelry into the sea, lake, or river. The English wash their windows, eyeglasses, and computer screens on May 28. The Irish drink.

Certain Nordic tribes considered trees to be earthbound angels who silently, dutifully interceded between Earth and heaven, and so sometime later, even after Christianity was introduced, people left their homes on the night of May 27 to sleep in the forest. In coastal communities, villagers would gather on beaches and wade together into the sea at midnight, where they shivered before a dawn that might never come.

Before Communism, the Chinese lit fireworks. To better illuminate the sky, fires were snuffed out and electric lights unplugged or else black drapes were hung over windows to hide the light. If not, neighbors would nail pictures of clocks on the negligent occupants' front door, reminding them that their days were numbered.

Orthodox Jews do not acknowledge the holiday. Conservative Jews recognize it as a kind of Rosh Hashanah–cum–Yom Kippur for gentiles. Secular Jews do what secular Christians, Muslims, and nondenominational folks do throughout the U.S., and that is order pizza.

Last Day was a late arrival to Japan, forced in with so much other Western culture, in the mid-nineteenth century. Today the Japanese celebrate with wild, extravagant spending sprees. Small family-run boutiques and huge big-box stores alike offer seemingly endless kegs of beer for their shoppers. Fueled by alcohol and nihilism, many Japanese households have plunged into financial ruin on this one night, causing many prudent wives to order holds on their husbands' credit and bank accounts for that day alone.

Consumption had little appeal for Yui, so he had to find creative ways to observe the holiday, which he was incredulous to discover was not deemed significant enough to be celebrated on the International Space Station. All day he ignored directives from Mission Control in protest. He tied his ankle to a toe bar in the Japanese laboratory, where he napped on and off. He watched the mutant baby mouse and marveled as the two heads took turns breastfeeding from their mother while floating in their plexiglass cage. After lunch and another nap, he flew, arms extended Superman-style, down to the American lab in the Destiny module and began drawing pictures on the walls in black Magic Marker.

"What the heck, Yui?" Bear gasped. In one image, lightning ignited a great fire teeming with the arms and legs of humans. A lizard's tail, bicycle wheels, ice cream cones, a startlingly precise handgun, all of it danced chaotically between the licking tongues of the blaze. Bear grabbed the marker out of Yui's hands. Without reacting, without even pausing, Yui unclipped another marker from his belt and continued limning his ghastly mural.

"*Mokushi hi,*" he replied. "The day of silent revelation. It is my Last Day present. I am drawing it for you, friendo."

"Thanks . . . but you can't . . ."

"I can."

"You're not supposed to." Bear hated how whiny he sounded when reproving Yui, like a high school hall monitor, a pedant and a fool.

Yui clung to the wall with his feet. His toenails were as long as talons. He must not have cut them in weeks, Bear realized. He wondered if it was part of an experiment. It was hard to tell with Yui which choices were recalcitrant defects of character also present on Earth, which had crystallized in the pressure cooker of space, and which were in the name of science.

Yui stopped drawing, placed the marker in his mouth, and gave himself a long scratch deep in his pants. A solemn look had sunk into his face. This mural was no act of rebellion. Or it was, but only in part. He had been struck all of a sudden with a bout of anxiety. He missed the comforts of home, his hydroponic persimmon tree, his skateboard ramp, his chauffeur, Asami, an elderly fetishist who regaled Yui with stories about the extramarital affairs he had with drag queens. He missed his brother, Tadeshi, so painfully he could not speak about it.

"I am sad, friendo," he pouted. He was now drawing a volcano spewing thick rivers of oozing, erotic lava. Bear squinted at the fine print on the marker, to see if it was washable or not. Yui embellished the streams of lava so that figures engaged in lurid sex acts appeared in the swooping arcs of its flow. Bear couldn't be sure, but it looked like there was some bestiality going on.

"In Japan, today is the day we celebrate the man who was born before man. He was born dead. What is the word in English?"

"Stillborn?"

"Yes. Stillborn. The gods had to start over. They went through many drafts. They failed. Sometimes man failed. Mostly man failed, but the gods were joking sometimes. They built man's asshole over his heart. They made a man with two penises—one in front and one in back. They made a man who was too dark to see at night. These men kept getting lost every new moon, falling off mountains, breaking their necks. Then they made a man who was so light he caught fire at sunrise and burned away. All these men wanted to live, like we want to live, but they had to die. That's why we celebrate today."

"That's cool, Yui. I never knew that about Japanese Last Day."

"It is not exactly true. Your American friendo Val Corwin wrote it. It might be true. Perhaps." He held the book in his arms like a teddy bear.

"Kitsch holiday," Svec said, appearing suddenly. Despite his thick fire hydrant of a body, he navigated the ship like a water snake.

"We believe what has meaning for us. Or what has meaning we believe. I change my mind. But, because I am confused, I know it is true." Yui smiled wanly.

"JAXA has been trying to reach you," Svec said with a tenderness that caught the other two men off guard.

"I know," Yui said, his gaze fastened to his mural. He was about to destroy its perfection with too many lines. He was aware of this yet he continued to draw fast, tumultuous waves undulating in the rock, in the lava, in the scorched earth bereft of man.

"Don't make me tell you," Svec said.

Yui capped the marker and let it float in the air. He pushed off the toe bar and glided toward the Kibo lab as if backstroking on the surface of water.

"What's wrong?" Bear asked once Yui was out of sight.

"His brother died," Svec said.

"What? How?"

"Don't know. Didn't ask."

"Whoa," Bear said, tracing his fingers over the mural. "Poor guy."

"Very sad," Svec agreed. They floated in silence for a moment. The only sound was the whir of the air ventilation system and the erratic ping of meteoroids striking the ship.

"Everything changes," Svec declared at last, "nothing disappears."

He squirted cleaner into a paper towel and with fast circling swipes erased Yui's dream song of the end of the world.

T HE LIBRARY WAS a modern, one-story building made of caramel-colored bricks. It wasn't the best-stocked branch of Boston's library system, though the staff there tried to make up for this by programming elaborate community events. Karen had grown fond of the librarians, who either didn't know about her past troubles at the main branch or had decided to allow her a fresh start. Either way, she was grateful and on her best behavior.

For Last Day the librarians had transformed the main hall into an exotic street bazaar. A banner in purple and gold announced their bleak and whimsical intentions: OH, THE PLACES YOU'LL GO—NOW OR NEVER! Large swaths of metallic cloth hung from the ceilings and draped over bookcases, creating darkened channels of mystery between the stacks. Stalls were set up throughout the lobby, each representing a different place, both real and imaginary, which library patrons were able to visit for the first and/or last time. As expected, the stalls were set up in alphabetical order. Algeria, Alice's Wonderland, Bethlehem, and China were all disassembling their stations by the time Karen arrived at quarter to four. Two dads and their geriatric-looking toddler walked toward the Jurassic Age, where a live iguana sat on top of a card table, placidly waiting to be adored.

Somewhere between Mexico and Mount Olympus, Karen found Joyce, her favorite librarian, wearing a sombrero. Joyce was passing out samples of mangoes with lime salt to children. She waited until their faces puckered, then snapped a picture of them with a Polaroid. Near her, a slim Chinese man in overalls sat barefooted on the floor playing the erhu. A little girl offered the musician her already-bitten slice of mango, but the man shook his head.

"He's fasting," Joyce explained to the girl.

"What's fasting?" The girl was around six or seven years old. She had been deposited there by a nanny, who was now napping in one of the leather armchairs by the front entrance, an Avon catalogue spread over her snoring face.

"It means he won't eat or drink anything."

"Why not?"

"To empty himself, starting with his belly, then his heart, and finally his mind, so that he can make room for the new world that might or might not come tomorrow."

A bolt of lightning made of sequins was stitched on the front of the girl's T-shirt and she picked at it avidly, flicking the tiny discs of silver and scattering them across the floor like seeds.

"I will eat macaroni and cheese for my last supper," she said. "My mom will eat Pinot Grigio. Daddy doesn't live with us anymore. He can eat shit, Mommy said."

"Even rage deserves a place at the table," Joyce said, patting the little girl's head.

Joyce was not foster-mother material, Karen knew, but she was on Karen's short list of people who would probably host her for a week or two in the near future while she found a more permanent home. But there was time for all that later. The celebration was winding down. Crumb-strewn platters were piled high with crumpled napkins and lipstick-stained cups, the paper corpses of a once bountiful feast. Mexico had one churro left and Karen shoved it into her mouth before anyone else could get it.

A row of potted Ficus trees marked the entrance to Xanadu. It was rigged up like a tent, or an elaborate blanket fort, constructed out of white bedsheets and hat racks. The entire Coleridge poem was silk-screened onto one of the tent walls. Several cones of pungent incense were burning on an altar. In the very center of the tent a chocolate fondu fountain bubbled, surrounded by skewers of fresh fruit for dipping. *This is what Rosette means when she says the Devil is always tempting her,* Karen thought. She wanted to dip her lips into the chocolate fountain and drink forever, but she needed to get onto the internet and time was running out. The system automatically logged you off after thirty minutes and made you wait ninety minutes more before allowing you the chance to go on again. The library would be closed by then.

"I have to look something up," Karen said, her mouth full of bananas, to Pam, her second favorite librarian, after Joyce.

"Be careful, sweetie," Pam warned. She was wearing a scarlet kimono, her black and gray hair swept up in a topknot. "We've been so busy creating this *spiritus mundi* that no one's had time to police the computer room. It could look like *Caligula* in there for all I know."

Karen did not know what *Caligula* was but she could guess.

The library's computer room, a way station for homeless men locked out of their shelters for the day, was not decorated at all. A brightly lit purgatory, it reeked of mouthwash, which the men guzzled in place of real booze, and the minty urine that soaked their pants afterward. Karen found all the usual patrons, bearded men slumped like statues of slowly melting wax, rapt in listless concentration as thick cocks thrust in and out of the raw, pink bodies on their various screens. Fluorescent lights buzzed reproachfully above them. The extreme wattage was meant to discourage these men, freeing the computers up for more civic-minded research. It didn't work. The exploding sun could not keep them from their porn.

Karen selected the sharpest mini-pencil from the box provided, both a writing instrument and a weapon in a place like this, and sat next to a man with a hole in his cheek. Each time he swallowed, his teeth flashed for a second behind the rotted hole. He either didn't notice or didn't care when Karen gaped at him; another moment of devilish temptation — Rosette would be proud that she had recognized it. Karen wanted so badly to ask this man a million questions, squandering the few minutes she had left. How did he eat? Was the hole self-inflicted? A piercing gone gangrenous? Oooh, maybe it was part of a scarification ritual. But, no, she had to focus.

Dennis.

She couldn't remember his last name, and so she began a search with her own name, quickly finding newspaper articles from the time of their rescue. Front page of the *Herald,* fifth page of the *Globe.* Those were the days of the early internet and much had been made of the innovations it brought to a very old form of evil. She saw her mother's name and felt a string being plucked inside her, ringing through the center of her body. Her hands shook, clumsy on the keyboard. Karen crumpled a wad of tissue and sucked on it until it was soft enough to swallow. She saw Dennis's father's name and her body clanged again. But this was no time for a seizure. She searched for Dennis Conhaile — his father's last name — and boom, there he was.

In a few moments more she had located his address and jotted it down on a piece of scrap paper. He lived just minutes away, according to the map. He had been so close to her all this time.

The man sitting next to her began to rub the outside of his pants as though vigorously wiping out a stain. Karen plotted the bus route as quickly as she could, and staggered back into the festival.

Most of the people were gone now. Tables were flattened and stacked next to a pile of drapery. Joyce was directing Pam with great, sweeping arm movements, and Pam ignored her, showing the remaining patrons a picture on her phone. Karen explored the last stalls in search of more food. Between the drinking fountain and the bathrooms was a station still standing, draped all in white. Lace and chiffon and satins were pleated together in thick, voluptuous folds. It looked to Karen like an enormous wedding dress. There was nothing else except for a white plastic chair.

"This one is Nowhere. It was my idea," Joyce said, appearing suddenly at Karen's side. "I wanted to capture the negative space that makes reality real. The *wa* in *konnichiwa*. I thought about making it completely empty, but we have too many elderly patrons who might collapse if they don't have a place to sit down." She folded up the chair and held it under her arm.

"It's really pretty," Karen said. Joyce frowned. Her face had a clayey texture that furrowed deeply, almost comically, with emotion. Joyce had been trained as a rare-books librarian but had a laundry list of gripes against her colleagues in that field, and a longer list still of vengeful machinations she'd plotted against them, only some of which she had gotten away with. She'd been exiled to this quiet outpost of the city library system as a result. It was her Elba.

"I didn't want Nowhere to be pretty," Joyce confessed. "That was all Pam. I wanted it to be stark, to inspire contemplation. To push people past the anxiety and fear, the grasping and desire, and into a place of sublime acceptance at the end of the world. But then someone donated all this lace. It is really pretty, though. You're right." She rubbed it between her fingers a little resentfully.

Pam waddled into the tent and unloosed her obi, where her phone was hidden. "Hey, Karen, did I show you the new love of my life?" Pam pulled up a photo of a miniature potbellied pig. It had black and white spots like a Holstein cow. Pam had driven to Vermont to buy her from a breeder. "She fits into the palm of my hand!" Pam squealed.

"Not for long," Joyce said. "There's a reason gluttony is represented by a pig."

"Joyce's just afraid she might feel something so base as to resemble affection," Pam said, and skipped through dozens of shots of her pig until she found one of Joyce cradling the animal like a baby, feeding her a bottle, a beatific smile on her face. "Ha! See?" she said, thrusting the phone in Karen's face.

Pam would be an ideal foster mother. And her home came with an alternative-mammal pet! If tonight didn't go well, Pam was a contender for plan B.

"We're ordering pizza and watching movies tonight while we try to house-train Pam's pig, if you want to join us," Joyce said.

Karen wanted all of those things very, very much.

"I can't," she heard herself stammer. "I have—a date."

"Ooh-la-la," Pam whistled. "Do you want a little color?"

Before Karen could ask what that meant, Joyce had unfolded the plastic chair and Pam was pushing her into it. Both women took a tactile inventory of Karen's face. Their fingertips were cool and smooth, as though softened by turning the pages of so many books.

"She has great bone structure. Very Nordic."

"What does *Nordic* mean?"

There were huge gaps in Karen's education. Though adequately intelligent—more than adequately, according to some tests—she had been relegated to special education classes her whole academic life because of disturbing, intractable emotional difficulties (tantrums, talking out of turn, obsessive attachment to inanimate objects in the classroom, inappropriate physical boundaries with fellow students, truancy). She could name the entire pantheon of Greek gods as well as list their salient character traits, but she could not locate Greece on a map. She knew what the word *perihelion* meant, thirsted for any opportunity to use it in conversation, but had only realized a few years ago that animals that lay eggs, such as birds, cannot also give birth in the mammalian way. For years she'd reasoned that chickens laid eggs for eating and then gestated baby chicks for progeny inside their stomachs. Karen's quest for knowledge was largely self-directed, and her interests were celestial, not terrestrial. She attributed this to having been born under a Libra sun.

"Your foremothers milked reindeer in the Laplands," Joyce said.

"They knew the direction of the wind according to the pitch of its howl, and could smell an approaching bear. When they smiled, these marvelous cheekbones of yours had the power to stop Vikings dead in their tracks."

"I like that story," Karen said. "Tell me more."

"We don't know that she's Lapp, Joyce. She looks Irish to me."

"Jesus, Pam. You think everyone's Irish."

Pam didn't argue the point. She rooted around her cavernous pocketbook and removed a pair of patent leather tap shoes, a flashlight, and the collected works of Philip Larkin, until at last she found a tube of hot-pink lipstick. She applied layer after layer on Karen's bow-tie lips, making her blot them on a tissue she procured from inside another of her hidden pockets. When Pam was satisfied, she dashed blush across each of Karen's ethnically contested, though highly esteemed, cheekbones. "You look hale," Joyce admitted.

"Go get him, tiger," Pam said, smiling.

THE SUN WAS blinding. The highway appeared to crumble atomically in its relentless light. Even with sunglasses, Kurt squinted to see, relying on reflexes to pull off the highway in the right spot. They passed a mini-golf course terraced into the hill that overlooked the highway. A long line of people waited to be admitted for eighteen holes of fabricated whimsy. Sarah could not contain her disgust.

"Who the hell would want to spend Last Day playing mini-golf?"

"Takes all kinds to make a world."

Kurt lived in a trailer park behind the mini-golf course. It was a shame to his proud, hardworking family, who subscribed wholesale to the American dream of ever-upward mobility, that their only son would elect such a conspicuous downshift.

"Fiberglass is for Gypsies," his mother had muttered over her steaming cup of tea when Kurt showed her the brochure for the home he'd bought for himself. "Your father is rolling in his grave."

His father had been a shipbuilder, a member of the guild, as had his father and grandfather before him. Kurt's two sisters, one older, one younger, had both gone to college and gotten jobs their parents could be proud of. The elder sister was a middle school math teacher and the younger managed all the food vendors at Fenway Park. Kurt was the name bearer, and what had he done with that name? Dropped out of art school after one year, then foundered for a spell as a gas station attendant before the accident and the stint in jail. He'd assumed his family would be happy when he was released early, but his homecoming had been treated as a silent disgrace.

Kurt was proud of his double-wide. He owned it. Bought it with money he'd earned himself. And he liked his trailer park neighbors, only a small fraction of whom identified as Romany Gypsies. There was a self-reliant economy here in which many outside needs were conveniently provided. Pot, plumbing, rat extermination, childcare, elder care, pirated internet, discount Indian reservation cigarettes, taxidermy, and tattoos were all bartered with a fluidity and friendliness that Kurt knew his self-reliance-loving family would respect if they could relax their classist hypocrisy. That hypocrisy was exactly what Kurt had been fleeing when he'd made the decision to buy his double-wide.

The bike motored up a short steep hill into the neighborhood. People were gathered in clusters around smoky grills, ambling in and out of each other's homes, celebrating the holiday. His neighbors waved and nodded when Kurt passed by on his bike, the men cocking an eyebrow at the helmeted young lady behind him. A pack of small boys were practicing bike jumps off a homemade ramp. When they saw Kurt approaching, they got serious and rode faster, popping wheelies. Kurt revved his engine in approval and the boys with their squinted eyes and sideways smiles raced off.

Sarah had never been on a motorcycle before. She'd never been to a trailer park, either. This day was taking an unusual shape, and though she was desperate to know Kurt's plan for them, she was playing it cool.

"They look like regular houses," she remarked, noticing the shutters on the windows and the hedges out front. She was expecting something bedouin, a vast network of corrugated metal huts and merchants on the road selling beaded jewelry and stolen cellphones. Most of the double-wides looked new. Their white siding was laced with a yellow fringe, the same buildup of pollen that plagued the wooden shingles of Sarah's house. It seemed like a requirement to fly a flag from the front door. The faded colors of many sports teams and veterans' groups and the good old red, white, and blue hung motionless in the thickening air. A couple of people had even hung Last Day flags, the tacky gold flame encircled by white doves set against a lavender background.

"They *are* regular houses," Kurt said. They'd pulled up into his drive-way. He also had a flagpole extending obliquely from the front of his house, but no flag was hanging. A giant spider web connecting the naked, outstretched pole to the side of the house sparkled in the early afternoon sun.

"Wow, that's the biggest spider web I've ever seen," Sarah said as she removed her helmet and got off the bike.

"It's a beaut, isn't it? Been there for weeks." He got off the bike with a little hop and started walking across the street. "I'll be right back," Kurt told her. "Go on in. Door's unlocked."

Sarah crouched in for a closer look at the web. Nothing, not even a gnat, was ensnared in the twinkling, translucent fibers. She flicked her fingers against the thickest spot and a spray of moisture flew into her face. A boy ambled toward her. He was barefoot and chubby, around eight years old, Sarah estimated. His hair was a curly mess. He looked at Sarah as though assaying her worth.

"Hello," Sarah said, creeped out by his silent stare.

The boy clicked his tongue in a soft, patient rhythm. *"Tich, tich, tich."*

Sarah wondered if the child was a special-needs case, though admit-tedly, she'd never been very good with children. Not even when she'd been a child herself. Suddenly the green underbrush sprouting around Kurt's front steps shivered and a small brown rabbit hopped out. *"Tich, tich, tich,"* the boy continued, and after a moment of consideration, the rabbit hopped straight into the boy's arms.

"Arturo the Fourth! He's still among the living?" Kurt said, returned now from wherever he'd gone.

"Arturo da Fift," the child lisped.

"Sorry. Arturo the Fifth. Josh's mother keeps getting these rabbits for him, but they always escape their cages and get smooshed by cars. Josh isn't standing for it, though. He went on a campaign, didn't you, *kimo sabe?*"

The boy pressed his face into the rabbit's fur and inhaled deeply. "I made signs."

"Posted them everywhere." Kurt pointed out the white scabs of paper still clinging to a few trees and lampposts. "Arturo the Fifth is an agent of change. He helps keep the speed limit down in this neighborhood."

The rabbit leapt from Josh's arm and disappeared into the shrubbery behind Kurt's trailer.

"Can I please have a cigarette for my mom, Kurt?"

Kurt tapped one out of his pack and tossed it. Josh caught it midair and ran away. The bottoms of his feet were pitch black except for the arches.

"He'd be a good runner if someone trained him," Sarah observed.

"Not a chance," Kurt said. "He's going to smoke that cigarette himself once he's out of sight."

"How can you let him do that?"

"You can't raise other people's kids."

He gave Sarah a little tour of his home. The kitchen was wood-paneled and underused. The living room was a dumping ground of pizza boxes and beer bottles. Clothes were strewn all around the floor of the bedroom. There was a damp, skunky smell that Sarah connected to the joint Kurt was rolling for himself and not to the cleanliness of his home, which was about average, she guessed, for a man like him. Though she had no idea what a man's home ought to look like, let alone smell like. Terrence's bedroom was the only categorically male space she'd spent any time in, and he suffered from the most tragic, strangling OCD she'd ever seen. Pens and pencils were stored in separate identical

Lucite boxes that Terrence cleaned once a month with Q-tips and rubbing alcohol, and all the venetian blinds on his windows were calibrated to hover at the same fraction of an inch above the sills. If there was an odor to his room, Terrence masked it with the earthy-smelling cones of burning incense that he arranged on a porcelain Japanese dish with painstaking, ritualistic care.

Poor Terrence. She wished that he were here with her now. It was such an odd longing, when confronted with a new romantic possibility—to want to retreat to an older, more familiar (though unfulfilled) one. Terrence was so safe. She never felt awkward when she disappointed him, because she could trust he would always forgive her when conflicts came up. His face would twitch and he wouldn't look at her, but within an hour he'd relax and everything would be okay again. It had happened like that a million times with Terrence. She could count on it. Not so with Kurt. She was so uneasy in his presence. He made her want to plumb unfamiliar parts of herself and present them to him as offerings. "Here is my secret fear of children," she might say, "here are my self-important prophecies, my latent, possibly nonexistent, sexuality. Have them. Have them all. . . ."

"It's way bigger than I expected" is what came out of her instead.

Kurt chuckled. "What were you expecting?"

"I guess an Airstream. Something you hitch up to a truck and go camping in." She tucked herself into the small bench behind the kitchen table, glad that half of her weird, spastic body was hidden for the moment.

"People live here. Permanently."

"So weird not to have a cellar." Was this a classist thing to say? Was *she* classist? It had never occurred to her before that she could have blind spots in her ultra-embracing worldview. She tried to recover. "But then again, cellars are, like, all about symbolic fears and rats. They're totally overrated."

She hoped this sounded supportive. She was taking this man as her lover, her first and maybe only lover, and though the trailer park was underwhelming, it was definitely *memorable*, which was a relief. In fact, this whole experience was already imbued with iniquity and enchantment. She would not screw this up.

"So here's the plan." Kurt pulled out a kitchen chair and leaned over his lap to face Sarah. It was something Dr. Vasquez-McQueen did during office hours and smacked of condescension. "I'm going to shave and change my clothes and collect some things for this amends I need to make. I would offer you a beer or a joint, but since you're underage, that is illegal for me to do. However, if you help yourself while I'm not looking, that's fine with me. You catch my drift?"

"I hate that phrase, but yeah. And I don't smoke or drink. Not, like, puritanically, I just, real life is weird enough, you know?"

"You're amazing, sweetheart." Kurt lifted her hand and kissed her knuckles, then hopped out of his guidance counselor posture and headed into the bathroom. Sarah sat at the table a moment, the fingers of her left hand still ablaze from his touch.

Kurt had rinsed and lathered his face when Sarah knocked on the bathroom door. "Can I watch?"

"Uhhh, sure."

She lowered the seat and the lid of his toilet, which was so disgusting she only allowed her eyes to skim the surface before sitting down. She watched in a happy trance as Kurt plowed away paths of speckled white to reveal the smooth pink skin underneath. She envied the way men could bear such totally different faces to the world in a matter of weeks. Kurt had an impressive scar on his chin, a deep diagonal line that glowed a little pinker from the brief attention of the razor.

"That's a cool scar." Sarah pointed.

"Hockey game."

"Actors always talk about having a good and bad side of their face, and I always thought that was stupid, but you actually have two distinct sides of your face. Like you're two different people."

"I am a Gemini," Kurt told her.

Sarah suppressed a groan. If she were a guy, her penis would totally deflate right now. She didn't know what the female equivalent of that was, but her brain was certainly losing its boner. Astrology was so, so unforgivably dumb. And ten times dumber when straight guys talked about it.

Kurt wiped his face clean, a new man. He patted Sarah on the head and went into his bedroom. She followed him, feeling bolder. Standing there as he sorted through the piles on the floor, she took off her sneakers, then crawled onto his bed.

Kurt ignored this and continued rummaging around the mess. Time for that later, he thought, if *that* was going to happen at all—she was just a kid, after all. He was still on the fence, still hoping that after his impending confrontation, where this girl would act as his buffer/guardian angel, something much better would work out for both of them independently later on in the night, and they'd part ways happily. And if they did end up in bed together, then, well, disappointments were better faced in the dark.

Sarah continued to lie in Kurt's bed, her anxiety growing by the minute. Was it her job to seduce Kurt, she wondered, or was she supposed to wait for him to move toward her? The rules of all this were confusing at best, unfair at worst. She lay there, trying to look cool. A full retreat, such as jumping off his bed, would give this moment a case of whiplash. Besides, her socks reeked and she needed to hide them under his blankets. She angled her body in what she hoped looked like a sexy pose and pretended to take a nap. There were more clothes tangled in his sheets. Errant socks and a pair of boxers she avoided touching.

It wasn't supposed to feel like this, Sarah thought; or maybe this was exactly how it was supposed to feel?

"Hey, I could use your help a minute," Kurt said.

He had gotten a hammer to take down an Indian tapestry nailed to the windowsill. The elephant god Ganesha sat on a golden throne in the middle of a woodland scene, proffering his own broken tusk in one of his many hands.

"I don't want it to get all ripped or frayed if I can help it."

Sarah climbed out of the bed. She caught the cloth as it fell and shook out the dust.

"Why are you taking this down?"

"I need to return it today."

"You've had it for a long time." She shaded her eyes against the light from outside.

"Yeah."

Her ponytail had gotten limp and a lock of hair fell into her face. Kurt reached over and smoothed it behind her ear.

"Okay," Sarah said, an answer to a question he didn't ask, her voice feathery and strange.

Kurt made a pile on his bed of things that he was collecting for his amends. The tapestry. A field guide to North American mushrooms, its pages waterlogged and crispy. A coffee tin that he sealed with a plastic bag and rubber bands.

"Are those—ashes?" Sarah asked.

"Some of it, yeah," Kurt answered.

Sarah was about to ask whose ashes they were when something stopped her. She heard a thump overhead and gazed up at the skylight. A mass of pollen and dirt had whorled together, looking kind of like the Milky Way. A cat scurried over the roof. The bottoms of its paws pressed into the window, leaving behind tracks in the thick yellow film.

Kurt moved his bed away from the wall and reached behind it to pull out a small painting mounted in a cheap gilt frame. It was a pinwheel of blue and green wings flying away from the center point, an ersatz mandala. Sarah judged it to be the work of a precocious but untalented teenager, someone her age but not as smart. She was hoping that was the answer. The signature at the bottom said *Mary*. Maybe a long-lost niece?

"My old girlfriend," Kurt corrected.

"Oh," Sarah said. "Did she die tragically?" She couldn't believe how much she wanted this to be true.

"Everyone's death is tragic."

MARY HAD BEEN the one bright spot in Kurt's life after he'd dropped out of art school. Kurt was nineteen when he met her and Mary was a sophomore in high school. She was a gorgeous earth child with large brown eyes and dark, gleaming hair, the kind of girl who wore sandals with wool socks in the dead of winter, who smoked like a chimney but wouldn't touch a plate with meat on it. She thought Kurt's illustrations of dragons and heroes were genius and she loved his family as much as her own. She hailed from a long dynasty of semi-important Americans—the last of whom was her uncle Bear, an astronaut—WASPs clutching desperately to relevance as their storied past collected more and more dust in the annals of local libraries.

"We were switched before birth," she liked to joke about Kurt. She fit in so much better with his German-Irish Catholic family, and in a parallel world, Kurt would have been much happier in hers. Mary's vague ambition to one day run a daycare center out of her home was applauded by Kurt's parents, while his artistic impulses—mostly ignored, at times derided by his folks—would have been nurtured to the fullest if he had been born into her clan instead. Mary was the first member of her family not to go to Choate. She said she'd bombed the entrance exam on purpose. But she would have done poorly regardless of her effort. She wasn't stupid, just simple, content with whatever knowledge landed in her lap, curious about her world, but only to a point. She felt no need to waste time reading that the woods were lovely, dark, and deep when she could just go there and see for herself. She was looking forward to marrying Kurt as soon as she was eighteen and wanted nothing more than to start a family.

"Her parents hated me long before the accident," Kurt told Sarah. "I don't blame them. I'd bring her home drunk or stoned, she'd have twigs and pine needles and sap in her hair. Those expensive sweaters they bought her would be all ripped. They'd say, 'What were you doing, Mary? Rolling around in the forest?' And she was so goddamn sweet she couldn't lie. To anyone. She'd look at them with her full-moon eyes and just say, 'Yes.'"

Kurt cleaned the dust off another picture frame he pulled out from under his bed and handed it to Sarah. It was a badly scanned photograph of Mary, printed at a drugstore, but Sarah could see, even in this slightly pixilated, desaturated form, how beautiful and unself-conscious the girl was. It was a picture of her smiling face, a scrap of shadow creeping up under her chin, suggesting Kurt, her photographer, hovering above her, probably in some delightful springtime field. She was so heartbreakingly pretty. Even the bump on the bridge of her nose was pretty, as though her beauty was so powerful it cracked under its own weight, becoming greater from the resulting flaw.

About two years into their relationship, Kurt had crashed Mary's car into a tree. They had just left Kurt's parents' house. He was drunk but she was drunker and so he reasoned it was better for him to drive. Rain pelted the metal roof like gunfire and the windshield wipers swung hysterically to keep up, offering brief, vanishing glimpses of the road.

He woke up in a hospital and was quickly transferred to South Middlesex Correctional. Mary had survived the accident, he would learn from his parents. He had no idea what kind of condition she was in, only that she was alive. After he'd served his time, her parents forbade him from seeing her. "You ruined her!" her father raged, his breath so saturated with scotch it could catch fire.

"What happened to her—it would have been better if she had died," Kurt said to Sarah, who was still holding Mary's picture in her lap. "A couple months after I got out of jail, her mother wrote me a weird letter. Said she'd had a 'spiritual awakening'—her words, not mine—and wanted me over to their house for lunch on Last Day. I didn't know what to expect."

Mary's mother had greeted him at the door with a vodka tonic, as if

Kurt were her husband coming home from work. Her actual husband, Mary's father, had left the country. "He's taken his grief into exile," Mary's mother explained, offering no more on the subject. They sat around drinking in the sunroom while the Azorean woman they'd hired to take care of Mary got her dressed and ready upstairs. Mary's mother offered Kurt a Librium, and when he refused, she told him, "I was afraid for so long that you were going to ruin her life. I hated you for that. And now that you have, and the worst has happened, I can't hate you anymore."

"Please, just let me see her."

"Get ready, young man," her mother warned.

What finally emerged from the upstairs bedrooms was a wild animal in the shape of Mary. A scar ran up the back of her skull and onto her forehead, a satin strip where the hair refused to grow back. Half of her face sagged and her eyebrows had grown bushy and uneven. Even her eyes had changed. It was as though the human light in them had been snuffed out.

"She started screaming when she saw me. Brayed, like a donkey. She hit herself in the face and wouldn't stop. The CNA had to force some liquid tranquilizer down her throat to get her to stop. Then we all sat in their goddamn sunroom and had lunch together. It was awful. Her mother drank and this nurse's aide pretended the spoon was an airplane and pushed tuna salad into Mary's mouth. She'd chew and then drool half of it back out. When she swallowed, the aide clapped for her. I wished that she had died. Or that I had died. That we could have died together. Then right when I thought things could not be worse, Mary shit her pants at the table. While her mother and the nurse were changing her diaper upstairs, I just got up and left and never looked back."

Sarah handed the framed photo back to him. Kurt placed it in a backpack along with the other effects.

"So we're going to see her again?" Sarah asked.

"She died, finally, two years later. Pneumonia. Her immune system was wrecked after the accident."

"Then where are we going with all this stuff?"

"To her sister. This belongs to her, not me. I should have done this years ago." Kurt folded his hands over his stomach for a moment. He looked scared. He rearranged the contents of the backpack so that everything fit and belted it shut. What Sarah thought were tassels dangling from the top flap turned out to be long strands of hair.

"It's a cool backpack."

"She made it. She's an artist," Kurt said, swishing the strands around with his fingers. "Her sister, I mean, not Mary. It's Mary's hair, but that could be a lie. Her sister is—look, Sarah, I don't want to go there alone, but I don't want to force you into something you can't handle. If you want, I'll drive you home right now, or anywhere else you want to go. It's been nice to have someone listen to me, someone who's smart. Not some drunk girl who's gonna end up causing trouble. Not someone who thinks she's cute and deserves a free tattoo."

He lifted up his motorcycle helmet and offered it to her.

"I mean it. No pressure. If you want to go home, I have a plan B."

"What's that?"

"Go down to one of the bonfires. Burn this stuff. Go to a bar and get drunk."

"I don't want you to do that," she said. "I'll go with you to make amends to this sister. But afterward, we're going to watch the sunset on the beach."

L ONG BEFORE THERE was sleep, there was night, Earth rolling away from the sun as a lover in a bed. But now such darkness is an old dream. The light of cities, of towns, and the highways connecting them, rupture the black hemisphere, bleeding through the membrane of night. Tokyo appeared to Yui as a great hemorrhage of electricity, and somewhere inside it his brother lay dead. Weeks of looking through these windows had taught Yui to recognize the particular patterns of Tokyo on sight, a homing mechanism that failed to soothe him as he floated now alone in the dark. He wished all the lights of Tokyo would shut off, then all the lights in Asia, so that the world could disappear into the black space surrounding it.

Right now the monk was sitting with Tadeshi's body. Yui had seen to that right away. His sister-in-law was too hysterical and had to be medicated. Yui had called upon Chiyo, his company's COO, to handle the details in his stead. The cremation could proceed but interment of his brother's ashes, Yui had instructed Chiyo, would wait until he returned. He'd given his sister-in-law permission to pick the bones out of Tadeshi's ashes along with an uncle neither Yui nor his brother had felt any special emotion toward, but who could serve as a representative of the generation that preceded the brothers, a link to their father, who had died a few years back. His nephews were too young and spoiled to be trusted with this task, and his own wife and children had always been resentful of Tadeshi, who was closer to Yui than they could ever hope to be.

Because of multiple failures in their connection, these arrangements had taken hours to discuss, with voices stilted and screens stalled, cutting off in the middle of a sob. At one point Yui had to confront the immobile face of his wife frozen mid-yawn on the screen of his laptop. He hated her for yawning, for feeling anything, for being so near his brother when he was not.

But it was all settled now. There was nothing left for him to do but float in the Cupola and look at the world spinning below. Mission Control had offered their sincere, uneasy condolences. They'd granted the three men a work dispensation for the next day. Yui was getting his Last Day holiday after all.

KAREN REMEMBERED THE day she met Dennis better than she remembered anything else that happened before or after.

"Pack for a trip," her mother had told her, thrusting a plastic shopping bag into her hand. Karen packed a sweatshirt, a bathing suit, a stuffed rabbit, an old cigarette carton filled with remarkable-looking rocks, a handful of crayons bound by a rubber band, and a pad of paper. She fell asleep in the car, so there was no way of determining how long or how far they'd driven. She woke up when her mother was pulling her out of the car to lead her up the stairs to an apartment above a convenience store. It was summer. She was done with school and eager to go back. The length of a summer was for her an immeasurable gulf, and *when* was an impossible question always dangling off the precipice of her mind—when could she go back to school, when was it time to go home, when would she be able to drive, when was Christmas, when was supper.

"When I say so," her mother always responded, and if Karen argued, she got pinched until a bruise appeared.

The air inside the apartment was hot and still. Dennis was there with his father, or the man Karen assumed was his father. She never actually knew, until this day, if that was true. His father was smoking a cigarette out of the corner of his mouth, blowing smoke out of his nostrils, grunting as he tried to heave an air conditioner onto the windowsill.

"Be careful, you moron, or you'll kill someone on the sidewalk," her mother said to this man. Like they'd known each other for a long time and she had earned her right to be annoyed by him ages ago.

The man said nothing. Neither did Dennis. He was sitting on a white leather couch, his eyes lowered, already ashamed.

Years later she would try to describe Dennis to people, but she never could. Sometimes when she lay awake at night, she would try to remember his face and falter. He had two eyes, a nose, a mouth. He had ears and hair, a chin. A way of walking all his own. A voice. She could picture these things in her heart but not in her mind, as though Dennis were a ghost that could be felt but not seen. He was Dennis. He looked exactly like Dennis. What more could she say?

That summer day so long ago, Karen had run around the empty little apartment with a last gust of energy, and for once her mother did not yell at her to stop or slow down. In the bathroom hung a set of new towels with the tags still on them. On the tank of the toilet sat an Easter basket Karen recognized as hers from earlier in the year, full of tiny motel soaps, strands of green plastic grass still tangled into the basket's weave. In the kitchen, there was a large gap in the counter where a stove should have been and a hole in the wall sprouting a few pointless wires. In the living room was just the white couch where Dennis sat.

There was nothing else, except the bedroom, which is where she and Dennis would remain for the next year. Some of the people who came brought them presents of candy or Halloween costumes and took lots of pictures. Others hated them for no reason Karen could ever discern. One man liked to cover their entire heads with a dark wool hat and call them by different names. Another spanked them, then afterward held them and cried. Their own parents seemed indifferent. But there were some visitors who said they came for love.

"I drove for miles just to see you," one man said. "After I saw your pictures, I got in a car and didn't stop once. I peed in a bottle. All the way from Ohio. Do you know how far that is?"

Dennis did and Karen didn't. Karen was seven, lagging behind in school because of so much absence, just beginning to master her letters. A was still a tepee in her mind, housing wild Indians intoning the vowel in a long, unbroken chant. Aaaaaaaaaaaaaah. B was a yellowjacket de-nuded of its stinger as it flew away from a painful welt. C was a cookie only partially eaten. K was a stick figure of Karen herself, but only half of her. Where was the other half?

Dennis was nine years old. He told her that he hated school, and of-fered no explanation.

After the apartment was raided, a foster family had kept Dennis and Karen together. It had seemed like the right thing to do, until it became clear that it wasn't. Karen was always sneaking into Dennis's bed at night. To stop her from kissing everyone with an open mouth, her foster mother, a Catholic, put red pepper flakes on her tongue and made her sit in the corner with her hands on her head to stop the little girl from touching herself so much. When it was time to start first grade, Karen was transferred to a new house. She hadn't seen Dennis since.

*R*EDEMPTION AS AN armband for the stocky war veteran who stubbornly, angrily, refused a free beer. *REDEMPTION*, one letter per knuckle, on the hands of the actor who'd recently given up on Los Angeles and moved back home to Boston. *REDEMPTION* written vertically down the side of the rib cage and onto the hip of the pretty young brunette who couldn't stop crying about someone named Hailee.

"I just miss her so much," she said. "I can't stand it. I don't want to live without her."

"Sweetheart, I've been there," Jake said to her. "Everyone in this shop has been there. Even the ugly old miserable bastards you can't imagine anyone touching, let alone fucking, have been there."

She blinked at him, the tears for one moment suspended, her sadness quivering in her eyes like the last dream to bring you from sleep into morning.

"Just tell me it's going to be okay," she said to Jake.

"It will probably get worse. But then it will be okay."

D EATH AND DISEASE didn't scare Kurt, but Mary's sister did. Whenever he'd spent holidays with Mary and her family, her sister had spoken to him in the same brisk tone her parents used, if she talked to him at all. Far worse was when she would walk away from Kurt and Mary in the middle of a conversation and not return. "What the hell?" Kurt asked Mary once. "Oh, she gets bored easily," was Mary's placid answer.

So it came as a shock when this witchy sister spent Mary's share of their trust fund, which had transferred to her, on Kurt's outstanding legal fees. Stranger still when she picked him up and took him home to her bed the night he was released from prison. He had always assumed she hated him before the accident. He would learn in the manic six months that followed that night that hate and love were indistinguishable passions for her, and that the expression of either was always for her a form of punishment.

She was the exact opposite of Mary, who was guileless and sweet, almost mentally disabled by optimism. What the sisters had in common was that they both recognized Kurt's talent, though the elder sister was less starstruck.

"You're a hand, not an eye," she told Kurt.

"What does that mean?"

"You've got skills but not talent. You're a craftsman, not an artist."

There was malice in her assessment, but a brutal honesty, too, which brought Kurt a tremendous sense of relief: he could finally accept his limitations and build from there. He'd never be in a gallery or a museum but he was good enough to start a tattoo business, and that was good enough for him. It was Mary's sister who had come up with the name Redemption Tattoo, and fronted him ten thousand dollars to start out, only to disappear a few days before the grand opening, hopping a flight to Guatemala without so much as a goodbye.

Every time Kurt had started to feel stable, the demons of his past muted to a low murmur he could mostly ignore, a message in his inbox would appear like clockwork from MorningStar76, Mary's sister, reminding him of all the things he had done and would never do, what he was and what he wasn't, how different, interesting, and real his life could be if he had never left her, as though the fact was not that she had left him. She'd haunted him with the unwanted details of her hateful sex life, tales of the poverty and squalor she elected to live in, the shantytowns in Africa, the South American slums, the weird cult-like ashrams in India where she was ritualistically molested by purported gurus. And always, at the end of each letter, she would urge Kurt to drop everything, to give everything up, and come to her.

Kurt refused to respond to these emails, though he read each one carefully, chewed on them until his jaws actually ached during many sleepless nights (the sleeping pills he took now more or less resolved this). But her most recent message had been different. It was terse and gentle, saying that she was in town for the Last Day holiday and that she'd love a visitor. Here was her address, if he wanted to stop by. He had sat on this prospect like an egg, waiting for the answer to hatch beneath him, freeing him from the true mammalian labor of birthing a decision himself. It was only this morning, in the fugue of nihilistic and ethereal hope that was the Last Day, that Kurt had been moved to write her back. He regretted it now.

The sun fired at the earth in invisible rays, striking the pavement so that it glittered like a large elusive fish swimming in and out of a net of shadows. Every traffic light on the way to her address winked green at his approach, and he wondered if her sorcery was responsible for this, as mindfuckery was her typical foreplay. He hoped Sarah would protest or offer up a new plan, a bunch of high school kids getting stoned in the woods somewhere, something, anything but this. But Sarah was agreeable, though a little tense, wanting only to follow him wherever he went.

"I haven't seen her in years," Kurt explained to Sarah as they parked in front of a convenience store. Kurt and Sarah searched the empty shelves of the store for a decent bottle of wine. They could only find beer, which he knew would disappoint her. As if on cue, the Last Day standard "I Just Called to Say I'm Sorry" by Winston Wonderful began playing on the radio from crackly speakers in the store. Kurt took Sarah's hand and squeezed it. He wasn't going to waste his whole day on a scavenger hunt, so he grabbed a six-pack of the most expensive beer in the store and got in line to pay.

The old woman in front of them was trying to pay for her cigarettes with loose change. Her hands shook violently as she separated the pennies, nickels, and dimes on the counter. Her hair was short, thick, and white, half of it a poof of curls, the other half flattened from sleeping.

"Let me buy those for you," Kurt said, slapping a twenty-dollar bill down on the counter. "A Last Day good deed."

"I want a lottery ticket, too," the old woman demanded. Her face was blotchy and bruised and her breath smelled like mold.

"And a lotto ticket for my friend here," Kurt said to the clerk.

"A quick pick," the lady added. "I don't have no luck with my own numbers."

"She didn't even say thank you," Sarah said after the woman left.

"It was sadder to watch her count coins." He paid the clerk, who was watching TV behind a plexiglass barrier.

They walked back outside to his motorcycle. Kurt stuffed the beer into the backpack he was returning. "I'm glad you're coming with me," he said, and slung the backpack over his stomach. "Once we get rid of all this stuff, we'll pick something up for dinner. And eat it on the beach."

The girl beamed back at him a dizzy smile. The bright-eyed elixir of teenage adoration made him feel smarter and more confident. Maybe a better man could do without all that, but not Kurt, not today. He had learned through much trial and error that it didn't matter what happened in the end, so he might as well surrender to his own idiocy. He took Sarah's chin in his hand and kissed her.

It wasn't Sarah's first kiss, but she decided right there to rewrite history so that from now on it would be. *We were standing on the sidewalk in front of this convenience store, it was Last Day. . . .* His lips were warm and very dry and did not linger long. A carbonated tingling erupted behind Sarah's kneecaps. Her wrists fell numb, useless.

MARY'S SISTER HAD just returned from another one of her pilgrimages. She was gaunt inside her pale gray T-shirt, and her jeans looked like a sack her body had rolled into. Kurt held her for a long time when he saw her. Neither one of them spoke, until Kurt pulled away, a sad look on his face, and said, "Jesus, Sarah. When was the last time you ate something?"

"I have some plums. They're mealy and taste like paper. It's not their season yet. I shouldn't have bought them."

Kurt shook his head. "This is Sarah. It's a day full of Sarahs, I guess. . . ."

"Sarah with an *H*?" Sarah Moss blurted out.

"It's the least interesting fact about me," her namesake answered. She took the younger girl's hand and squeezed it as hard as her bony fingers were able.

The only feature she shared with her sister, Mary, Sarah thought, comparing the figure in front of her to the photograph she had seen earlier, was their nose, though on the elder sister it looked ugly. This other Sarah had unnerving blue eyes set far apart on her face, giving her the vigilant look of an animal.

"Could I have a glass of water?" Sarah Moss asked.

"Of course," the woman answered and walked as though in great pain toward the kitchen. Her black hair reached down to her waist and was streaked with white strands.

The apartment she had sublet was unfurnished except for a long wooden picnic table on which she had arranged a series of photographs.

"So you were in Asia this time?" Kurt lifted a photograph from the table and winced at what he saw. Sarah inched closer to him and looked over his shoulder. All the photos were portraits of people peering directly into the camera. The one Kurt held was full of little children squatting in a darkened doorway. Their mouths were ringed with erupting pustules, and tears streamed clean tracks down the filth of their faces.

"That one's called *The Impetigos.* Isn't the light perfect?" the other Sarah called from the kitchen sink.

Kurt returned it to the table and picked up another: a man with a mangled half of an arm held a chicken by the throat with his other, intact hand.

The other Sarah handed Sarah Moss a mason jar of lukewarm water teeming with particles. Sarah Moss sipped it warily as she watched the older woman stack the photos to make room for her guests at the table. "That man lost his arm as a teenager. He chased a soccer ball into a thicket where an unexploded ordnance was waiting for him. There are thousands of them left over from the Vietnam War."

"You work for an NGO?" Sarah Moss asked.

"No, I don't believe in activism. The idea that people's lives are supposed to get infinitely better is the very barrier holding our species back from true fulfillment."

"Sarah's got a trust fund," Kurt quipped. "So she can afford to be radical."

"Not anymore." She lowered herself to the floor and folded her long, willowy legs into a tight lotus. "I spent the last of it this year. I bought this girl out of sexual slavery." She reached up for the cigarette Kurt had just lit for himself, and without looking or even thinking about it he gave it to her.

"She was sixteen and had a severely lazy eye. I mean, the thing looked like it was going to roll out of her face at any moment. That one lazy eyeball had seen more in its sixteen years than most of us see with both eyes in a lifetime. It had had enough, was ready to abandon ship. 'Let the other guy do the witnessing,' is what that eye was saying. I liked her lazy eye. I liked her, too. I took some amazing photographs of her, then erased the data from my camera. I wanted to stipulate that this prostitute never wear sunglasses again, but my Thai is fluent only to a four-year-old, and you can't make stipulations when bargaining over human lives. I paid a gigantic sum to her pimp. Emptied my trust fund."

"That's a kind of activism," Sarah said.

"I just wanted to see what would happen. I wasn't trying to save her."

"No one would accuse you of that," Kurt said, lighting another cigarette he kept partially cupped in his hand, as though hiding it from her.

"What happened?" Sarah Moss asked.

"She went back to her pimp. Not even a week later. But it was my goal to get my bank balance down to zero, so I succeeded."

"Sweetheart," Kurt began, but the conclusion of that thought was too sad for him to finish. He excused himself to the bathroom.

What was the attraction? Sarah wondered. This elder Sarah was frightening and came off as even more asexual than she was. Then, as if she'd read the question gleaming in Sarah Moss's eyes, the woman offered this:

"It might not appear so, but I do love that man. In my own way. And he loves me, though he can't admit it. Not anymore. It's like the darkness within him recognizes the darkness within me. A negative *namaste*."

Sarah wanted to run out the door that very moment, to leave this witch forever, but she would not let this woman win Kurt's love. Not today. She picked up a photograph and asked about it, trying to change the subject. "What's going on in this one?" It was a picture of a dead tiger hog-tied to a stick being carried by two slight, stern-faced men.

"That was in Indonesia. That tiger killed a little girl in the village. The villagers took it really personally, which I found fascinating. We see natural disasters as blameless, senseless tragedies. Typhoons and earthquakes are emotionally fraught but simple at the same time. Not like the bulk of life's traumas, caused by some human being's fear. But these villagers regard the realm of nature on the same level as any other human endeavor. So when nature strikes, they first propitiate the gods they offended and then seek vengeance. They stalked that tiger for a month before they caught and killed him. I was there the day they took his corpse on a parade for everyone to see."

"How did they know which tiger did it?"

"I wondered the same thing. Animal faces are as distinguishable as human faces to them. They're all neighbors. They were confident it was him."

"I feel bad for him. If it was a him," Sarah Moss said. "The tiger."

"The only thing left of the girl was her arm. The tiger left it at the edge of the village as a kind of offering. Like a house cat leaves a dead mouse on the doorstep. It was a hell of a parade."

"I bet." Sarah Moss wanted to cry. It was taking all her strength to maintain this posture of cool immunity.

Kurt returned from the bathroom and it was obvious right away to both women that he had been crying. "What do you say, Sarah? Should we order a pizza? My treat."

"Thank you," the woman said, gazing up at him. "No."

"You got to eat something. You're disappearing."

"I know." She unfolded her legs and gathered them into herself. She rose slowly from the floor and walked her imperious, exhausted body over to the window, where she sat again and stared. For a long time no one said anything. Sarah Moss began flipping over the photographs so that she and Kurt wouldn't have to see them anymore. When she was done, she looked at Kurt and tapped an imaginary watch on her wrist, telling him that she was done with this adventure. He smiled at her. That's what he had brought her there to do, to let him know when it was time to leave. Without her, he would have stayed all night, trapped in this abyss.

"So," Kurt said. "I wanted to return these to you." He unlatched the fringed top of the backpack and took out the can of Mary's ashes.

"Don't," Sarah said from the window.

"They don't belong to me." Kurt pulled out the items one by one. "It wasn't right for me to keep them."

"Guilt is a waste of time," she started to argue. "It's a—"

"Yeah, yeah, I know your intellectual arguments very well and I don't need to hear them again. I feel bad and have felt bad for years now because she made this painting for you, and I didn't think you deserved it. I didn't want you to have it. I didn't even want you to have her fucking ashes. So I took it all from you. Even though I couldn't look at it, either. It was under my bed, for Christ's sake."

"It doesn't matter—" she groaned.

"Yes it does. She loved you. She made this for you. I was spiteful and selfish and I'm sorry. That's why I'm returning it to you."

He placed the painting on the floor and slid it across the room to where she stood by the window. Sarah Moss was scared that the woman would do something horrible, like throw the painting out the window or drop her pants and pee on it. But she didn't do anything; she didn't even look at it. She continued to stare at the sky.

Sarah Moss looked out the same window. The uppermost branches of a tree were wiggling a little in the wind. Beyond them, nothing.

"Happy Last Day. Until night falls." Kurt took Sarah Moss by the hand. "Come on. We're leaving."

"Wait." The other Sarah pulled herself out of her reverie and walked up to Kurt. She put her hand on his cheek, and kissed him. It was a long, slow kiss that Sarah Moss could see involved tongue.

"Thank you, Kurt," she said at last. "I'm grateful that you took such good care of these things. I've moved around so much over the years. I've acquired and lost so many possessions, some of them, I'm loath to admit, quite meaningful to me. There's no way I could have been a good steward of her ashes and effects. But you were. And I'm truly grateful."

"Jesus Christ," Kurt whispered, his eyes tearing up again. "You're too good for this world, sweetheart."

"We all are, Kurt." She opened the door for them. "Goodbye."

The door shut behind them with a bang followed by the clatter of multiple locks.

The air outside had cooled quite a lot. The sun was not ready to set but its light was thinner, almost watery, as it prepared to swim away.

"Thank you for coming with me," Kurt said, wiping his eyes with the backs of his hands. "She was always weird before, but not like that, not so—"

"Sadistic?"

"Maybe." Kurt remembered the last time he'd slept with her. She'd said things he shuddered to recall now.

Sarah fished her sweatshirt out of her bag and wrapped it tightly around her body. She looked up at the wan blue of the sky. A thick tower of cloud was disintegrating fast like something on fire. If there was proof of anything mystical—answers, explanations—she couldn't think of a dumber place to look for it than the sky.

"IT'S FUNNY," BEAR said, "she doesn't look all that far away."

"I am surprised every time I come here and see that she is so close."

The green tangled veils of the aurora borealis rippled over the North Pole. The ISS made another lap around the world.

"He was supposed to be here," Yui said, following Bear to the galley.

"I read that."

Yui and Tadeshi had both trained to become guests in space. Their ultimate goal was to go together. Tadeshi, who was six minutes older, had offered ridiculous sums to JAXA, NASA, and Roscosmos to allow for the first time not one but two non-astronauts concurrently on the mission. Even the desperately underfunded European Space Agency had refused their offer. The Yamamoto twins had never been separated like this before. They were a study in cooperation. They had been since they were born, and probably before then. Yui would not drink from his mother's breast until his brother latched onto the other. When the boys started their schooling, their tutors learned early on to give them identical grades, an easy indulgence as their test scores often *were* identical, or near enough. The woman who became Tadeshi's wife had first approached Yui for a date. She'd been a silent stalker of his at university, claiming that she alone could tell the twins apart from across the street, a boast that was probably true given the amount of time she spent staring at them. Yui had spent their only date combing through her friends' online profiles to find a girl he could claim was prettier, confabulating a story that he liked her friend instead, so that she would like Tadeshi better. In a standoff of kindness, each of the two brothers, both engaged, stalled his wedding plans so that the other could have the honor of marrying first and offering his bride their mother's wedding ring. In their company, they assumed separate roles—Yui was the artist and Tadeshi the businessman—but drew the same salary. They were competitive only in their ability to surrender and sacrifice for the other. When Tadeshi won the first seat on ISS Mission 47-48, his brother was overjoyed that he would not have the burden of taking it from him. Then, two weeks before they were to fly to Moscow, Tadeshi tore his Achilles tendon getting out of a Jacuzzi.

"I demanded to see the MRI. I thought Tadeshi was faking, to give me the trip. He was not faking. But the injury was intentional. Definitely. I know."

Svec had smuggled several pints of vodka on board, which he now offered to Yui. He had been saving them for his last night on the ship— this would be his last mission in space, he was planning to announce his retirement once he landed—but the death of a twin certainly called for drinks, no matter what that punctilious American said. The vodka was hidden among all the other beverages in soft plastic pouches, suggesting some outside cooperation with the team that had packed the Soyuz that had brought them here.

"It might not—" Bear stammered when he smelled the alcohol on the other men's breath. "I mean, I suppose it's okay, on Last Day. But don't you think drinking, and whatnot, will interfere with our mineral balance tests?"

Svec swigged without apology. "This one here"—he pointed at Bear—"was not supposed to be on mission, either. Greg Koehler was my left-seat man. He got sinus infection before launch."

"That's true," Bear admitted. "Greg's a good man. A great astronaut. I feel sorry for him, missing out on this."

"Greg is like brother to me," Svec said.

"Do you have a brother?" Yui asked Bear.

"Two sisters," Bear said.

Yui sobbed, but without gravity his tears could not fall, forcing him to blink like a maniac in a grand mal seizure and blot his face constantly with a towel.

"My older sister lives in Boston. My younger sister just moved into a group home there recently. She's special needs."

"What does she need?" Yui asked.

"She has Down syndrome."

"My son," Svec began, then stopped. A meniscus of water pooled over his eyes. It took very little—the opening bars of "Ochi Chernye," a single line of Pushkin—added to a few milliliters of vodka to make Svec cry. He threw the remainder of the empty carcass of his liquefied dinner in the trash and pulled a laminated index card out from under his shirt. It was held in place by two clamps attached to a chain of tiny metal beads around his neck, like a Christian scapular. "He made," Svec said, smirking again in that expression Bear now realized was involuntary, not ironic. On the paper, printed in messy Cyrillic scrawl, was the name and birth date of every single man and woman who had ever orbited the earth in space, Svec explained. "Maxim cannot be in school. He is not normal. But loves astronauts. Knows everything. More than me! He can recite this list without looking. Like machine."

"Oh." Bear held the plastic sheet in his hand and smiled. "He's autistic."

"He is good boy!" Svec slapped his hand hard on the table.

"Tadeshi choked to death."

"Terrible. Terrible."

"He was alone. Eating at his desk. I suppose, eating too fast. Why was he rushing? I wonder."

"Best not to think about it."

"He had a mole. On his left buttocks. I do not have this mole."

"Okay, Yui. It's going to be okay—"

"If the crack in the buttocks is the equator, Tadeshi's mole would be somewhere near Madagascar."

"Which orientation are you using?" Svec asked.

"All right, fellas, let's be careful with this stuff." Bear took the vodka pouch from Yui and saw that it too was already empty. Yui and Svec laughed and opened another pouch that they passed back and forth to each other. Ripples of laughter flowed into rushes and within minutes they were out of control.

"Svec, you have girls, too. Daughters, am I right?" Bear needed to take control and steer this ship in a different direction.

"Whores," Svec said, his eyes squeezed shut, trying either to hold their image in his mind or prevent it from entering. "Like their mothers."

"I love whores," Yui sighed. The very thought calmed him immensely.

"Oldest daughter is dancer. Not real dancer. How do we say? Strip dancer. Whore dancer. Her mother is, too. I tried. I send her to good school. I give her good advice. Always give her mother money. They don't care. They like to take their clothes off. Her grandmother was whore, too. Mother's mother. It's in their blood. Nothing can be done about it. Second daughter, from second wife, she is lesbian. She has hair like you." He pointed to Bear. "And ring in nose like bull. She hates me."

"Tadeshi has a gay son. Masami. His mother wanted a girl and gave him a girl's name and now he is fully gay. This is how it happened."

"It doesn't work that way," Bear said.

"My sons are little assholes," Yui said, then doubled over laughing until he was spinning in place.

"Kids can be tough," Bear offered. "I know I certainly had a hard time with my girls. And once they hit the teen years? Phew, it was tense. Everybody about to burst into tears or rage at any second. My wife, my ex-wife, she was a mess about it. Crying and screaming right alongside the girls. I was so glad to go to work every day back then, I'm telling you. Pack it on, I told my project manager. Anything to get me away from their mood swings. But now they're both in college, my girls. One's in graduate school, for special education therapy. The other is studying economics at UCLA. They're great girls. I really feel like they are my buddies now. Like, if I met them in some other context, if they were my interns, I'd be really impressed by them, and interested in what they had to say. But man oh man, the road here was a rough one."

"My sons were born little assholes. It is their destiny."

"But you love them, right?"

Yui sucked the vodka out of the pouch until the package crinkled and folded in on itself. "Yes, of course. I love them. But I love Tadeshi more. No one can compare."

"I understand," Svec said, opening another pouch. "I feel same about Greg Koehler. He is my truest friend. Like brother. I would die for him."

"I would die for my brother," Yui said. "I feel one emotion right now. Just one. I am furious Tadeshi did not let me die first."

Bear wasn't sure how long he could babysit his colleagues as they drank. The porthole window offered a glimpse of Australia, a fat, stunned rhinoceros marooned in the middle of the sea. A meteoroid sailed into the atmosphere and burned up like a cigarette tossed out the window of a moving car.

"I should send a few emails out before I hit the hay," he told the men, but they were not listening to him.

After settling into his CQ, Bear opened his laptop and began typing in his journal. He used to think he would die for his wife, that she was his partner in every sense, that his success depended on her nurturance, and that without her, there was no point in succeeding. Then she left him for a pharmaceutical exec from Boston. And his daughters? Would he die for them? They were self-sufficient, resourceful, tough. He'd raised them that way, and so never, not even in their childhood, had he loved them with the vertiginous pity so many parents feel toward their helpless young. His daughters could survive anything; they didn't need their dad's even hypothetical, metaphorical pledge to give up his life for them. And besides, they had chosen their mother in the divorce, had followed her across the country to Boston, treating Bear like a beloved uncle they patronized with visits not more than twice a year. He loved his sisters, but he would never give his life up for them.

Bear wrote in his journal that if he died tomorrow, there would be no lingering resentments. No unfinished business. He had been a good husband, and then a compassionate ex-husband, a great son and brother, a loving father, a dependable friend. But there was no one he would die for, like Yui's Tadeshi or Svec's Greg. *Is this a fundamental failing of mine?* he wrote, his neck perspiring. *There is no one, not even my children, whose life I value above my own.*

"Hotel of Bad Dreams. That is where we are. That is the name I will give my new game. Because that is the name of this place," Bear heard Yui saying to Svec outside his CQ. A long silence followed, floating like matter, carrying weight and dimension. What were they doing? Bear wondered. Then at last he heard each of the men crawl into their crew quarters.

"Name of this world," Svec answered.

THE BUS STOP nearest Dennis's address was at the bottom of a hill in a neighborhood Karen had only ever heard of on the news, and never for a good reason. Trash cans were lined up on and around the sidewalk, standing expectantly, like children waiting for the school bus. In the distance, at the top of another, even taller hill, sat a power plant surrounded by a few straggly trees. The sun sank behind it, streaking the sky like a chemical explosion slowly burning off its rainbow of gases.

She continued down the long street. It looked like all the other streets in the neighborhood. Rows and rows of triple-decker apartments, each building a different shade of Easter egg pastel, with wooden front porches that sagged in the middle, on the verge of collapse. Karen came upon a lean woman in a conical straw hat picking bottles and cans out of the trash. The woman wore a surgical mask and purple rubber gloves that spanned almost the entire length of her slim arms. She reached intrepidly into the barrel, practically disappearing inside, then resurfaced with a bottle that she shook empty and stowed in one of the many plastic bags tied to her grocery carriage. It was an elaborate system, Karen could see, separating items by material and size.

"Get out of my trash!" a man yelled from his porch. His hair had been shaved off and was growing back in patches over his white skull. No one, certainly no immigrant, which this trash picker probably was, had a right to touch his private property, even if it was private property he didn't want. He yelled at the woman more and she yelled back in her language, some kind of Chinese-sounding tongue whose very tone infuriated him.

"It's a friggin' holiday. Even God took a day off." He nodded at Karen, as though they were in agreement.

Could this be Dennis? Karen wondered. She double-checked the address she had written down at the library. No, Dennis lived ten houses down, she was relieved to see. The man took a last drag of his cigarette, wincing as though it hurt him to smoke it, then flicked the still-burning ember into a bucket of murky, brown water standing on the small front lawn. He looked at Karen with a knowing leer, and she froze in that old, old way, grinning back at him like a scared animal. Sometimes men could just tell. They knew all about her just by looking at her, and before she knew it, they were unbuttoning their pants. She had to be careful. She and Nora were working on boundaries. "You have choices," Nora was always saying.

"I have choices," Karen repeated to the man, her voice quavering like a pool of water disturbed by a tiny leaf. She prayed the house would reabsorb this man, suck him back into its hideous belly. She held her breath. "Go away," she whispered. The man rose and returned inside, letting the screen door slam behind him.

Of course that was not Dennis. Karen rebuked herself for even thinking it might be. Dennis was her brother. Well, this wasn't really true, but it seemed *spiritually* true. They'd shared a kind of womb together. A terrible one.

In the distance Karen heard the train approaching. The tension of its arrival rattled the ground. Pulses of silver, splashed with graffiti, swam fast behind the houses like a school of fish. She was glad Dennis lived near a train. It would make traveling to and from this place easier for her. She imagined a whole future in which she lived here with him, in this neighborhood, in the house she had yet to reach, a house she was fast furnishing with the frills of her own imagination. The thoughts were unspooling too quickly. Rip by rip she ate a brown paper napkin her fingers found at the bottom of her purse.

Would she marry him? Yes, she would. She would ask Rosette to be the maid of honor at her wedding. Dennis would stroke her hair every night until her eyes closed. He would get cancer and she would have to nurse him to health, but it would never be the same. Such is life. They would survive until the end. Just the two of them, sitting on the cement foundation of a house that had been burned down along with everything else in the great undoing of a Last Day far in the future.

She kept walking, the numbers on the houses ascending. By now, a deep blue darkness had gathered above the great pillowy clouds, a si-phoning point where night was slowly being released. And then she was there at Dennis's house, number 60. There was no front porch, only a cement step without a railing. Three names were listed next to the buzz-ers, but not one of them was Dennis's. A strip of duct tape covered the doorbells but Karen pressed them anyway. The tape felt sticky and the buttons inert. When no one responded, she opened the front door, which, she discovered, was unlocked.

Loud Spanish music rattled through the first-floor apartment. She heard voices on the other side of the door, talking and laughing. The door opened and a man emerged holding a tray of uncooked hamburg-ers. He said something to Karen in Spanish. It sounded busy and con-gratulatory. Karen peered behind him. A Last Day party was in full bloom: a bouquet of gold and purple balloons tied to a chair, a toddler bouncing on the hip of a woman in a purple dress. The woman leaned over a table of food to kiss a man who was uncorking a bottle of wine. It was a nice little scene, and Karen was distantly satisfied to see that no matter what happened to the earth tomorrow, these people were leaving it in joy. The man in the hallway finished whatever he had to say to Karen, then headed down the hall to the back deck. Karen climbed the stairs to the second floor.

The door to this apartment was open only as far as the chain that locked it would allow. A woman appeared in its frame at the sound of Karen's heavy feet on the landing. She was an erecter set of bones bound in pale yellowing skin, wearing a loose gray T-shirt. Two bare feet protruded from beneath the thickly folded cuffs of her jeans.

"You're not the delivery service, are you?" she asked Karen, in a grainy, colorless voice.

"No. I'm sorry," Karen said.

"Don't apologize. Colloquially, people attach the words *I'm sorry* to the word *no*, when a simple 'no' is enough. It cheapens the whole English language when you toss an apology into a conversation where it doesn't belong."

"I'm sorry," Karen repeated, feeling sweaty and uneasy in her green dress.

"Fine," the woman allowed. She leaned against the doorframe and rolled herself a cigarette. She picked bits of tobacco off her lips and tongue and tucked the cigarette behind her ear. Her hair was long and black, with silvery white strands. Karen remembered her fifth-grade teacher telling her that all human hair longer than one and a half inches was just a string of dead cells swinging uselessly off our heads, and that if aliens ever landed on Earth and met us, they would think our habits disgusting.

Karen lingered on the stairs, transfixed by this opinionated ghost of a woman. "Today was a really pretty day. A good one to go out on," Karen offered.

"I haven't left this apartment since—I can't remember. Thursday?"

"Oh. Do you have one of those ankle bracelets that go off at the police station when you leave?"

"No."

Karen wanted to know whether the woman behind the door was pretty or not, but she could only see one narrow slice of her at a time. Almost every face in the whole world was gorgeous if you looked at only one small piece of it, especially if that piece was an eye. All put together was where most people's beauty fell apart.

"I'm testing myself. It's an exercise," the woman said. She waved the smoke away from her face, stirring the white tendrils into a messy cloud.

"Like, for losing weight?"

"How much can we live without? At what point does isolation force us into connection? At what point does something become everything?"

"Yeah." Karen had no idea what she meant. "Does Dennis live here?"

"I think there is a guy who lives upstairs with that hog and her piglets. I'm just subletting. I don't really keep track."

"I'm going to see him now," Karen explained.

"I am ready for it to end," the woman said. Her voice came from a well, not a fountain, Karen decided.

"Okay." She was getting anxious now. And hungry. She hoped Dennis was friends with the Spanish-speaking family downstairs and would want to go join them for hamburgers.

"Could you do me one last favor?" the woman asked.

A last one? Karen was scared that she had inadvertently agreed to do a first favor and had already forgotten it and failed.

"If you pass by a bonfire tonight, could you toss this in?"

She held up a backpack, and before Karen could assent the woman was cramming her bundle through the four-inch space her chain lock allowed. It took a lot of finagling. Whatever the bag contained, it must have been a collection of things small enough to rearrange themselves into an agreeable shape with one large thing that wanted to cause trouble. Karen immediately pictured a human skull, a man's. The woman pushed with her weak, malnourished arms and Karen pulled. The bag popped through at last. It was made of tan canvas and the top flap had been threaded with what looked like long strands of human hair.

"It's heavy," Karen observed. "But not too heavy."

"Good."

"What's in it?"

"It's bad luck to ask."

"I'm sorry."

"I forgive you," the woman said. Karen couldn't be sure, but she thought she saw the woman wink at her.

SHE HEARD THE sound of a baby wailing as she reached the landing of the third floor. This was something she had not considered—that Dennis might already be married, that he would have gone and started a family without her.

She knocked on the door. At first no one answered, so Karen knocked harder. A scurry of feet and sulky moans and the continued cries of a baby were the only response. A low-pitched "Get it" blasted through the noise and at last the door opened. The little boy who opened it immediately ran away from her, his job done. He wore underpants decorated with cowboy hats and guns, and a pair of thick glasses that magnified his eyes. He leapt onto the couch where a young girl, presumably his sister, also sporting thick, goggle-looking glasses, was reading a magazine. The boy grabbed the magazine from her and threw it behind the couch onto the floor. The little boy was around seven, Karen guessed, and his sister a bit older but not much. The baby she'd heard crying was nowhere to be seen.

Karen entered the apartment, closing the door behind her. "Here you go," Karen said, picking the magazine off the floor and returning it to the girl, who did not look up or thank her. It was a back issue of *Famous, Etc.*, a weekly periodical reporting on famous people doing banal things and banal people doing extraordinary things. This issue, which Karen had read in Nora's office months ago, featured a TV actress talking about her lactose intolerance and a teenage girl who had given birth to a baby in the middle of her school's field trip to the Bronx Zoo. The teenager had washed the baby in a bathroom sink, cut the umbilical cord with a plastic cafeteria knife, and left her son swaddled in her jeans jacket at the entrance to the reptile exhibit. Later she changed her mind and wanted the baby back, and through a surprising amount of legal mercy, she was now reunited with her baby, who was doing fine, the article said. The TV actress talked about her battle with gas and bloating, a hereditary response to milk, but admitted that she indulged in goat cheese every once in a while. The magazine in the girl's hands had the address square ripped out of the cover, a telltale sign of a doctor's office magazine.

"My therapist is named Nora. Who's your therapist?" Karen asked the girl.

"Hillaria," the girl answered, still not lifting her enlarged, bespectacled eyes from the glossy photos of infant abandonment.

"Do you like her?"

"She sucks."

"Oh. I'm sor—" Karen began, "I mean, that's too bad. Where's your dad?"

"I don't know. Probably jail. You can ask Ma when she gets home from work. But be careful. Sometimes, just mentioning my dad puts her in a bad mood."

"Jail?" Karen's heart rattled inside her chest. "Is your dad named Dennis?"

"Dennis is in the bedroom," she said, and pointed with her chin to a dark hallway behind the kitchen.

The boy was busy building a fort out of towels and blankets that stretched from the kitchen table to the couch where his sister read. He yanked a cushion from behind her head and she swatted him like a puppy with the magazine. The front window of the apartment was blocked almost entirely by a large television, the big boxy kind Karen thought of as old-fashioned. At Heart House they had a flat-screen TV. One of the rich absentee relatives of a catatonic named Aimee had bought it to make herself feel better about never visiting. Karen felt a little bad for these kids, living with such an unwieldy, obsolete piece of machinery. On the TV a cartoon mouse was traversing the vast landscape of a dining room table laid out for a banquet. Karen remembered watching this same show when she was a child.

The crying baby emerged from beneath the draped blankets of the fort. He was not the same race as the other two children, Karen observed. The older kids were white, pasty even, and the baby looked African American, but maybe not, as Rosette was always assumed to be Spanish or Brazilian when she was in fact from the Azores. Rosette felt these distinctions mattered a lot but Karen had read that race wasn't even real so who cares. This baby was cute, for sure, with round mournful eyes and a loaded diaper about to fall off his little hips.

"He fucking smells. Change him," the middle brother instructed his older sister, who groaned as she hauled the baby into her arms and carried him down the hall.

"Dennis is in there," the girl said to Karen as she went, kicking at the second door of the hallway with her foot.

Karen followed the girl down the hallway and tapped at the bedroom door. "Hello?" she said softly, and turned the knob. Another giant television—this one flat and new—occluded the only window in the room, and towels and black trash bags were tacked to the sill, covering what little light might sneak in from the edges. A video game stood idle, the crosshairs of a gun's scope trained on a blank expanse of desert. The sand shimmered like the great sea that had once covered it. Karen recognized the game immediately. Jared, the Sunday overnight counselor, liked to play it. Karen knew the game's pause music all too well. It was intense, like a beating heart over an electrical storm of guitars. The volume was up so loud and Dennis—her Dennis—was fast asleep in the bed. He lay on top of the blankets, a jumble of pink comforter and sheets, the joystick a few inches from his inert hand. He had a large round belly lopping over his boxer shorts, his face covered by a bunched-up sheet. Karen remembered, when they were together in the apartment as kids, Dennis would hide his face inside his shirt when he cried. Even when they were alone. If he wasn't wearing a shirt, he would pull a pillowcase over his head. Once he'd used a paper bag. If she touched him in these moments, he would slap her, but that had never stopped her from doing it again. She hated when Dennis cried. It hurt more than when she cried.

"Dennis?" Karen whispered.

With the controller she turned the volume of the TV down to just one bar. She knelt by the side of the bed and peeked under the sheet. His breath was hot and smelled polluted. It was too dark to get a good look at his face. Karen stroked his ear with her fingernails. Dennis did not move. He was breathing, his swollen belly expanding and contracting in an even rhythm, but he did not wake up.

Under the bed was a pile of magazines. Pornographic and amateurish, full of poorly reproduced snapshots of young, not very pretty women. The sheer number of magazines was staggering to Karen; there were maybe as many as a hundred.

"You can't help it," Karen said to her sleeping love. "You've been so lost for so long. So have I. But it's okay now. I'm back. I'm here."

She decided to let him sleep and get to know his children a little better. They would be her children soon, in some way or another. She would be their stepmother. Or step-aunt? She kept tossing herself back and forth between the two roles, hoping one would choose her rather than the other way around.

Karen closed the bedroom door quietly and took a seat on the living room couch. The boy was staring at the TV now, his eyes lulled by a violent fight between cat and mouse. Their scrambling bodies rolled into a cloud that bounced across the screen.

"Excuse me," Karen said to him, and he jumped into alertness. "What is your name?"

"Miles," he answered.

"I'm Karen."

"Okay," he said.

"Do you know what today is?"

"It's Last Day," Miles said proudly.

"That's right. Do you know what that means?"

"God doesn't love us anymore. He's sick of our bullshit. He said we can either act better and not hit each other and not say swears or he will get rid of us all and start over with new people."

"What?" Karen cried.

"He goes to kindergarten at Catholic Charities," Miles's sister chimed in. She was leading her baby brother by the hand, his diaper changed. "I go to Centerville. Because I'm gifted."

"No, Tianna. Sit on the floor." Miles swung his legs out over the empty cushion beside him so that his siblings could not share the couch with Karen and him. It was a transparent display of dominance that thrilled Karen more than she was comfortable admitting.

"Do you know the story of the Selfless Knight?" Karen asked.

Tianna picked up her stolen magazine and began copying pictures of famous people in a thick spiral notebook. "I know it." She licked her palms and tried to smooth down her thin, straight hair. A very white, disciplined part was combed down the middle of her scalp, bisecting her head with astonishing precision. "But you can tell the story to Miles. I don't care. Hopefully it will shut him up for five friggin' seconds, so I can get some work done for once." She slumped down on the floor at Karen's feet and shaded in the jawline of the actor slated to play Zeus in the newest mythological blockbuster franchise.

The girl *was* gifted, Karen admitted with a jealous pique. The likeness of her portrait was incredible. The baby, whom no one bothered to call by name, found a dusty remote control under the couch and began gnawing on it.

"Once upon a time . . . ," Karen began, skipping over the pre-Gregorian-calendar history of the tale, in part because she only knew the broad strokes of that history: that once upon a time, Last Day was a populist response to the second Sacking of Rome and the barbarian belief that the old gods of antiquity took better care of their people than the one true Christian God, and that the tradition had blossomed and spread for a thousand years, surviving suppressive orders from the time of Augustine to the Knights Templar, the latter being the involuntary sire of the tale's protagonist; but mostly because she loved the invocation of those words—*once upon a time*—and the way it lulled children into a spell. ". . . there was a selfless knight who lived in a kingdom far away."

Miles inched closer to Karen and began sucking his thumb.

"The knight was in love with his king's only daughter, but she was betrothed to another prince in a kingdom very far away. Do you know what *betrothed* means?" Karen asked.

"It means get married," Tianna said.

"Oooh," Miles squealed. "She's going to show him her penis and boobs."

"Don't be an idiot." His sister rolled her eyes. "Girls don't have penises."

"Yes they do!" He stood up on the couch and lifted his T-shirt up to his neck, slapped the rippling bones of his chest, then yanked his shirt back down, sat back on the couch, and hid his face in Karen's arm. She could feel his eyelashes fluttering against her skin.

Karen decided not to address the outburst, which triggered too many of her core issues contained in several social contracts drafted by Nora, so she continued as though nothing had happened.

"The princess was going to get married and go so far away that it would be impossible for her to ever come back home again. They had no technology back then."

"That's not true," Tianna piped up. "Technology doesn't mean computers and stuff. A wheelbarrow is technology."

"Yeah, but in olden times, once you went away, you went away for good. Right?"

The girl rubbed her eyes. She sighed. "Yeah. Fine."

"So, the morning of the Last Day, the princess fell ill and everyone thought that she would die. The Selfless Knight loved his princess so much that he rode for miles and miles to a sorcerer at the edge of the forest to ask for help. At first the sorcerer argued with the knight. He said, 'Once she is married and gone, she will be as good as dead anyway, so there is no point in saving her. And if the sun does not rise again tomorrow, there will be no one left, not even you, Selfless Knight, to mourn her. Go, my son, go back to your parents and eat one last meal at their table, drink with your brothers, enjoy these precious hours that you will never have again.' But the knight insisted. Do you know what *insisted* means?"

"I don't care!" Miles said, his owlish eyes delighted.

"Okay." Karen smiled a toothy, subservient grin. "But the knight cared a lot. That's what *insisted* means. He cared so much that he said he would rather spend his last day on Earth in service to his princess. If she died because of his selfishness, he did not want to live anyway, he told the sorcerer. And if he was able to save her, and the world turned again tomorrow, then he would be happy knowing she was alive in it, even if she was betrothed to another prince in another kingdom out of his sight. The sorcerer was so touched, he shed a single tear that he wiped with a handkerchief. Then he dropped the handkerchief into a boiling pot of soup. Sparks of purple and gold light flew out—"

"That part is from the movies, the purple and gold," Tianna interrupted. "It's a modern part that we only just started including. In the olden days, the colors didn't matter."

"I like purple and gold," Karen said.

Tianna rolled her eyes and noisily flipped the pages of her magazine. She was finished with Zeus. A pop star who had recently gone to rehab was her next subject. She was a bleach blonde with dramatic, black eyebrows and a fake mole above her lip. The actress was feeling better than ever, her picture's caption asserted.

"But I guess you're right," Karen conceded. "It doesn't matter."

"And it's a cauldron of magic potions. Not a pot of soup."

"I know that," Karen said. "I just wanted to help Miles understand."

"I hate soup!" Miles cheered. "I hate doctors and soup and doo-doo diapers and my sister. I like you, though."

He took a fold of Karen's Easter dress into his hands and stroked it lovingly.

"I love you, too!" Karen wasn't supposed to say that to strangers. It was a direct violation of Nora's provisions in another of their personal and emotional safety contracts. But it was a holiday, possibly the last holiday ever, a day that stood outside of the temporal world and so should not count under contractual agreements.

"Tell him what happened next," Tianna said. "They don't get to learn this stuff at his Catholic school. They don't learn anything over there."

Tianna sat up on her heels and gently removed Miles's glasses from his face, which she cleaned with spit and the hem of her purple T-shirt. When she was finished, she cleaned her own glasses. Her eyes were tiny and dark without them, the color of burnt wood, and her sockets were ringed with addled, exhausted shadows.

"The sorcerer agreed to help the knight but said that first the knight must fetch him three important things. 'Anything you ask,' said the Selfless Knight. 'Bring me a flame from the fire at the top of Mount Elder,' instructed the sorcerer, 'a leaping frog from the Lake of Days, and a stone from the Great Wall of Dreams.'"

"Those things change in other countries' versions of the story," Tianna said. "Sometimes it's the feather of a special wild chicken. Or a fish or a mushroom protected by an ogre. It just shows what's important to people in different places. Like farming or mining or forests or fishing."

This girl was a lot older than Karen had guessed. Or maybe not. She was staring at Karen with her ancient-looking eyes. *How old are you?* Karen wanted to ask, but she was afraid of the glare cutting through those thick glasses. What came out of her mouth instead was, "How many freckles do you have?"

"That's a stupid question," Tianna answered.

"I have a freckle on my bum," Miles said.

"Don't," Tianna said with a quiet ferocity that hushed the boy, body and soul.

"Okay." Karen laughed nervously. "Where was I?" Her stomach hurt badly. She'd noticed an array of pill bottles on top of the bureau in Dennis's bedroom. Maybe he had something good. "The knight went to fetch these things for the sorcerer. He learned a lot of lessons along the way. To keep the flame from Mount Elder alive, he had to ride slowly on his horse, because if he went too fast it would blow out. To collect the stone from the Wall of Dreams, he had to wait for gravity to release one. If he pulled one out himself, the whole wall would come tumbling down and crush the village of elves living beneath it. The frog could only be lured from the Lake of Days, because the water was so cold that if he touched it, his hand would freeze and fall off. So the Selfless Knight sat on the banks and sang frog songs until a frog hopped out and joined him."

"It's about patience," Tianna added.

"Yes, thank you." The child's intellectual gifts were starting to annoy Karen. "The knight delivered all these things to the sorcerer, who had fallen asleep. When he woke up, he'd forgotten who the knight was, and what the whole task was about."

"This is my favorite part in the movie," Tianna said, sitting up tall. "The live-action one. Not the cartoon version. The cartoon version is stupid."

"I like the cartoon version," Karen said. It was older than she was and illustrated in a palette of Day-Glo colors popular in the era of its production. Watching the animated Selfless Knight always made her wish she had been born sooner.

"I like the cartoon version better, too," Miles said.

"He's never seen either." Tianna shrank back down and twisted little curls in her glossy hair, which unwound immediately. "His attention span is too short for movies."

The story itself bent time in a way that was allegorical, as it would be impossible for the knight to complete even one of those tasks, on horseback, in the span of one day. It begged questions of time and relativity, calendars and clocks, a leitmotif of a holiday that compressed the whole spectrum of human emotion into an amorphous span of hours, not quite one day, not quite two, a fact of the tale that Karen and the children took for granted.

"What happens next is funny," Karen told them. "The sorcerer tells the knight, 'Look, I don't know who you are or what you're doing with this rock and frog and flame, but if your princess is sick, feed her a bowl of porridge made with cold milk that is one day old.' 'That's it?' cries the knight. 'Are you crazy? I could have done that ages ago! I thought you were going to use all these things I got you as ingredients in your magic potion.' He was furious. That means very angry."

"I know what *furious* means," Miles said.

"Of course you do, sweet boy."

"Get to the end!"

"Sorry," Karen said, meaning it more than ever now. "'My son,' said the sorcerer. 'You can yell at me all you want, but the sun is rising on the Last Day and the world may end at any moment, and you yourself said you wanted to spend your last hours in service to the princess.'"

"And the knight says, 'So you *do* remember!'" Tianna yelped. "Sorry. I can't help it. It's my favorite part."

"It's everyone's favorite part," Karen said. "The sorcerer smiled and poured himself a drink from a certain bottle into a certain cup and said, 'I always drink wine from this bottle in this cup at the dawn of Last Day.' He offered the knight a drink, but the knight refused. Instead, he dashed for the door, hopped on his horse, and rode like lightning back to the palace. It just so happened that the handmaid of the princess was a friend of the knight's from childhood, and he told her how to fix the porridge that would save the princess. The handmaid made the porridge and spooned it into the blue lips of the princess, who was very near death. The princess got out of her bed, vomited, and stood up tall. She was all better. The castle rejoiced. The king put out a banquet for the whole kingdom. Everyone ate and drank and danced all day and into the night. The next day, the sun rose again, as it has done every day and every year up until now. The world did not end, but the princess set sail for her fiancé's new land soon after. The Selfless Knight, along with everyone else in the kingdom, went to the port to watch her ship set sail. The princess waved from the bow, crying and smiling. A gust of wind blew the handkerchief wet with her tears out of her hand and into the air. It landed in the knight's hands. As he walked home that day he saw an old hag squatting beside a fire, struggling to keep it burning. The knight dropped the princess's handkerchief into the fire. He was sad to see his princess go, but knew she would always be a part of him, that he didn't need her handkerchief to remember her. He also wanted to help the old hag keep her fire burning. He was, after all, a selfless knight. Just then, purple and gold sparks flew out of the fire and it grew warm and strong. The hag turned into the princess, his princess, and they kissed at last before the beautiful setting sun. The end."

"Wow!" Miles leapt into the air and fell into Karen's lap, his forehead banging hard into hers. "Wow wow wow!" he said.

"You don't even understand what it's about," Tianna scolded.

"Yes, I do!" He turned his face into Karen's stomach and screamed, "You're a motherfucker, Tianna. And a meanie!"

He began crying and kicked the sofa with his dirty feet.

"I'm sorry, Miles," Tianna said, offering her hand to her brother, letting him slap it repeatedly in penance. "Want to make cookies? I'll let you lick the spoon."

Miles considered this for a length of time Karen found to be astonishing. Why wasn't he screaming *Yes, yes, yes*? The boy was deeply hurt and could not seem to shut off the flow of his rage.

"I want to make cookies by myself," he said with a pout.

"You can't do that," Tianna said, with what Karen sensed was a little frisson of power. "Only I am allowed to use the oven. You need me to help."

"This lady can help. She's big."

The baby, who had been napping peacefully on the carpet, woke up with a vague whimper.

"That notebook is exactly the kind of thing you should burn in the bonfire tonight," Karen told Tianna.

"But I love this notebook. And it's not finished yet." She fanned through the many white, lined pages, showcasing its potential.

"That makes it even more perfect."

"No, I should burn something bad I want to get rid of. To make room for something good."

"Not in the olden days. Back then people burned all kinds of things. Good things and bad things and things they'd had forever and things that were brand-new. Just to make a point."

"Like what?" Tianna was clutching her notebook against her chest. The lights of the TV twinkled in her glasses.

"Like baby horses and ball gowns and gold necklaces and all kinds of things. Anything you can think of."

"That's stupid," Tianna said. "Gold wouldn't even burn in a regular fire."

Karen wasn't sure if this was right and reproached herself for not knowing. She'd studied the symbols for alchemy, had made flash cards and everything. The one for gold looked like the left eyeball of a subtly powerful bird. But melting gold, what that involved, she had no idea.

"Why would they burn a baby horse?" Miles's voice cracked. His lips trembled as he tried bravely to contain this question and its inscrutable answer, but within seconds he was in tears. Karen had miscalculated. That parable was meant to shame Tianna for her snobbery and prideful attachment, but Miles was the one who was wounded. The sacrificial horse Karen had spoken of was something she had seen in a medieval triptych by a German painter. It was called *Last Day Offering*. In the painting, a whole procession of barnyard animals waited to be torched. Red lightning cracked the flat black sky so that it looked like a broken plate. The humans had stern faces and foreshortened limbs.

"Now that I think of it, the horse might have been a pony, not a baby."

"A foal," Tianna corrected.

"Stop it!" Miles cried. "You're lying." He was inconsolable, recoiling now from any gesture of affection.

Telling the whole truth had clearly been the worst idea in this situation. But how could you tell only half the truth? Wouldn't that make things more confusing, like offering someone half a story?

The sound of jangling keys pulled the attention of all three children toward the door with a magnetic force. Their mother was home. She was very tall for a woman, and also very fat, which lent her overall presence a distinct power. Her feet fell like cement bricks across the floor. She was wearing purple hospital scrubs. A pair of white, sparkly sunglasses pushed back her burgundy hair. Her face was freckled like Tianna's, though much tanner, and her cheeks sagged as though her prettiness had been pawed off her face by her children.

"Are you going to just sit there, Tianna? Jesus . . ." The woman dropped half a dozen rustling plastic shopping bags at the threshold of the door and stepped over them.

The baby rose to his feet and toddled warily toward his mother. "There he is," his mother sang, her voice, her whole body, softening as soon as the baby was in her arms. "No one gave you a bath today? Like I asked them to?"

Tianna was struggling to lift every single grocery bag at once and carry them en masse to the kitchen. She got as far as the living room couch, where she implored Karen to help her. "She loves Avonte the most because he's the baby," Tianna observed. "He isn't any cuter than Miles was. He's just the newest."

Their mother, who had yet to acknowledge Karen, a stranger in her home, carried Avonte into the kitchen, where she opened and slammed shut a succession of cabinet doors.

"Why is Miles crying?" she bellowed.

"She told us a scary story," Tianna yelled back.

"I'm Karen. I'm Dennis's old friend. We used to be in foster care together." This, Karen decided, was the best explanation of herself, under the circumstances.

"Is he even up?" their mother asked Tianna. She couldn't have been less interested in Karen. But the feeling was mutual. This woman would be a distant memory soon. Miles could come with them if he wanted, wherever she and Dennis decided to go, but Tianna would probably stay behind. They would have her every other weekend and holidays, but not all of them, she hoped. The baby looked like too much work. And it was best to leave a baby with its biological mother anyway.

"He's been out cold all day," Tianna answered in a tone that belied her pleasure in this report. "I made breakfast and lunch."

"Figures."

Their mother disappeared with the baby into the bedroom where Dennis was still asleep. No, they would not be staying here at all, Karen decided. It was a nice enough building, adjacent to the train, friendly neighbors, good natural light if they moved the televisions to different spots, but she and Dennis needed a fresh start. They couldn't go back to Heart House. Overnight guests were not allowed and it was only a matter of days before Karen herself was kicked out. They would have to stay in a motel. The very thought sent shivers up and down her legs.

"Tianna!" the mother bellowed from the bedroom. "Get your brother dressed."

"Are we going to the bonfire?" the girl asked. She eyed her notebook lying on the floor and shot Karen a look so caustic it could peel paint.

"Yeah, after I drop you off at your grandmother's. She's gonna take you."

"Is Miles coming with me?" Tianna explained to Karen, "We have different grandmothers. Mine lives in Dorchester. His lives in Roslindale. Avonte's grandmother lives in Maryland. Our mom's mom is dead."

"Just do what I ask and stop badgering me. I don't have the stomach for it today."

Tianna took her brother to their bedroom in the back, leaving Karen alone. She flipped through Tianna's notebook of celebrity portraits. The girl had an accurate but light hand, her pencil strokes a faint whisper over the pages. Among the faces were lists of words in alphabetical order, spelling lists, obviously, and they too were printed as though by a ghost who could not manipulate the pencil close enough to the page to make real lines.

"It's you."

Karen looked up from the notebook and saw Dennis standing before her. He was awake, barely. His eyes were small and sunk deep in their sockets. His lips were pale. There was a yellowish tint to him. A yellow aura was not good, Karen remembered dimly. Her mind had drained its vast catalogue of information and she could think of nothing to say. So she repeated him.

"It's you."

Dennis sat down in the armchair diagonal from her. His gaze was loose and slow to catch focus. He looked at Karen, but only for a moment, then languidly turned his attention to the TV, or the window behind it.

"Is it cold out?"

"I don't know," Karen said. "It was nice out today. It was getting cooler as the sun set, but not cold."

"It's Saturday?"

"Yes, it's Saturday. It's Last Day. That's why I'm here."

"Forecast was good for this weekend, I think."

"Dennis, I have so much to tell you. I had a good job. At the YMCA. But then they fired me. And I have to move. I'm scared, but also really feel that this is all part of a bigger plan. What about you?"

Dennis mumbled a response. In volume it was the most he had said to her so far, though she couldn't understand a word of it. The phrase *disability benefits* came through.

"I get disability, too," Karen said. "And social security. I have a lot of friends."

"Good," Dennis said. "Good."

She wanted to touch him. Her hand lifted to reach the arm of his chair, then stopped midway and returned to her lap. She felt that her body was not her own anymore, that it would act out of turn, that even though she felt no urge to pee, at any moment she might wet her pants.

"Are you happy here, Dennis? Do you ever miss me?"

"Karen," he said with a troubled certainty. "It's really you."

"That's right. I'm here."

"The one and only . . ." His voice trailed off again.

"I've missed you so much, Dennis. I think about you all the time. A lot more lately. I don't know why."

"Do you have a job someplace? Where do you live?"

"I just told you, I had a job at the Y but I got fired. I live at a group home in Allston."

"Ooof. The Green Line. Rough. Worst transit line in the city. Walking is faster."

"Are you married? Is that woman your wife? Are those your children?"

"We're engaged." Dennis smiled and lowered his eyelids until they were nearly shut. "Engaged to be engaged." He laughed but did not explain the joke. The laughter sputtered out like a tiny mechanical toy whose battery was nearly spent. His head dropped suddenly and he fell asleep.

How could Dennis, her Dennis, have ended up here engaged to this woman? Karen had never been in a romantic relationship, outside her imagination, that is, and could not imagine the workings of such a utilitarian partnership: that the children's mother, Amanda, had a steady job with decent healthcare coverage, and Dennis offered disability benefits, food stamps, and free, if not quality, childcare; between the two of them they had enough connections in the world of pills to keep each other high and living comfortably, something neither of them could achieve alone.

"Dennis," Karen hissed. "Dennis, come with me. Let's get out of here. Let's go."

"Oh, yeah?" he answered, his head still slack, his eyes closed.

"Don't you want to come with me?"

"Okay."

"Okay," Karen whispered. "Okay, then. You'll tell them? Or should I?"

"Let me rest a minute." He reached over to pat her knee but missed and nearly fell over. Karen caught him, felt the weight of his shoulder against her hands. He was so heavy, like a bag of wet cement. His shirt had no sleeves and his arms were covered with a rash of pink pimples. There was a tattoo on his biceps, a Chinese symbol, each stroke like a sword balanced to build a complicated, unstable house.

"Aw, shit. Did he fall?" Dennis's fiancée shouted from the kitchen. "He's on all new meds. He'll probably just stay in tonight. You're welcome to hang out here with him, but I'm leaving. The kids are going to their grandmother. I have the night off for once and I'm not wasting it laying around at home."

"Can I use your restroom?" Karen asked.

"We call it the bathroom. And sure. Be my guest," she said in mock grandeur.

Karen propped Dennis up with a pillow until she was reasonably sure he was stable, then she excused herself to the bathroom. There was no window in the bathroom, but the door locked, which put Karen at ease. She splashed water on her face, then washed her hands. This fiancée had what Karen considered to be an alarming number of perfumes. They crowded the dingy, gold-flecked Formica counter. Further proof, Karen saw, that this woman was cuckolding Dennis, her purported life partner, covering the stench of her betrayals and lies with so much cherry-vanilla body spray.

Dennis had to know that he was not the father of any of those kids. He deserved better than this. He probably had diminished self-esteem, after being traumatized the way they were as kids, and then who knows what had happened to him afterward in his spate of foster homes. Karen was lucky. She'd been seeing Nora for years, and that had helped her self-esteem a lot. She wanted Dennis to start seeing Nora. She wanted all the best things for him. But first they had to leave this place.

When Karen emerged from the bathroom, Tianna and Miles were dressed and ready to go, waiting by the door, while their mother consulted her reflection in the microwave's door to apply mascara.

"Oh, good. Finally," she said, foisting the baby into Tianna's arms and taking her makeup bag into the bathroom.

"I'm going to burn Viscount Darkdoom," Miles said, holding up a plastic figurine of a homely, well-dressed man from some cartoon show or movie Karen had only vaguely heard of. "He's a bad guy," Miles explained.

"He's starting to get it," Tianna said proudly. "I talked him into it." She had put on a purple ruffled dress and a pair of cowgirl boots. Her face was clean and Karen detected a layer of gloss on her lips. "I'm going to burn my old bunny," she told Karen. The toy in question was a limp carcass of blue plush fur stained on the ears with an awful, crunchy brown matter. "Avonte puked on it and the smell won't come out, even though I washed it."

"You'll have a nice time," Karen said weakly. "Bonfires are fun."

"This one has face painting," Tianna informed her. "Too bad you're not coming."

"Come with us!" Miles said.

"Maybe Dennis and I will meet up with you later."

Both children shot her a dubious glare. Dennis had slumped over his knees in the recliner, his palm extended as though to receive alms.

Karen had the backpack that the woman downstairs had given to her by the front door. She picked it up and handed it to Tianna. "Can you do me a favor and burn this?" Tiana hoisted the bag onto her shoulder.

"It's heavy," she sighed, and adjusted the straps. Her own overnight backpack she slung across her chest.

"Okay, let's go," their mother shouted. She had done a lot to herself in a short amount of time. A purple leather skirt and chunky black heels exposed her legs, which were long and nicely shaped. A green shamrock tattoo floated above her ankle. Black, spidery lashes fringed her eyes, which were watering from the purple contact lenses she'd put in.

"Hey, Prince Charming, I'm going out," she shouted at the recliner. Dennis made no reply. "If you end up leaving him here," Amanda told Karen, "make sure the door's locked." She took the baby from Tianna and herded her brood out the door and down the stairs.

"Dennis." Karen took his empty hand in hers and squeezed it. "You don't have to stay here. Maybe you feel guilty. I don't know, but I think they'll be fine without you."

Dennis rubbed his eyes. "What time is it?"

Karen scanned the room for a working clock. "I don't know. It's getting late."

Dennis sat back and pulled his phone out of his jeans pocket.

"Six fifty-seven," he said. He found a crumpled pack of cigarettes in another of his pockets and lit one.

"You look like your dad when you do that," Karen said.

"I don't remember what he looked like."

"He smoked. I remember that." She sneezed three times in a row and Dennis said nothing. "Let's go, Dennis. I don't want to stay here anymore."

"Okay." He reached over again to touch her knee and this time his hand made contact. Karen felt a jolt like a rubber band snapping against her skin. He was looking into her eyes now, his cheeks sunken and his eyes glazed.

"Want to watch a movie?" he asked. He was looking right through her, at something behind her. She turned around to see what it was.

"Yeah, that's right," he said. "Back there. In my bedroom."

He got up from the chair and Karen rose to follow him.

He was barely undressed when his penis sprang out of his underwear all pink and flushed as though surprised. He pushed Karen backward onto his unmade bed. Dennis squeezed his eyes shut the whole time. Was he shy or ashamed? She couldn't tell. He didn't want to talk, which was all Karen wanted to do. She didn't even realize how much she was talking until he put his hand over her mouth. "Dennis, I can't breathe," she tried to say, but only thick, low notes escaped her. Finally he groaned and collapsed next to her.

"Dennis," she whispered. The sheets were wet and sticky and quickly getting cold. "Dennis?" she said again, and when he didn't answer, she shouted.

"What."

"I want to go now," she said, crying. "Please say you're coming with me."

"I'll meet you there," he said, drifting off, away from her.

"But where? I don't even know where we're going. I was hoping you would know. That you'd have an idea, at least."

"Okay." He patted her thigh.

"Dennis?"

She found her dress bunched up between the mattress and the bed-side table. Her underwear was on the floor near the foot of the bed. She dressed in the dark of Dennis's bedroom, a red orb glowing on the bottom corner of the TV pulsing slowly, too slowly, like an alarm that knew it was already too late.

The top of Dennis's bureau was covered with pill bottles. Tall ones. Fat ones. Orange with white tops. White with no tops. Most had labels but only some were labeled for Dennis. If the occult could have been Karen's college major, psychopharmacology would have been her minor. She was practically fluent in medical Greek. Anything ending in -*done*, like its sound suggested, rang her soul's deepest gong and produced an almost immediate sense of calm and well-being. It was false, Karen knew. She did not like to abuse drugs. They interfered with her intuition. But her stomach was twisted hard inside her, a legitimate pain. And eighty milligrams equaled eighty dollars: who was she to turn away from a tiny pot of gold so clearly delivered by the universe? Karen selected three half-full bottles and put them in her purse. Then she found Dennis's phone and dialed the only number that made sense at the moment.

"Rosette? It's me, Karen. I need you. It's a real emergency this time. I'm dying."

MANY PEOPLE SUBSCRIBED to the once-a-decade Last Day apology, including Kurt's own father, who believed that anything more than that was excessive and prideful. Though Kurt's father also thought painting the family's last name on their mailbox was excessive and prideful. Kurt remembered going on a Last Day drive with his father when he was still a boy so that his dad could make amends to a former colleague. The old friend lived in his mother's basement, Kurt's father explained, and without a word more Kurt understood that this was a shameful state of being.

"I've owed him this money for ten years," his dad said on the drive down, "but I didn't think it mattered. He'd just blow it at the tracks. I thought I was sparing him the trouble a wad of cash would cause. But fair is fair, and when you owe someone money, you pay it back, no matter what a son of a bitch that person is."

It was a rare moment of mercy in an otherwise relentless life. Kurt wondered whether, if his father had lived longer, the old man would have made amends to his son one day, too. Kurt was the spitting image of his father, a genetic jackpot closer to a psychic spittoon, as Kurt was the target of all his father's bile. They had the same square face, the same light brown eyes, the same sour stomach. Their little league stats were a weapon of comparison, which his father trotted out often, almost daily, as though meaningful. Kurt had been a decent outfielder but the old man's pitching bested the son's squarely. That Kurt's batting average was slightly higher was a point seldom made, not after Kurt realized that making it caused the whole family, especially his mother, to suffer come the first drink at nightfall.

But gravity is one of the great miracle workers, softening even the most obdurate in old age, and perhaps, Kurt speculated, his old man's persistent scrutiny and unforgiving appraisal of everyone, especially his son, would have broken down over time as his body did. In time, if he had lived, Kurt's old man might have mellowed into a tolerable guy. It used to bother Kurt, all the acid his dad spat so expertly into his eyes; then one night while still in prison, after suffering the requisite abuse of the day with the stoicism that was another of his father's genetic gifts, he figured it out—*Dad hates me because he thinks I am him*—and he never took the old man's vitriol personally again.

Kurt kept his distance from then on, noticing from afar that once his father had lost his son as a punching bag, he began to push away first Kurt's older sister, then the younger, the baby of the family, who had always been Daddy's girl. When the first grandchild was expected, the old man had a last surge of bitterness. Kurt's older sister had married a Pakistani man, a Hindu, a religion their father could not differentiate from Islam, which he could not defuse from a primatological alarm system that sounded "Threat!" despite all logical arguments to the contrary. He refused to allow his wife to host the baby shower at their house and he grumbled unintelligibly when friends congratulated him on the new grandchild. It looked like things were beginning to relent as the grand-baby, a boy, grew up and showed an interest in backyard baseball. Then his father dropped dead at fifty-seven of an aortic aneurysm, and there was nothing left to say.

At forty-two, Kurt had never made amends to anyone in his life. From every angle, the tradition appeared to him as supremely selfish, a conversation that dredged up a painful or forgotten or wished-to-be-forgotten past in the hope of relieving the perpetrator of the burden of guilt at the expense of the victim. The few amends he'd received had followed this pattern. Megan Brown's amends had been more like a one-woman show without a stage. Another former girlfriend had written to him apologizing for the way she'd used her affair with Kurt to get revenge on her husband. Kurt hadn't even known that she was married at the time. Not that he would have cared. It was just a pebble of information he could have done without. Another woman had approached him at a crowded Indian restaurant hosting an early morning all-you-can-eat Last Day buffet. She was drunk and spilling her plate of chicken saag on the floor. He didn't recognize her at first until she announced in her inebriated, too-loud, South Boston bray (that voice he could not forget), "I made your, uh, your *dysfunctions* all about me. It's clearly the cancer, or stuff that happened in prison, or whatever. Not your fault, not mine. But I'm sorry." Kurt bought her a beer and sent her back to her table of delusional, supportive female friends, all of them hungover or still drunk from the night before.

Kurt was freely able to admit that he'd been a bastard to certain women he'd slept with, but he was an honest bastard, and so any hurt they still felt was their morbid toy to play with. With his male friends he was quick to back away from a fight before it even started. His sisters loved him in their distant, emotionally convenient way, and he loved them back when circumstance (their father's funeral) or calendar (Thanksgiving dinner) demanded it. To force anything more out of these relationships would be dishonest, as all the past harms—that time he knowingly left the gas tank on empty when his sister had a soccer tournament to get to, the broken promise to pay back that now trivial sum of money—had been ironed out of time by many more small acts of unspoken kindness. It was not his family's way to talk critically about their actions, let alone their feelings, and to foist such a conversation onto his sisters, merely because of a kitschy holiday, would be unfair. His mother was in Florida now with her new husband. She was enjoying a warmth of climate and companionship she had never gotten in the first half of her life, and the best amends Kurt could make to her was to be happy for her.

His entire relationship with Sarah Clark-Davenport had been a perverted amends to Mary; further proof, he thought years after he'd extricated himself from *that* shitshow, that the whole institution of reparations was faulty at its core. And yet, now that Mary's ashes and everything else attached to her were no longer under his bed, he felt freer than he had ever known possible.

"I've never made amends on Last Day," Kurt said to Sarah Moss as they pushed a grocery cart around a supermarket. "I mean, ever. In my life." Clouds of mist sprayed intermittently on the slanted stacks of apples. "It's incredible. There's like a runner's high, or something, that comes along with it. I finally get why people do this. Do you have any amends you want to make?"

"No," Sarah said.

"I'll drive you anywhere. I'm serious. I want you to have this experience." He wrapped an arm around her shoulder and guided the direction of the cart she was pushing. "What am I saying? You're too young to have hurt anyone. Too sweet." He gave her shoulder a little squeeze, then bounded across the aisle to grab some oranges.

It was a long ride to the beach. The sky was a vapid shade of blue full of lumpy metastasizing clouds. Behind them the sun was setting in all its tacky grandiosity. Sarah refused to look at it. She hated that she had to hold Kurt's body now, that she had to synchronize with his every lean and sway. Motorcycles were stupid. Dead Mary was stupid. Sarah, sister of dead Mary, was stupid. The idea that Kurt had had sexual intercourse with other people ignited nothing inside her, but that he could love someone as clearly as he loved this evil harpy Sarah was the absolute stupidest thing in the world.

"What's wrong?" Kurt asked her after they parked at the beach. She pulled off her helmet and revealed a scowl.

"Nothing."

Nothing. That little two-syllable word coming from the lips of a silent, brooding woman was the grenade of all pronouns. Kurt had heard its lethal frequency a thousand times before. It didn't matter how old or young or pretty or ugly or proud or insecure they were. Women always wanted to fight. He assumed they were born that way.

A vendor in the parking lot was selling cords of firewood at a criminal markup, five dollars extra for cords of driftwood, for the Last Day bonfires. Kurt bought two bundles and trudged over the dunes toward the beach.

A long row of shoes had been left at the entrance to the boardwalk by dozens of other holiday revelers. It was considered good luck to walk barefoot on the beach on May 27, and many people left their shoes behind in a show of solidarity. If the world did not end, Sarah knew, her shoes would still be there tomorrow. Yet she couldn't help feeling apprehensive about this tradition. She'd had this particular pair of sneakers for years, they'd been through a lot together, and here they were, getting abandoned moments before the world ended. Maybe she should burn them? But then what if things turned out fine? She'd have to ride Kurt's motorcycle with bare feet.

She held her sneakers close against her chest and followed Kurt's path in the sand.

"If it were possible to divorce myself, I would," Sarah grumbled.

A woman with a magnificent Afro overheard this and laughed. She was crafting a photograph of all the shoes with a very large professional-looking camera. She was dressed in a lot of wheat-colored linen separates cut on a bias. She asked Kurt and Sarah if she could take their picture, too. She was writing an article for a national travel magazine, she said. This beach had become a popular spot for Last Day.

Kurt put his arm around Sarah's shoulders, felt her stiffen at his touch, and arranged the tender, unsmiling face he always used for pictures. The photographer looked at the image she'd captured and winced.

"Great. Thanks. Do you want me to send it to you?"

"I'm fine," Sarah snapped. "I don't need to document every single moment in my life with pictures and post them online for digital applause, thanks."

"Sure," Kurt said. "You can send it to me."

He and the photographer exchanged cards and Sarah rolled her eyes.

"Until night falls," the woman said. Sarah watched Kurt watch the photographer walk away.

They trudged onward in silence over the high dunes. The sand was cool and uncooperative, and each step was difficult, sapping the wind from their lungs so that even if they'd wanted to talk, they were too out of breath. Then, all at once, there it was: the ocean, beautiful and indifferent.

They walked by a teenage boy vomiting into a rusty trash barrel. Sarah recognized him immediately as one of the boys on the train ride from Edgewater that morning, though he was too ill to recognize her. He held on to his dirty white baseball cap in one hand and with the other gripped the barrel.

"I'm so wasted, man," he said to Kurt. He did not remember how he had ended up at the beach. It was a bush-league move, to get so wasted before midnight. "But I am not a bush-league drinker," he insisted.

Kurt took the boy's hat, gave it a hard shake. Sand issued from inside the empty dome and slapped against the barrel with a pleasant sound. Kurt replaced the hat on the boy's head so that it wouldn't fall off.

"I puked out of my nose. My nostril. How does that happen?"

"You don't want to know the answer to that right now," Kurt said to him.

"I . . . am a phe-nom-enom."

"We all are, brother."

Sarah could just as easily choose to be happy. Or at least accepting. But she didn't want to. The simplicity of anger was its most attractive feature right now, a slash-and-burn approach to all the problems this night was presenting. It made her feel better for the moment. She chewed on the inside of her cheek until she tasted the metallic tang of her blood.

"Look at them all," she said, still chewing, nodding in the direction of the crowds setting up camp for the night. "The way they're all clumped together in one spot. It looks like a microscopic slide of bacteria. That's the human race. A sophisticated disease."

"You're too young to be this cynical."

"I'm an old soul, apparently. My guidance counselor told me. She claims she can read auras. I hate her."

Kurt handed her a can of soda from the bag. After a few sips Kurt offered her a splash of whiskey, which she accepted. Why not, she decided, it can't make things worse. The whiskey tasted like a punishment. There was no way she could finish the can, but she didn't need to. Very quickly there was a sensation that the screws holding together her cranial apparatus were now just a little bit looser. So this was the draw of alcohol, Sarah thought. It was kind of nice.

Kurt walked in front of Sarah, his path hugging the shore. The sand gleamed like a sheet of melting ice. She watched his tracks imprint, then vanish. She could not lift her gaze above the ground. Kurt, his stooped shoulders, the last light of day glimmering on the water—it was all too much to take in. The tide crept closer and the water sent a chill up from the soles of her feet to her knees. The sound of voices began to fade behind them. The shore was studded with seashells, some of them really stellar specimens, a perfect whelk, a razor clam with both valves still attached, its opalescent inner chamber flashing in the slanted light of dusk. Sarah wanted so badly to collect them all in her pockets, but what could be more pointless than hoarding seashells at the end of the world? She was about to cry when Kurt's voice snapped up her attention.

"Look," he said.

The sun was scattering its colored light all across the sky. Deep shades of pink stained the scalloped underbelly of the clouds. Gold clasped unevenly to the edges of a dark, stormy-looking mass. The blue sky was a mess, with white blooms and streaks, clouds growing tall as buildings, clouds stretched thin as old, threadbare rags, clouds like the tracks of animals dotting the horizon.

"Wow," Sarah admitted.

"Beautiful."

"That one cloud there looks stormy."

"It's blowing out to sea."

"How can you tell?"

"Look at the birds."

Seagulls were flapping their wings against the wind, holding fast in the air as though frozen. Sarah looked at Kurt. He was powerless and kind and nothing he did or said to her would make the world end or keep it going. In fact, it was a lot of pressure to put on one man, and it wasn't fair. She wanted to apologize for this, but also to punch him, and maybe kiss again? She looked back down at the wet sand. Pink and gold light spilled into the puddles made by the anxious digging of her feet.

"You said I was too good for this world. But you said it to her, too."

"I don't have a defense against that, and I don't think I should have to. If you're so mad, I can bring you home now. I thought we'd have a nice night together. But we don't have to be nice and we don't have to be together."

"Did you love her? Sarah, sister of your dead girlfriend Mary?"

"Christ, I almost married her," Kurt said, realizing his mistake a moment too late. He meant it as a declaration of gratitude for a bullet dodged, but this young girl was a coiled viper right now.

"You almost married that horrible woman?"

"You don't know her—it's complicated. She had a really messed-up life. You don't want to know the half of it," Kurt tried to explain.

"You're right. I don't. I don't care about her tragic life. It doesn't make her special."

"Why do all girls do this? Hate each other for no reason. It must be exhausting. Hopefully you'll outgrow it."

"Nope!" Sarah said. She drank as much of the whiskey and Coke as she could stomach, slugged it dramatically, as she'd seen actors do in movies, and when she felt she was about to gag she poured the rest in the sand, drowning a collection of barnacles floating in the sugary foam.

"Do you feel better now?" he asked her.

"A little, yes. Thank you."

"Let's build a fire."

He dropped the cords of driftwood into the sand and began arranging them in a cone. Sarah wanted to argue about the dioxin released from burning driftwood but she kept her mouth shut, instead ripping up her issue of *The Economist* and the unused pages of her journal for kindling.

"Why did you love her?"

"She was beautiful and smart and mean. She took care of me when I had no one."

"Did you love Mary more?"

"Maybe?" He blew onto the flames, urging the ropes of blue fire to latch onto the wood. "Probably. I was a kid. She was a kid. Who knows. We might have grown out of each other. I felt like such a loser, like everything I touched turned to shit, including Mary. Sarah seemed to reverse that. For a time. She was a sociopath, but she was brilliant, and she believed in me. In a really basic way. She believed I would kick cancer when I was sure I would die, and she was right. She believed I could make a career as a tattoo artist when it seemed like a pipe dream. When I got well again, when I was stable, she dumped me. Even that was a gift because then I was free."

The fire burned a pale lavender color that neither of them had expected to be so pretty, so enchanting. When Kurt was satisfied that it would burn without his coaxing, he sat on the sleeping bag Sarah had laid out and together they watched the waves cross each other in wide, endless X's, watched until even these subtle hatches were rubbed away by the night and the waves were nothing but sound. The bluish-purple fire crackled softly in the dark.

"There's no moon tonight."

"It's a new moon."

"I hate how no moon is called a new moon. It's a fucked-up name."

"You're hungry. Time to eat."

So they ate. They ate every single thing they'd bought at the store.

Two packages of chicken sausage, an entire bag of marshmallows, an extra-large bag of barbecue potato chips, two slightly sour oranges. Kurt swigged his pint of whiskey straight, saving the last sip for Sarah, who drank it, shuddered, then fell into his arms. Kurt turned his face toward hers like she was the last thing left to eat. He chewed on her neck, her earlobe, the sides of her face. The actual coitus part did not hurt the way Sarah thought it would. From Lindsey's accounts, the first time was supposed to be so painful you almost died, and if the pain didn't kill you, the hemorrhaging would. There was none of the fabled bleeding. The only thing that hurt was her face from kissing. Kurt's beard had clearly started to grow back a couple of hours after he'd shaved (*Oh!* she thought, *that's where the phrase* five-o'clock shadow *comes from*), and the stubble abraded her skin. His teeth kept clanking into hers, a collision more uncomfortable than painful. Kurt's penis felt like a sweaty hand that had fallen asleep against her upper inner thigh. He struggled to get inside her, and once he did he didn't stay there long before slipping out again. Some people walked by—they could hear the voices approaching in the dark. Kurt pulled the corner of the sleeping bag over them and covered Sarah's face with his. When the people had passed, he kissed her on the forehead and tried again to work his way inside. Finally he made a sound like choking and she felt the warm trickle of his semen on her stomach.

"Huh," Sarah said when it was all over.

"Yeah," Kurt sighed.

"Is it always like that?"

"Sometimes." He pulled his jeans back on and rolled himself a cigarette. "You don't shave at all?"

"Only in the summer."

Kurt crouched by the fire and fed more logs into its snapping flames. Sarah's underwear was knotted up around one ankle. She pulled them on and let the cool air chill her body. She still didn't know what to feel. Was she repulsed, piqued, or suddenly insatiable? No. But she felt fine. With or without orgasm, the mere concentration of sex, its focused physicality, had a calming effect. At least for the moment. She gazed at the black sea shimmering beneath the opaque black of the sky and was so grateful to have had this experience at this exact location, at this time, with this person. It was nothing to write poetry about, but it was nice being so close to someone, trusting him to care for her body and knowing he trusted her to care for his. If he asked her for more, she would probably consent, but if they never did it again, that would be fine, too. As long as he wanted to lie next to her and hold her, protecting her again like he had when those strangers passed by.

"There are no stars, either," she said. "Are you sure there isn't a storm coming?"

Kurt looked at the dark folding over the sky.

"It's okay. It will blow over."

She wiped her stomach off and put on her shorts.

"We should burn something. Each of us. Here." She handed Kurt her journal, her scattershot dissertation on names, birds, time, sex, and the cosmos, all the hopes and anxieties of her life so far. "There's some pretty important stuff in there," she added, as though he had contested the worth of her offering. "Stuff I won't be able to remember or repeat."

"Sounds good," he said. He took a check out of his wallet. It was for $350, from a customer getting a full-back piece that he was paying for in installments. It was a toss-up whether or not the check would even clear. Kurt threw it into the fire.

"It's cozy over here," Sarah said. She shook the sand off the sleeping bag and smoothed it with her hand. "Come back."

"In a minute. Got to keep this going." He poked at the burning logs.

"In love," Sarah's mother had once said, "there is always the one who offers the kiss, and the one who offers the cheek." She had never elaborated on this. Sarah wondered which thing her mother offered, which her father did. Sitting here now, she couldn't even venture a guess. Sarah had had several major epiphanies so far in the protracted crossover from childhood to adulthood: that her parents were once kids with dreams of being something different from what they actually became; that she had lived with them for a decade and a half and that there were things she would never know about them, nor they about her; that all people were fundamentally unknowable; that her body had pretty much reached the size and shape it would always be for the rest of her life as long as she took care of it; that if she was lucky, she would be with her parents when they died, and if she was unlucky, they would outlive her. Intellectually, she'd figured it out a long time ago, or most of it—what it meant to be an adult, to grow up. But there was still so much she didn't know. She had imagined that sex would be a portal to more answers, but it was only another question.

"Come over here," she said again. Kurt continued rearranging the burning logs, reaching into the flames. "Be careful."

"Don't worry."

She considered her parents again. They definitely loved each other. Perhaps they loved each other more than they loved her. Growing up, she'd never felt a lack or a longing. Being with them, sitting at the dinner table, all three of them content, paying attention, making jokes—it was good. But she was a discrete object outside of the force field created by their composite energies. Not left out, just outside. There was a standing invitation for her to join them, but it was her choice, and for reasons she was just beginning to understand, she chose not to. She didn't want to live inside their love, because it was theirs, and she wanted her own love. Was this it? This feeling for the man tending the fire that kept her warm on the last night of the living world? Was this love?

Maybe it was not about a biological balance of immunities, but about one body of knowledge compensating for another. What he knew, what she understood, his observations, her readings, the way two of them together annealed each other's mental weaknesses, leaving them with a greater wisdom.

"Do you remember the email I sent you? About the formation of the universe?"

"Yeah." Kurt tossed his cigarette into the fire. "But remind me. I forgot some of it."

"That's okay. Because I want to tell you about the part I cut out. It was too long already, and it seemed irrelevant, but it was actually the most relevant part of the story. In the first microsecond of the universe, as all the gases were cooling and expanding, the intensity of heat and radiation formed quarks, which bundled together according to mutual attraction. The positively charged bundles are called baryons, and the negatively charged baryons are antibaryons. They existed at a precise ratio of one billion negative to one billion and one positive. If they had been perfectly balanced, their respective charges would have nullified each other, ending in total annihilation, which would have produced such expansive, diluted radiation that no new particles could be formed. Instead, because of this imbalance, we got atoms, which later became matter, which became the universe as we know it. Isn't that amazing?"

"Pretty cool."

The fire was roaring now. Kurt returned to the sleeping bag. He collapsed next to her, wrinkling the blanket she had so carefully smoothed out, and making rivulets of sand pour in again.

"Come closer," she said. "I'm cold."

Kurt lay next to Sarah and held her in an uneasy spoon pose. Then he rolled away and she remained, their backs facing each other and radiating heat. The stars were still absent from the sky, a fact neither one of them wanted to point out. They dropped in and out of sleep, their bodies softening, giving up, then jolting back from the accidental touch of the other's arm or a foot.

"Look. They're back."

"What's back?"

"The stars."

A few of them, at least.

The sound of the waves softened and they fell deeper.

"They're gone now."

Which one of them said this? Sarah didn't know.

"I love you," she said, unsure if these were her last conscious words or the first ones uttered in her dream.

THE NEXT MORNING, they let Yui sleep. Svec gladly conceded to Bear first dibs on the treadmill, though he was otherwise unbothered by his hangover.

"I'm amazed," Bear said to him.

"We train for this," Svec said, his typing like rapid gunfire on his laptop. "How to drink in microgravity. No Russian has ever thrown up in space."

"Really?" Bear adjusted the harnesses and belts strapping him into the treadmill, then increased the speed and lengthened his stride.

"No," Svec said, smirking again. "Joke."

It was seven o'clock in the morning for the astronauts, eleven in Star City, and 2 A.M. in Houston. Mission Control never slept, and if there had been raucous partying in any of the command centers (there had been), the crew on the ISS was shielded from it. That morning they downloaded the customary schedule, broken down in certain places to five-minute increments. Bear spent the morning taking pictures of colloidal particles in the Destiny module, and Svec added to the database of bioproductive ocean areas. They worked alone, in silence, with the contentment of men doing what they were put on Earth to do, in their case, to study her from afar.

Bear finished earlier than Mission Control had predicted and decided to spend his surplus eleven minutes of leisure time eating a Last Day snack, a bag of pizza-flavored corn puffs. Svec had also hit a major benchmark in his work and was treating himself to some jelly beans as a reward.

"You know what, comrade," Bear said, "these puffs have both the ideal structural integrity and volume for—"

"I know what you will say," Svec interrupted. "But some of us actually prefer to be challenged."

Bear was already constructing lariats out of dental floss, one each for him and Svec, who examined his, then threw it in the trash. "Will make my own," he said.

"Practicing your dribbling with a tennis ball can improve overall handling in basketball," Bear submitted. "Popcorn rodeo is good for the rookies. To get them warmed up. But I'm talking about the big leagues here."

He tossed a corn puff into the air and flicked it gently, giving it spin. Using their floss lassos, he and Svec took turns trying to harness the burnt orange morsel and return it to their mouths. Svec made contact on his first try but tugged a little too hard and lost the puff five inches in front of his face. Bear failed several times to lasso the corn puff, but once he did manage to get it, he drew it to within two inches of his mouth.

"I win," Bear said.

"*Nyet*. We both fail."

"Jesus." Bear chomped the air until the puff was in his mouth, his top and bottom teeth clanging too hard against each other.

"We should wake him up."

"I don't want to go near his pod. It smells."

"Loser must get him to lunch," Svec said, setting a new corn puff in motion. Mission Control murmured into their headsets and both men ignored it. Svec hung his floss lariat gingerly onto the puff and pulled it in a slow, downward motion to his open mouth.

"Do not forget to tell Yui to record my victory in notebook," Svec offered.

Yui's crew quarters smelled brackish on a normal day, but Bear was assaulted by a much more noxious scent as he now approached it. Grief, he decided, remembering the particular stench of his clothes as he'd undressed every day that he'd visited his teenage niece in hospice years ago. It was a pituitary nightmare, pain sneaking out through his pores in total defiance of the stolid, supportive presence he was hoping to provide to his sister and brother-in-law during that time. Hygiene was no picnic on the station and forgiveness was critical, but this was something else. Yui would need to do a thorough wipe-down and fast. Maybe even dispose of the clothes he'd been wearing that night. Broaching this would be a psychological challenge, one Bear was not looking forward to, but he rationalized that it would yield interpersonal insights he could use later when debriefing new astronauts before their missions.

"Hey, friendo." He rapped on the plastic sliding door of Yui's CQ. There was no answer, only the horrible smell. "I know, friendo," Bear confessed. "You want to go home, and barring that, you want to stay in bed and dream about it. I want to do that, too, sometimes. We all do. But you need to get up, have something to eat, and, um, clean up."

He was holding his nose now. The smell was overpowering.

"Did you get sick last night, friendo?" There was no answer. "I'm going to open this door now. Okay?"

Yui floated in a sleeping bag strapped to the wall, with his arms crossed over his chest. It was how he always slept, how Tadeshi slept, too, though Bear could not have known that. His skin looked like a mixture of ash and milk, and his eyes, wide open, were not moving. Only his hair floating on end around his still face gave the impression that he had once been alive.

"He's dead," Bear told Svec.

The permanent striations of Svec's mimetic muscles twitched.

"I don't know when. Or how. Or—"

"None of that matters. NORAD reports that debris from meteor storm is coming toward us. We need to maneuver station out of way."

"Roger that. Yui's body can wait."

"He will be patient."

"Yes, he will. Poor guy."

Svec made the executive decision to handle one crisis at a time, and postpone telling Mission Control about the onboard fatality. The two men got to work and in short order had shifted the orbit of the massive station out of harm's way. Once the station was reoriented, the internet shut down and the satellite connection was lost. This happened from time to time, and while disruptive, it was no crisis. Svec told Bear to connect to CAPCOM via the ham radio.

"No response."

"Try again in ten minutes."

He did. Nothing.

They were cruising over the shadow line now, an orbital path where the sun seemed to drift in a restless circle alongside the earth, neither rising nor setting. Bear had always been curious what this orientation looked like, and now that his wish was granted, he felt uneasy. They tried again to reach Mission Control and again they could not connect on any platform. They had never experienced a break in communication this long before. Svec decided to use the time to exercise. He loaded his music player into the sound system and blasted his favorite heavy metal album, *Chornoye Utro*.

"Self-titled album. Very best one. After 1990 they were shit. Freedom ruins heavy metal. Need iron fist—bad father, bad dictator—to make true metal." He panted and smirked, sweat beading up on his skin like crystal dewdrops as he pushed his feet down on the treadmill.

"I don't know what they're saying," Bear sighed, biting his tongue to keep from adding *and I don't care.*

"This song is about woman. Bigger breasts, bigger problems. It is true."

"I'm taking some R&R in the Cupola."

The sound of disconnection hummed low and steady in their headsets. It threatened to seep into the crimped tunnels of their brains, implanting the tiny, psychic seeds of madness such isolation can wreak. Watching the sun as it slowly circled, never crossing before or behind the earth, refusing to offer that one supreme metaphor of renewal—this was madness. Strapping oneself into a treadmill, running toward nothing—this, too, was madness.

Dᴜʀɪɴɢ ᴀ ʜᴇᴀᴛ wave last year, a man at Rosette's Kingdom Hall of the Jehovah's Witnesses claimed to have received a vision from God. Alfred Guy was a Haitian émigré who worked for an HVAC company, a man as sober and staid as his job, too boring to be selected by God for spiritual ascendancy. But God did come to Alfred, he reported, in the dark of early morning last August, in the form of a man cloaked in blinding light.

"Burn everything you believe," the monsieur spoke without moving his lips, his face as explosive and formless as time. With his long arm like a ray of the sun, this deific stand-in set fire to Alfred's Bible just by pointing at it.

Alfred produced the scorched *New World Translation of the Holy Scriptures* as evidence to the elders at the Jehovah's Witness Kingdom Hall in Cambridge, where Rosette was a faithful sister. The leather cover was black and crispy.

The elders told Alfred to go home and get some sleep.

Alfred tried again before a larger audience the following Sunday. They were reading about Peter on the Sea of Galilee, his boat so full of fish it would sink. Alfred leapt to the dais and cried before the other Witnesses, "It's coming. We are not ready." His lips were wide and dry from smiling. "It's time to give up."

Within minutes the elders were escorting Alfred out the door. Rosette remembered the hush, the feeling of shame that unfurled across the hall, causing many to bow their heads. But a few people could not bow their heads and Rosette was among them. Paralyzed for a moment, she was incapable of looking away from Alfred, a tall handsome man whom she had somehow never noticed before.

One by one, folks left the Jehovahs and joined Alfred, who had spent his own money to rent a space above a Cambridge strip mall between an office-supply chain store and a discount sports clothier. He declared himself Pastor of the Last Kingdom on Earth, which is to say he sat in a left-behind office chair and talked about his vision for the coming end to anyone who came in through his open door.

There was nothing to fear, he promised. The end would be brief, total, and complete, a heartbeat in time, almost merciful in its efficiency. There would be no pain for the wicked; they would die instantly. Then it would all be over.

"And then what?" they asked.

"I don't know," Alfred replied.

"But, but, but . . ."

"Don't try too hard to know," he implored them instead. "If you can help it."

His lessons were short, often monosyllabic. Sometimes, when plied with existential puzzles, Alfred would offer no more than a sigh. His congregants, however, made up for his silence. That was the point of the Last Kingdom—to fill the last days of this world with a joyful noise. They batted around their stories all at once, talking to and at and over and through each other. The dominant story at Last Kingdom was that there would be a blast that would scorch the earth to ashes, and after everything cooled off, new plants and animals would emerge, hardier and more beautiful than before.

"Or not," Alfred offered, inspiring a frenzy of discussion, babble, and song, all at once.

"That actually makes a lot of sense," Karen said when Rosette tried to explain all this to her in the car. "Forest fires are wicked good for the soil. It's because of the sulfur."

"Never mind the sulfur," Rosette said, leaning hard on the horn. "Aye! *Puta!* I'll fry your ass in a rusty pan!" She slammed on the brakes and flung her arm across Karen's chest as though this alone would prevent her large body from hurtling through the windshield. It was the most maternal of gestures. The seat belt could barely contain the wild beating of Karen's heart.

"People in this city are crazy. They think we can read minds. Turn left whenever you want but don't signal to the other drivers. Lord have mercy . . ."

"I'm hungry, Rose." Karen had said this three times already. They had been her first words when Rosette had arrived in Mr. Cox's big silver Lincoln Town Car at Dennis's address. Mr. Cox was asleep in the back seat. "We could stop at McDonald's but I'll have to pay you back," Karen suggested.

"You can eat at Last Kingdom," Rosette said. "I made my mother's octopus stew. The best in the world."

They arrived at the shopping center around nine o'clock at night. All the stores were closed for the holiday, their windows papered with purple and gold banners advertising their grim sales. BUY NOW—BEFORE IT'S TOO LATE! Rosette unlocked a glass door that led to a staircase filled with a plasticky, chemical scent. The walls were a pale gray bearing perfect squares of a clean, lighter shade of paint where pictures had once hung, the ghostly reminders of vacated businesses. Even those that had remained in these sad office suites were halfhearted operations—a party rental company that was in actuality a front for Mafia interests; the headquarters of a nearly bankrupt, poorly attended French Canadian film festival; and the Last Kingdom on Earth Parish.

The music of Last Kingdom could be heard all the way down the hall. It was an office space like all the others, furnished only with what the previous occupants had left behind, half a dozen high-backed, rolling office chairs and a conference table pushed against the far wall, lined with aluminum foil trays of food. Only the elderly were seated. They rocked back and forth in the wobbly chairs as the music washed over their subdued faces. Everyone else was standing barefoot. Rosette removed Mr. Cox's and her shoes at the entrance and Karen did the same.

"We stand a long time. Hours and hours," Rosette explained. "It's hard on the feet. No shoes is better. Let the body balance the way it is designed to." She plopped Mr. Cox down in a chair but he immediately stood up, his chest full and proud.

"I'll be fine sitting on the floor," Karen said.

"No. We are greeting our Maker standing."

Karen angled toward the food table, but it was blocked by three guitarists blasting a long, improvisational song. The faithful numbered close to thirty people, exiles from the Jehovah's Witnesses and the stragglers they'd collected along the way. The music was loud and electric and seemed to have no beginning and no end.

Everyone was talking at the same time.

". . . I am so grate-ful! I am so grate-ful! I am so . . ."

". . . and you knew. You knew exactly what you were doing. You left me alone with wolves. I was a child—a friggin' child . . ."

". . . *pleine de grâce. Le Seigneur est avec vous* . . ."

". . . *hold me, hold me, never let me go until you've told me, told me* . . ."

". . . and a dishwasher and a mudroom and a fireplace and central air . . ."

". . . two three four five six seven eight nine ten one two three four five . . ."

". . . Doug can burn in a fire. Amber can explode. Shep—actually Shep's whole family—they should be eaten alive by lions. No, by maggots . . ."

". . . that's an insult to wolves. Wolves are ten thousand times kinder than the monsters you . . ."

Whatever came to their minds, whatever moved their spirits. Theirs was a faith uncluttered by mytho-historical characters and poorly translated verse. It left a lot to the imagination. It got very personal. The true language of God was spontaneous and perishable, they believed; recitations by rote were another faulty life-preserver in the floods of deception. Or so they assumed. Alfred had never actually told them any of this, but he'd implied it.

"Can anyone hear each other?" Karen asked Rosette.

For no reason she could discern, a man at the center of the rabble lifted his arms up in supplication. His long fingers reached all the way to the drop ceiling.

"Yes or no, *oui ou non, sí o no, sim ou não* . . ."

The lead guitarist ripped a lawless, boiling lick, nodding his head as if in response.

"Pastor Alfred," Rosette said, nudging Karen. The supplicating man was almost as broad as he was tall. For years he'd tried to make himself fit into the small enclave of Haitian immigrants in Boston, a place that felt no more his rightful home than Haiti had, and so, he'd decided, home must be a notion that simply did not exist in this world. What he'd found instead was a people so battered by weather and addiction, fear and pride, that the sheer pragmatism of Armageddon made perfect sense. Exhaustion was the best motivator, and so they all decided to stand until they dropped.

It was a tenet of this new church that the drama of the coming apocalypse not overshadow its message of surrender. Alfred tried, in his passive, lazy way, to discourage discussions of fire and nuclear winter, horsemen and demons. They were beside the point. Passion needed to be conserved for the awe and splendor of whatever was coming, and though Alfred did not purport to know anything for sure, he mused aloud that histrionics would probably irritate the Supreme Being burdened with such a brutally complete task of search and destroy.

"Chill," he urged his parishioners when they lapsed again and again into talk of blood-black rivers and fire in the skies.

They came every Monday and Wednesday night for lectures, stream-of-consciousness rants from Alfred that expounded on the finer points of his utilitarian hopelessness. He had few concrete ideas himself, which allowed his congregants to come up with the details, approved by a simple majority vote. Thursday nights were for meditation, a practice in which members stood in two rows facing each other and stared, eyes wide open, into the eyes opposite them for a full ten minutes, then they switched, square-dance style, to a new partner, until everyone in the fold had been "seen" by everyone else. Friday nights were for cooking and resting in preparation for Saturday, when, at sundown, their weekly vigil for the end began. It was a twenty-four-hour ritual, with members coming and going, though most stayed for the entire saga, joint pain be damned.

Karen watched the whole circus in amazement. While not in their Sunday best, most folks looked as if they'd put thought into their clothing. They stood and swayed, hollering their prayers to and at each other and whatever God they hoped was listening. There were no Bibles at the Last Kingdom. No hymnals or pamphlets. The word of God could not be trusted coming from man, Alfred had warned them repeatedly. That this included him was a fact he fully acknowledged.

"This happens to be where I am waiting for deliverance," he said, as though he had heard Karen's thoughts and was responding in kind. "Don't mean you have to wait here, too."

A pretty young Korean woman in a floral, grandmotherly dress started jumping up and down. "I am so grate-ful! I am so grate-ful. I am so gra-a-a-a-te-FUL!" she sang in an almost petulant, schoolyard tune. "How can I say thanks for all that you have done for me? All this life we don't deserve! Lord, take it away from me!"

"It was never ours to begin with," the pastor said in a natural tone of voice. Sweat pooled in the thick folds of skin at the back of his neck. Despite the heat, Alfred wore a brown wool suit. A white man with hairy knuckles removed a handkerchief from his suit pocket and dabbed the pastor's neck with it.

"Thanks, brother," Alfred said.

"Don't mention it, Al," the hairy man brayed.

It was an unusually diverse crowd for Boston. There were a decent number of nations represented, considering the size of the sample. The lead and rhythm guitarists were brothers, Adiel and Anildo, Cape Verdean high school students wearing thin neckties and crisp, collared shirts tucked into their sagging jeans. They would have joined Last Kingdom even if their parents hadn't belonged, such was their sweet fatalistic fervor. They liked the idea that nothing mattered but God, as the majority of stuff in their life—their grades, their skin, their sex prospects— was so unruly and frustrating, the source of all their pain. The message they gleaned from this new religion—forget it all!—met the paradoxical needs of their adolescence: to feel both totally powerful and completely taken care of at the same time.

The pastor rewarded their commitment by giving them free musical rein on Saturdays. Their bassist, Nate, was a white boy with shoulder-length hair and a nose that looked broken too long ago to be fixed. After nineteen years, his life felt long enough. The maintenance manager of this office complex, he lived in a squalid apartment with two disrespectful roommates he'd met online, and he worked long hours to pay for this tiny scrap of undignified freedom. Until he'd befriended Adiel and Anildo and joined the fold, he had been on the verge of suicide.

The three of them stood together at the edge of the crowd, playing shifting melodies that swelled with feeling, then drew back.

"I really friggin' hope God sees us, sees our love and devotion," shouted Moira, a deliriously smiling white lady. In her early fifties, she was decked out in black jeans and a black sweatshirt that had been cropped at the waist and the neck, exposing the tanned, very wrinkled skin of her shoulder, where a wobbly, amateurish shamrock had been tattooed a long time ago. Moira held her hands over the eyes of a small girl, Shayla, standing by her side. Shayla had dressed herself in boyish hand-me-down gym shorts and white athletic socks that were scrunched up at her slim ankles. New breasts pushed disconcertingly into the billowing, man-sized T-shirt she'd chosen to hide them in. Moira guarded her fiercely.

"Can God see us?" Moira was crying now. "We are giving Him friggin' everything."

Alfred folded his hands over his stomach. At heart he was an antinomian. Good works, he believed, were just another currency in the bankrupt economies of human faith, a way for man to barter his way into salvation. The greatest sin, the only sin, Alfred believed, was trying to make a mystery make sense. But he didn't want to be dogmatic about any of this. If his followers got the finer points, great. If those parts were lost on them, well, that's just how things go. They liked to take his words letter by letter. It was what they were used to doing and he had no delusion about breaking their habits in this lifetime, not with the deadline of a looming apocalypse ahead. That's why he tried to say as little as he could get away with. It was easier to let them make their own meaning. And anyway, half the time he couldn't remember what he preached from one day to the next. There were wild inconsistencies in his sermons, he was sure, which worked toward the ultimate good. It gave everyone less to hold on to.

But they wanted an answer and they wanted it now. He'd already forgotten the question.

It hurts to love you so much, he wanted to tell them.

"It's a shot in the dark," he said.

Rosette grabbed Karen's hand, kissed it, and held it enjoined with hers in the air.

They went on like this for hours, straight through the midnight hour, when the Great Hush of Last Day unfurled across the Eastern Standard Time zone. House lights switched off, restaurants got dark. Voices everywhere reduced to a whisper, uttering only the sibilant command, "Shhhhh, shut that off, shut up, shhhhhh." Light withdrew in stutters and voices darkened to shadows. People mouthed their last words, voiceless confessions offered up for the sky to swallow. They muted their kisses, softened their breaths, paused the music and the dancing, ceased their chewing, drinking, urinating, lovemaking.

"Lacrimosa dies illa
Qua resurget ex favi—"

At Symphony Hall, the conductor dropped his arms and all the musicians and singers stopped. They sat and waited.

Up and down the eastern seaboard, radio frequencies did not so much mute as morph into an otherworldly buzz, the hiss of cosmic inhalation, a slow, deliberate breath measured one time zone at a time. TVs still blared their regularly scheduled commercials, though a few stations offered a quiet, though not entirely silent, thirty-second spot of holiday greeting at the midnight hour. In New York's Grand Central Station, only the four clocks, hidden behind its garish holiday flags, could be heard ticking. Even the vagrants, the ones who were awake, knew to hold their tongue.

The sound of cars on highways swam in their ceaseless current. In just a moment, the lights would stutter back on. Voices would return to their normal levels. Some would scream their way out of the silence, howling and whistling like a victory had been won. In São Paulo, Atlanta, Brooklyn, and Belize, men on rooftops would shoot guns into the air. Throngs in Times Square would cheer and throw their hats, their cups, their lighters, whatever they had in their hands, into the blind, invisible sky.

But not yet. For this moment, all was quiet, dark, and still.

Time twitched and the bottomless stars grew brighter.

Outside the window of the Last Kingdom office parish, the lights of the parking lot went on a timed hiatus. The wind pushed trash across the pavement. For sixty seconds all was dim. Inside, however, the band played on. Last Kingdom did not recognize holidays, Christian or secular, and so at the stroke of midnight on the Last Day the congregants continued to hold forth and wail at and with each other. Then it was over. The lights of the parking lot came back on.

Karen had many times tried to witness the Great Hush of Last Day but was foiled year after year by her meds, which knocked her out into an almost vegetative state not long after dinner. Now her eyes strained to see what, if anything, was happening around her that was different or special. In the ceiling just above the window a stain like spilled coffee flowered outward from the corner of the room. Karen's eyes, tired from straining, lost focus, until she saw in the perforated drop ceiling a face emerge. Smiling and blotchy, it pushed itself out of the ceiling stain, taking shape in three dimensions, until Karen saw—she swore she was seeing, swore on her heart, on Nora's heart, on the hearts of all the kittens in the world—the tiny, hovering face of an angel.

"Do you see her?" Karen asked Rosette, who was still holding Karen's upraised hand in hers. "She looks like Glinda the Good Witch. Do you remember her?" Karen pointed at the ceiling.

"Oh, my sweet girl. Sweet, sweet, crazy, crazy girl."

"No. Look, Rose. There she is. Tell me you don't see her."

Rosette shook her head. "It's time to eat," she called out, and Pastor Alfred threw his arms in the air and shouted, "Amen!"

The musicians unplugged their instruments and sat on the carpet along with everyone else. An assembly line of women formed to plate and deliver food to each parishioner. A bowl of stew was put in Karen's hands. She ate it so fast she cracked a tooth on a chunk of bone floating in the thick broth.

"Mmmm," she said, pretending to wipe her mouth with a napkin so she could spit out fragments of her tooth. "What kind of meat is this?"

"Goat," an old woman answered.

"I've never had goat before. It's delicious. Did anyone else see that angel?"

The angel had disappeared. Squinting at the ceiling stain, Karen could almost make out a two-dimensional likeness of the face, but she wasn't pushing it. You couldn't force astral communion, or else everyone would be doing it all the time, and then who would there be to drive the buses and check the chemicals in the pool and perform vital surgeries?

"No such thing as angels here, hon," Moira said, picking her teeth with a plastic fork. "The real God don't need all those accessories."

"Rose? You saw her, didn't you?"

Rosette held her hand up to Karen's face. She was listening to the messages on her phone. When she was finished, she fixed Karen in a flinty stare. "Babygirl, is there something you are not telling me?"

Karen could only blink at her. Where to begin?

"Your home called me. Asking if I had seen you. You are a missing woman tonight. . . ."

"I've finally found a faith that works, Rosie. I'm ready to join your church. You can't make me go back. Not yet, anyway."

Everyone was looking at them now. What a moment! This was the drama Karen had longed for. She sensed serious potential for applause. If only Rosette were not the antagonist in the scene. She considered Rosette a kindred spirit, a big sister. No matter who Karen got to foster her, and there were plenty of new options here at this church, Rosette would always be family. Karen had always imagined that in a past life, once upon a time, she and Rosette had been crushed under the same heavy stones for the same crimes of witchcraft/generally disruptive female power, that their spirits were forever entwined as they followed each other into successive lifetimes.

"I can make a major contribution."

"I don't believe anything you say."

"No, really. Look."

Karen produced one of the three bottles she had taken from Dennis. She shook it like a little maraca. "Like last time, Rose. Except this time you can give my half of the money to the church. As my initiation fee, or whatever."

"Crazy girl!" Rosette said under her breath. She snatched the bottle from Karen and hid it in her pocket. "You are crazy in the head. Half intelligent, half stupid. How can you be so stupid?"

"You always say the meanest things in whispers," Karen replied. "Just because it's quiet doesn't make it hurt less."

"What's the problem, Karen?" Moira asked. She had never liked Rosette. Didn't trust her.

"I want to join!" Karen cried. "I want to be in your church."

The congregation gathered around Karen and Rosette. Someone said, "Let's ask her the Central Questions," and everyone murmured in agreement.

"Sister Karen, do you believe in one all-powerful God?"

"Do you accept His will totally and completely, even if it means you are going to die in the fiery hell of Armageddon?"

"Even if you are not among those elected to be saved?"

"Are you willing to give up everything? To give it all to Him?"

"And admit that no matter what you do, no matter how good you are, how hard you try, it might not amount to a hill of beans?"

"Do you promise to die trying?"

Karen was not at all willing to agree to any of these terms. She could not accept a world in which she was not a co-creator alongside the Divine. She had seen too much—portals to unknown worlds in every puddle of water, winking omens in the highway lights, dented cans baring to her their souls. There wasn't just one God who took everything away greedily; there was a web of intersecting lines like spider's silk connecting the souls of all things living, dead, and inanimate in a giant inescapable whole. It was never-ending, and she definitely had the power to affect it by her thoughts and energies and actions. And it wasn't fair that some people got to go to Rosette's God's party in the sky and some people didn't. She looked at the faces staring at her now, these variegated masks of humanity, all wanting her, all offering her this covenant.

"Yes!" she cried, and everyone cheered.

Shayla ran up to Karen and hugged her hip. She reached into her pocket where she had been saving a single package of cherry fruit leather. She ripped off the wrapper and tore it in two, offering Karen half.

"Cherry is the best flavor," Karen said.

"It's the only one for me," the girl agreed.

"Don't just stand there, girl. You think because everyone is clapping for you, you are some princess now. Hmmph. Clean out those coffeepots," Rosette said to Karen.

Everyone was collecting the plastic bowls and spoons to be wiped clean for another use. How nice, Karen thought, that despite the end of the world, these folks were still recycling.

It was just before dawn when the parish of Last Kingdom arrived at the YMCA. The sky was a flimsy dark tinged by a veil of green. They parked their cars in the handicapped spots, the members-only spots, the fire lane. It was Last Day—who was going to stop them? But Karen urged them and they agreed to file in quietly. There was no need for stealth. Everything they were doing was being recorded on a closed-loop surveillance system. For all her powers and ambitions of vision, Karen had never noticed the cameras installed outside and inside the Y.

Today she was going swimming with her thirty new best friends! A super-secret pool party at the YMCA. It was a fantasy she had spent hours describing to Nora as they tried to construct a psychic safe place where Karen could retreat to when disturbing memories were triggered. Nora had given her full poetic license in this fabrication, suggesting trip wire and laser guns to keep out bad guys, for comfort a basket of kittens who never ever peed, the visibility and vantage point of a high mountain lair surrounded by a moat teeming with loyal alligators. But for once Karen's mental landscape remained firmly rooted in reality: the place she always returned to in these therapeutic exercises was the YMCA swimming pool with its high, echoing walls, its pistachio-green tiles, the milky light pouring in from the frosted glass of the windows; and presiding over everything, sitting way up high in the lifeguard chair, solid as a caryatid in an ancient temple, inviolable, loving, and stern, was Rosette.

Nothing ever hurt in the pool. Here she was neither fat nor clumsy. She was never cold, never hot, and hours could pass before she realized she hadn't eaten. It was a place where all her limitations and needs dissolved. She looked at her green dress rippling like an anemone around her legs. This dress had been through so much today, and now it was being bathed in chlorine. She would wash it in perfume and fabric softener when she got to her new home, wherever that would be.

"Pick a song everyone knows," someone instructed Karen.

"Everyone?" she cried. "I can't—"

"Don't think about it. Just sing."

"*Happy birthday to you*," Karen began, and everyone else joined in. This was her baptism! The acoustic effect of the whole congregation in the pool was stunning. Karen felt her blood thicken and slow, the rush-hour pumping of her heart ease, the water surrounding them flatten under the command of their chorus. Musically they harmonized about as well as a flock of shorebirds at sunset, but it was a powerful invocation. As a welcoming ceremony, Karen had to admit, it was working. Maybe the God they believed in was capricious and snobby, but their encouragement was sincere.

"What do I do now?"

"Go," Rosette said, splashing her. "Go swim under and come back up."

Karen dove headfirst under the water and swam as deep as she could. She opened her eyes and saw a million fractured beams of light flashing everywhere, like a star had fallen from the sky, broken open, and scattered too fast to dissolve in the water. She felt the pressure around her building, trying to lift her to the surface. She flapped her arms, fighting to stay underwater. She thought about Dennis. Just his name. She thought about her mother and how she had floated anxiously like this inside her once, wanting to be born but waiting for her mother to push her out.

Dennis was never going to be okay, and neither was she. No one was. This moment was as good as it was ever going to get. If the world ended right now, Karen thought, it would be okay, but it needed to happen quickly. Right now. *I don't want to be here anymore. Come take me. Us.*

Come, she said in her head, until it was no longer a word. Her eyes were burning. The pressure was building inside her lungs. *Come right now. Right now.*

"Baaaaah," Karen screamed as she surged to the surface.

"Sister Karen," an old Haitian man shouted. *"Byenveni lakay ou."*

"Look at her."

"Did you feel it?" Rosette asked.

Karen, gasping for air, dog-paddled weakly to the side of the pool. She threw her arms over the edge and held the concrete side like a favorite pillow in the aftermath of a nightmare. She didn't know what was real anymore. Everything she believed in this life had drained out of her body, been siphoned through the pool's filter, disinfected, and pumped back out invisible as water.

"I'm still here," she said, unsure if even this was true.

IN FRENCH, LAST Day is called *le jour d'infini rien* or, more simply, *le jour rien*. In Italian, *giorno di nient'altro*. In Spanish, *el día de la entrega*. In Japanese, *mokushi hi*. In Slavic tongues, some variation of *the gate of no dawn*. In Nordic cultures, *the day time takes a nap*. Tom tried his best to spell these words right, to angle the strokes of the kanji appropriately, but he was very drunk and very tired and even letters in English looked alien as he scraped them into people's skin.

THAT NIGHT SARAH dreamed she had a baby with no body. It was a large smiling head she kept swaddled in a yellow blanket. She was ashamed of her genderless little imp but filled with love for it, too. A mutant and a mistake, it had her eyes and nose and mouth, and it was so happy, its smile inextinguishable. "Cantaloupe," she named the baby. "You can't name a baby Cantaloupe," Kurt said to her; he was ostensibly, in the logic of the dream, her baby's father. "Please?" she said, but he was walking away from her and into the vaporous corridor of her unconscious. "Please?" she kept shouting in the empty hallway, until the sound of her own voice woke her up.

She was on the beach. The sun was a muted white light behind a screen of clouds. The ocean was churning, the color of dull utensils. It was day, and she was still alive. But Kurt was gone. She peered into the horizon, as if he had walked on water and would be waiting for her at the edge of the sea. She shook herself more awake, stood up, scanned the length of the beach left and right. In the far-off distance, she saw the abandoned campfires of last night releasing strings of smoke into the morning air. Kurt's helmet was gone. A fresh pile of sand had been poured onto their fire.

THE FIRST RAYS of morning seeped through the cloudy glass.

"We used to baptize everyone at Carson Beach," the hairy-knuckled man explained to Karen. "This is much better. You think we can use this pool from now on?"

"Definitely," Karen promised. Carson Beach was home to used tampons, syringes, and plastic bags containing the occasional mobster body part. Even the seagulls who fed there looked disgusted and ashamed.

She practiced her butterfly stroke for a few laps, then decided to join Moira and her grandchild Shayla in the shallow end, where they were pretending it was the Olympics.

"Rate my handstands," Shayla begged Karen. "But take it serious. Grandma is bullshitting me because I'm a kid. I'm not playing around here. I need a real friggin' judge. *Capiche?*"

Each time Shayla's head plunged underwater, Moira fired at Karen rapid disjointed installments of her life story. There were three ex-husbands, a dead son, a daughter in assisted living because she'd overdosed so many times she'd lost her gross motor skills. Shayla was not even her biological granddaughter. Moira had inherited the child from—

"How was that one? Were you even paying attention?" the child cried, eyes burning red with chlorine.

"Good, Shay. Do another one."

"Eight point five," Karen said, an honest assessment, which the child took as a personal challenge to try harder. She dove under again.

"So, that was the last time I bailed his sorry you-know-what out of jail," Moira went on. She was a petite muscular woman with long blondish-white hair and a gold hoop in her left nostril. Her skin was inscribed all over with shamrocks and mermaids, clipper ships and anchors. One tattoo inked onto her shoulder was a lot brighter than the others: the image of a sapling, spindly and leafless, embracing with two branch-like arms a two-by-four board of knotty pine bearing the yellow price tag of a hardware store.

"Got that one for free nine years ago," Moira explained. "Couldn't choose the picture, just had to accept what I got. Never met the artist before in my life. Hardly said two words to him, but he sure knew me all right." She kissed her fingertips and pressed them against the little sapling on her shoulder.

"Oh," Karen said. She had so much to say but couldn't find her voice. It had slid down her throat and was curled up and hiding somewhere beneath her stomach. Tears fell down her dripping wet face but for once she couldn't make a sound.

"Come here, sweetheart," the old woman said, and pulled Karen into her for a long, weightless hug. Karen felt her feet slipping down at the drop-off point where the deep end began. She held on to Moira.

"I never had a real mother," she whimpered.

"I know, baby," Moira said. "Neither did I. A lot of us here didn't."

If Dennis died, which she knew he would, probably soon, would she feel his soul leaving the earth, or would it get lost in all the garbage floating around, the lies people told and the hateful things they said? Even the spiritual realm was vulnerable to pollution, and it was getting worse every day.

"Rose," Karen called, her voice smacking against the walls and bouncing off. She spotted Rosette and Alfred pulling a stiff and soaking Mr. Cox out of the pool. They laid him on the floor beneath the life-guard's chair. There were so many voices caroming off the tile, colliding into each other, expanding in air. "Rosette!" Karen shouted. Karen tried to run to her, to run across the shallow end of the pool. Her legs dragged behind her. She'd had dreams like this. Was this one of them? Rosette was crying, wringing her hands, and Alfred was whispering to her. He knelt down by Mr. Cox and pumped his chest. Through the windows Karen saw a blue flashing light. Then red. She heard the single chirp of a siren, turned on and then just as suddenly turned off, as though by mistake.

"I KNOW THE ham is working," Bear said when he returned, "but I'm not getting anything back. They can hear us, we just can't hear them."

"We should not wait for CAPCOM. Need to handle his body."

"Agreed."

"The MELFI locker is cold. He will fit in there."

"We'd lose all our samples. That's a lot of data."

"Could jettison his body. What I would want if I died in space."

"But we don't know that is what he would want. We have his family to consider. And JAXA. It would be an international disaster."

"Even in cold locker, we will have smell."

"The new crew is coming in two weeks. We could preserve him in a spacesuit, tether him outside, until we can send him back with the return capsule."

"Like bad dog? On leash?"

"Heck, I don't know."

"Okay. For now we wait," Svec said.

He wiped the sweat from his body and took off his shirt. Over his heart was tattooed in blocky Cyrillic *MAXIM*.

"Never knew you had a tattoo."

"You like?"

"That smirk, man. I know you don't mean it, but it just looks like you're making fun of me."

"Never. Here, comrade." Svec handed Bear a plastic pouch of vodka.

"How many of these do you have?"

"Enough."

"I don't drink. I told you that months ago."

"Today is exception. Today is too much for any man. Even you."

"You don't understand," Bear said. "My father died in a drunk-driving accident."

"My father, too." Svec sucked on the nozzle of the drink pouch, tempering the ridiculous indignity of the apparatus by his audacious sense of comfort and ease with it. "Crashed car into brick wall."

"Well, my father *wasn't* drunk. Someone's selfish drinking took his life. I won't mess with this stuff."

"Think of it like medicine." Svec held the pouch out to Bear. "To Yui. Our fallen friendo."

Madness, Bear thought, and took the drink.

"Yowww!"

"Now you feel fire. Good. Fire burns all rubbish. Make you new."

The men drank their way through one pouch and opened another. It was a mutiny, Bear thought, vomiting into his favorite baseball cap. There would be hell to pay once they got linked up again to the ground.

It was still possible, Svec countered, to put in a half-decent day's work, and Mission Control would be none the wiser. He fiddled with a spectrometer for a few minutes and began to laugh. "I don't know what we are measuring with this thing. Probably trying to make new weapon. To destroy U.S.A. To kill your whole family! Ha-ha!"

"I don't know what half of our experiments are doing, either. They told me it was intentional, so I don't fudge the data. But we're probably trying to kill you guys, too." He grabbed the pouch of vodka out of Svec's hand and pulled hard. "I like the beginning of drinking, when I feel like all the screws in my brain just got blasted with WD-40. I do not like the end of drinking, when I—" He wretched some more, shuddering in the hollow places of his body, heaving from what felt like the bones of his feet.

"If you drink often enough, it is never beginning or end," Svec explained. "But is harder up here. Vestibular system already confused. Me, I do not vomit in test flights. Not in parabolic flight. Not in high-G training. Okay, comrade. I will help to clean you now."

Bear was pawing at the bullets of floating bile he had managed to produce. His eyes were the color of ripe strawberries and brimming with unmoving tears. Svec dabbed Bear's face with a soft towel. He captured the wayward stomach matter and disposed of it, made his friend a batch of weak reconstituted grapefruit juice, and instructed him to sip slowly.

"I'm going to the Cupola," Bear said. "I always feel better in the Cupola. Just saying the word *cupola* makes me feel better."

"Okay, comrade. You go. I will clean some more."

Svec wiped down all the places where Bear's vomit might have splattered. He wondered about his life in retirement. He'd spent so much time striving toward one goal or another. What would he do now? Of course he would always be a representative of Roscosmos, talking to people about space, delivering speeches and lectures, cutting ribbons, shaking hands with men who envied him. But beyond that? There was nothing. Only life, which, as far as Svec could see, boiled down to eating. You chewed on the thread of life until you met your end. He could spend his days hunting big game. There would always be a tiger or a bear to stalk and kill. But then what? Stuff it? Hang the dead thing above a fireplace? It was disrespectful to turn an animal like that into a decoration or a toy. He could chase young women. It would not be so different from the bears and tigers after a while. His mentor, Gregori Borisovitch, had died three months into his retirement. Without a mission to prepare for, his heart had grown weak and stopped beating in his sleep. *This is what will happen to me,* Svec said to himself. *I will go home and be dead in three months.*

"Come quick, Svec. You got to see this."

"Your face is white."

"Just look."

Bear grabbed Svec's hand and tugged him along like a child pulling a parent to the site of his latest accident. Svec tried to free himself but Bear would not let go. They entered the Cupola one at a time and there beheld the earth they had been unable to reach for several hours. Flimsy clouds swirled in tatters over Central America.

"What?" Svec asked.

"Just look."

The clouds disintegrated and blew apart, revealing what looked like another layer of clouds beneath them, brown ones, piling up and spreading in liquid spurts over the horn of Brazil. All of North and South America, every square mile of it, was covered with brown suppurating sores. They oozed and dribbled in thick brown rivers, swirled in brown eddies, spilled into the sea.

"There's no rain forest. We used to be able to see the rain forest."

"Maybe there was fire?"

"Over the whole continent?"

"It is everywhere."

They checked the photos captured earlier in the day. At 13:41 P.M. GMT the brown clouds had begun mushrooming all over the earth. If there was a point of origin, Bear and Svec could not find it.

HARDLY ANYONE WAS looking at the sky when it happened. That posture of curiosity and awe was reserved symbolically for the night before, May 27, when heads tilted upward in waves across the globe as darkness descended one meridian at a time in the Great Hush. It was a reenactment, conscious or not, of the moment those terrified Babylonians had watched the sky in the aftermath of the eclipse that they were sure was ushering the end. May 28 was devoted to more timid celebration. Pouring water on the ashes of last night's fires, cleaning the syrup of spilled drinks, munching on cold pizza, nursing hangovers, running a commemorative 5K.

But An Chu was staring at the sky. It was evening in Hong Kong, past her bedtime. She knew that today was special but she did not know why. She was exhausted by the past two days of celebration, vacillating between elation and rage. The sugar in her blood had spiked and fallen in rapid cycles from all the candy she'd been allowed to eat. When the doorbell began ringing with another round of holiday guests, she slapped her nanny across the face. An was done with them, and her nanny kept insisting, as her mother had instructed, that she give each guest eight kisses for good luck.

An Chu's nanny, Dai, hated An Chu. She hated the child's flat-faced mother and her ubiquitous string of fat black pearls. The father was a grumbling suit who did not strain his eyes even to glance in the nanny's direction. Dai was saving up to get her teeth fixed. They were crooked and irregularly sized, as though Dai's mouth had been assembled with spare parts. Her top right incisor sprang out with the alacrity of a diving board. That night, waiting for An to fall asleep, Dai calculated how much longer it would take, in terms of hours, days, months, before she would have enough money to get her teeth fixed. The thought so depressed her that she lay down beside An on the bed, and as the din of the party outside rose to a clamor, she cried herself to sleep.

An watched her nanny's face soften, listened for the delicate gurgle of sleep to take over, then climbed over Dai to the floor. She put on her shoes without buckling them—buckles were still beyond her—and stepped awkwardly into the fray outside.

"Until night falls," she repeated, not knowing why everyone laughed in response. It had been the refrain of last night, so why not tonight? The adults touched her head and face, tugged on her pigtails, and told her she was pretty. She'd heard this so often—how pretty she was—that the sentence felt like a long surname. *Hello, my name is An Chu the-Prettiest-Girl-in-the-World.*

She skated across the polished wood floor in her shiny unbuckled shoes, navigating the crowd of giants, not finding her parents among them.

The sliding glass door that led to the deck was open. An knew as well as she knew anything else in her flowering, inchoate mind that she was not allowed to go onto the deck alone, but she was doing it anyway, a cerebral explosion between impulse and thoughtful decision-making inching her closer to autonomy.

A strong wind lifted the strands of hair that had fallen out of the elastics Dai had wound so tightly just a few hours earlier. Her cheeks were pink and warm. The sky was a cloudy black stained blue at the horizon where day smoldered on the other side of the world. The moon was a filament of light outside of An's line of vision. She watched, instead, the billboard across the street blinking purple and gold. It was a sign for a parking lot and was made of twisted neon bulbs, an antiquated spectacle in the largely digital lumisphere of the city.

The light blinked on and off from the top stroke of the first character to the bottom, pausing at dead bulbs where the neon had burned out, a flickering that transfixed the child. She noticed how the purple and gold light reflected on the glass of her building, and kicked her foot in a confounding ache to be closer to the pretty sparkles reflected on the window below. Her shoe flew off her foot and tumbled from the balcony, falling thirty-seven stories to the ground below. An looked down in terror, then back at the parking lot sign as if its mysteries would now be revealed. She looked behind her into her apartment. A man grabbed a woman by the hips and pulled her close; the woman pulled away from him, arching her torso like a wind-bent reed. An Chu looked out again, down at the ground, then up at the sky.

NICOLE JOHNSON MET the man of her dreams at a bar with a broken neon sign. Six years later she married that man, Luke, and two years after that he left her for another woman. Luke had been walking their dog, a chocolate labradoodle named Tallulah, when a car on their street got rear-ended, spun out of control, and crashed into a retainer wall. The car immediately burst into flames and Luke, letting go of Tallulah's leash, dashed into oncoming traffic to pull the driver out to safety. He rode in the ambulance with her to the hospital, Tallulah long gone, never to be seen again, and after the woman had been stabilized Luke continued to call the ICU to check on her.

Nicole watched her husband fall in love with this woman over the next six months, like another car accident happening, this time in slow motion. She'd told herself she was paranoid, she was insecure, she should have a baby, she should not have a baby, she should be sexier, she should focus on her career, she should be empathetic, she should trust.

Nine months after the accident Luke had moved out and filed for divorce.

Now Luke and this woman were getting married in Palm Springs, on Last Day, Nicole had learned from a bout of social media stalking. Of all the clichés.

She drove around for hours that night, making herself sick. Even her car was now tainted. She had bought it with Luke when a much less dramatic accident had totaled her old car. They'd brought Tallulah home from the breeder in that car. They'd made love in the back seat once when Luke's parents were visiting from Ohio and they had nowhere private to go. It still smelled faintly of Tallulah's fur, like a mixture of corn chips and rainwater.

Nicole had to get rid of it. Now.

She pulled off at a dealership called Hugo's that every year hosted a famous Last Day sale, plastering the city with ominous billboards, signs, flyers, and airplane banners, always a bleak biblical nightmarescape of the end and the words IT'S NOW OR NEVER AT HUGO'S. Nicole traded her Honda in for an even older Toyota, plus two hundred dollars in cash. Worth it, she felt, her heart clanging against the bones of her chest like a prisoner with an empty tin cup. This new car smelled like Lysol, fake cherries, and ash, someone else's ghosts.

She drove past all the Last Day parties she'd been invited to, past all those pitying, insistent friends who'd vied to be the one to hold her together right now. None of them understood that she didn't want to be held—she wanted to disintegrate, she wanted everyone and everything to break apart. Thinking about it did not depress her at all. The Last Day holiday had never made more sense.

She stopped to refill her tank, get a Diet Coke, pee, then hit the road for another two hours. If she ran into traffic on the highway, she got off at the very next exit without caring where it led. She traced asymmetries all over Los Angeles, following a tangle of invisible lines.

At one point she thought she saw Tallulah being walked by a fat teenager juggling the dog's leash and a slice of pizza.

"That girl is me," Nicole gasped, wondering if her life was being lived in a multiverse and if her body, in this car driving around in unfinished circles, was its nucleus. She'd seen something like that in a creepy documentary Luke had made her watch years ago, about time and space and particles and intentions. There had been a bit about jars of water expressing sadness and rage in the arrangement of their molecules, and earnest talk of the possibility that every living moment of your life was occurring simultaneously on different planes of existence. It had given her nightmares, she remembered, and Luke had had to rub her back so she could fall asleep. Right now she wished it were all true, that on some plane of existence she was in bed, dreaming this last year and a half, and that she would wake up and Luke would still be there holding her. If she only kept driving she might find the portal back to him and then, back home.

And where was she when this realization dawned? Right smack in front of the bar where she'd first met Luke. She parked her car in front, the same broken pink of the neon sign glowing in the window. It was around six o'clock in the morning. The world had not ended. The bar was still open. She sat at the same stool she'd sat at years ago.

"Do you have anything to eat?" she asked the bartender.

He was reading on his phone and refused to look up, pointing with his elbow toward a stack of pizza boxes on a side table. Nicole opened each box and found only chewed-up bits of crust until she reached the very last box at the bottom of the pile, where a single slice was left. Pineapple and chicken, her favorite.

"I just don't know what I did wrong," Nicole said to the bartender. He wasn't the same man who had tended bar the day she'd met Luke. Even though no one else was there, she had to ask him twice for a glass of water. The bartender all those years ago had been old and bearded, not terribly big but saddled with a fat, round belly, a tired, dispirited Santa Claus sort of man. This kid was barely old enough to drink. His hair was shaved to a pale golden-white fuzz except for a long swoop of bangs that fell into his eyes.

"Luke is half-white and half-Korean and I'm half-black and half-Mexican, and that both matters a lot and doesn't matter at all in our breakup."

At hearing the word *breakup,* the boy looked up and flung his bangs out of his face with a sudden jerk of his neck. His eyes were light and colorless and Nicole was febrile and exhausted.

"She's white. The other woman. Just white. And not as pretty as me, but younger. Though only five years younger, which isn't *that* significant, right?"

His bangs had returned to his face, shielding his impassive, unearthly eyes once again.

"I was a good wife. I stayed in shape. I kept things interesting in bed. I looked up exotic recipes for dinner. I cooked, for God's sake! I said yes to sex even when I was exhausted. I did that thing with the scrunchie all the women's magazines say will 'drive him wild'. . . ."

"What's a scrunchie?"

"It's a glorified rubber band." It amazed her that she was talking about all this in complete sobriety and not a single tear was in production. Maybe she'd finally cried out her life's allotment of tears and now there were none left. She felt chalky inside, as if her bones could be rinsed away by a light rain. Her head clanked. Maybe she'd spent her life's allotment of love and there was none of that left, either.

"Sometimes I wonder if I am being punished for something, and I have to make it right, which I'd do, gladly, if only I could remember what it was I did wrong."

The bartender stabbed the ice in his drink with a straw, his face solemn and intent. She couldn't tell if he was even listening. He harpooned a maraschino cherry at last and slowly, patiently dragged it to the lip of the glass. He balanced the cherry on the straw and brought it to his mouth without dipping his head to meet it.

"The universe doesn't care enough about any one being to punish it," he said after he'd swallowed. "You need to think bigger."

"Yeah, but—" she began.

.   .   .

IT WAS NOT Last Day on the island of Bali. Last Day had never been celebrated there. It was simply the evening of May 28, time to set out the last *canang sari* offering of the day. A woman shook the branches of a Japon tree and collected the fallen blossoms in her shirt. She added them to the folded-coconut-leaf dishes full of betel, lime, cigarettes, and gambier, decorated with plumeria and marigolds, and laid them before her doorstep and on the dashboard of her husband's parked car. The smell of incense drifted through the air, mixing with the smell of burning trash. A stray dog ambled down the street. He lifted his leg to pee on the *canang sari* that had just been laid out. A little boy watched him and laughed. A black butterfly took flight.

IT WAS MIDAFTERNOON in Addis Ababa. Zelalem Jember slumped over his piano with his head in his hands, scratching an itch that did not exist. Somewhere beneath his hair, the dermis of his scalp, and his obdurate skull, the music wriggled between his synapses, little electric eels of melody stinging him with one note, then vanishing, leaving him bereft, in that simultaneous longing and dread known to all artists in the middle of difficult work.

"You have no idea what it's like to compose an opera with the sound of giants pounding behind you!" he had screamed at his wife before she'd left for the day.

She couldn't stand him when he was like this. "You do this all the time. Why don't you try relaxing?" she'd suggested as she tied the lacings of her shoes. "Listen to some Kebede. Take a nap."

Zela did exactly as she'd said, in part to spite her, to prove that she was wrong and her advice inane and futile. The great Kebede scowled at him through the speakers of their stereo. *You simpleton*, his bust of Bach mocked him, *oaf*. Yared's framed portrait simply shook his head, his face wrinkled with disappointment. Specters of the great composers hovered

around him as he lay writhing on his bed. He had won a sizable international grant to write an opera about genocide. It was to be his magnum opus. Now the prize money and the unfinished second act
conspired to strangle him. For the past month he'd refused all social
engagements, eaten too little, slept like the dying, clinging to his sandy-
eyed insomnia as though the skeins of life itself were unraveling before
him, and he had no choice but to bear witness.

But he was not dying. He was just a disgruntled fifty-nine-year-old
man slamming up against the limitations he'd created out of fear. This
nap was not helping. The masters were not inspiring. He couldn't wait
until his wife returned, so that he could tell her that she was wrong.

It was the opera, Zela decided. Who wouldn't be angry, miserable,
hopeless, spending hours a day amid the hell of humanity? And yet he
loved this opera so much, even its slow, painful birth. How could he love
something so elusive, so violent, so heartbreaking and out of control? A
sweet breeze lifted the dark curtains in his bedroom window, and the
sizzling light of day flashed for a moment like a young girl offering a
glimpse of the thighs beneath her skirt.

Zela yanked himself out of bed and trudged to the kitchen, where he
stood slack-jawed for a long moment. He opened a tin of cookies and
shoved them into his mouth two at a time. He wasn't hungry, he just
wanted to feel something churning in his stomach besides envy, despair,
and fear. "You're too dramatic," his wife said all the time. Instead of replying, "You're right," which he knew she was, he said, "Then you were
a fool to marry me."

He ate two more cookies, hardly tasting them. In the apartment next
door a baby was shrieking. Zela chewed and listened to the pulsating
wail. *Whatever it is, baby, it will pass and then return*, he thought. *Pass
and return.* He reached for another cookie but just held it in his hand.
"Feed that baby a lullaby," he whispered to the desperate parents on the
other side of the wall. *Pass and return.* He hummed to himself and
walked to his piano. He would not work on his opera today, Zela decided. He would write a lullaby instead. A lullaby for the world. He

began pressing chords into the keys. But the fear returned, the despair, the futility. No, not for the world, he sighed. Just for a baby, that baby on the other side of the wall. The song was flowing through him.

VAL CORWIN HAD a satisfying, almost mystical sense of her work as an artist: stories and pictures came to her from worlds unknown and she set them free on the populace just as soon as she was able, urging them, like children of a certain age, to live a life of their own, apart from her. While there were plenty of accolades, there was just as much censure, some of it nasty and personally damning. To keep working was her only goal, that and enough money to pay her half of the bills, and this was best accomplished by insulating herself from certain social scenes. But she was by no means reclusive. She was on her third husband—the one, she joked, who just might stick around—and they had lived together for forty years in an apartment on Manhattan's Upper West Side. She had two grown sons and a network of stepchildren, former and present, who had given her five biological grandchildren and sixteen more she doted on without any legal or biological reason. She and her husband traveled several months of the year, visiting family and friends across the country and abroad, and attended about one-third of the parties they were invited to, depending on their energy that day.

There were so many rumors surrounding the reclusive author, including the mythology of reclusiveness, that when Val Corwin was awakened that morning by a phone call from her agent, her first instinct was to ignore it. "Did you know you are a man?" her agent had said, laughing, many years ago. "Breaking news, Val: you are actually a gay man," he informed her years later. She was a Communist, a Canadian, a Trappist monk, and a fugitive. It was mostly funny, but in her eighties now, Val was tired and wanted to sleep in. When she didn't answer the phone, her agent called back immediately, something he never did, so Val, her mind up and running already, answered him at last.

"Val, they're giving you a Pulitzer."

"La-di-da," Val said, and hung up.

THE CONGREGANTS OF Last Kingdom dripped large puddles all over the beautiful parquet floor of the YMCA lobby. Her boss, Roberto, was going to be so mad about that, Karen thought. He was obsessed with these floors. He tended them like an orchid, blocked off the lobby and its entrance every winter in order to protect these floors from the salty, sandy trudging of shoes.

"I really need to wipe this up," Karen said to the police officers buzzing around. "Can I go get some towels? I'll come right back. Promise."

No one answered her.

The parishioners had been instructed to remain quiet while the interrogations proceeded, but it was as if none of them spoke English, Officer Stone said. "It's like the Tower of Fucking Babel in here, am I right?" he sneered.

"I think they speak English just fine, they're pretending not to," Officer McCarron replied after he'd radioed the precinct for a couple of interpreters. "They're all out of their gourds is what they are," he concluded.

Karen saw a police officer handcuffing Rosette and leading her to the door.

"Rose!" she yelled, her heart throwing itself again and again against the cage of her chest.

Rosette's foot slipped in an invisible puddle of pool water that had collected near the front entrance. Karen rushed toward her and caught Rosette by the shoulders before she could fall. "Today is a day that's never been before, babygirl," Rosette said to Karen as the police pulled her away.

.   .   .

THE OCEAN WAS a dull mirror of the sky, the tide sweeping sideways across the sand. A flock of noisy shorebirds milled around its wake. Laughing gulls and herring gulls waddled together in the shallow water; oystercatchers ran on their absurd legs and startled each other into flight. Perched on a stone, a cormorant spread its wings to dry in the sun. Cormorants were Sarah's favorite shorebird. They were impressive hunters, and their turquoise eyes were proof that there existed a breach in the world of magic and fairy tales into this one. But Sarah was not looking at any of it. She was staring directly at the sun, holding it in her gaze as long she could stand it, hoping to go blind.

How long would it take before that actually happened? she wondered. It was one of life's precepts—*don't stare at the sun*—and like many others, it was something that assumed understanding while the nuances were never fully explained.

Sarah stared at the sun a while longer, then blinked away the glare and looked at the birds. *Whatever*, she thought, blindness was only cool if you were musically gifted, and Sarah hadn't been able to get through six weeks of guitar lessons—the strings had hurt her fingers. Now she was giving up on blindness, too.

She trudged back toward the entrance of the beach. The sea was an unvarnished sheet of silver pocked by nodes of white light. Wind pushed paper trash and empty cans from the night before in crab-like patterns across the sand. Here and there, extinguished fires had scarred the sand black. She'd had sex for the first time; she'd been dumped for the first time: now she was alone and full of feelings that were at once ancient, almost inherent, and also brand-new. She didn't know what to do next.

As she walked a long path to the entrance of the beach, Sarah tried on a sunny little delusion for size—maybe Kurt was coming back? Maybe he had simply gone for coffee and would return any minute now with a steaming cup for her, black with three sugars, which he didn't know she liked but he would guess it about her and be right. But that was exactly the delusion that had gotten her into this situation. He'd packed up all his things when he left. He was gone.

The only thing worse than being dumped was being dumped via the biggest cliché in the world. Young girl gives virginity to older man who hightails it out before she wakes up the next morning. I mean, come on! That was supposed to happen to those other ordinary Sarahs, she thought, the kind who wore high heels and different varieties of underwear and burst into song when they drove around in cars together. Those girls were well equipped for this moment. Sarah had expected a lot of disasters, but not this. The worst-case scenario she could come up with before this was that Kurt's heart would seize up in the night, the completion of love having an arresting effect on him, and he would die in her arms; the next morning she would light his body on fire, and later face the police brave as Electra, answering to a higher law. Or they would fall more deeply in love than she could even imagine and live a long, interesting life together, their intimacy so powerful they would feel each other's illnesses and hunger and stubbed toes from the next room; they would be childless and grow old, a sculpture garden they built together their legacy after death. That and some swans. They would raise swans.

It pleased her mildly that her storm prediction was right, and annoyed her still that Kurt had doubted her and wasn't here to acknowledge it. The sun tucked itself behind a wispy gray cloud that was fast erasing color from the sky. The temperature had dropped since she'd woken up. In the distance Sarah saw a very fat man in a black wetsuit followed by two golden retrievers lumber over the dunes and into the water. He was as big as a walrus, with short, sausagey arms and a small bald head settled into the deep folds of his neck skin. He had a thick black mustache and a rubbery smile, the kind seen only on the faces of the very religious, the mentally slow, or those recently returned from a brush with death. The man tossed a ball into the ocean and the dogs darted over the sand and raced into the waves to fetch it. He waded in after them, lobbing the ball again and again as he swam deeper, his dogs paddling nearby.

The spangled surface of the water flattened suddenly, as though hushed, and the first raindrops fell, cool pricks against the skin, stippling the dirty-looking sand. Sarah dropped her backpack and walked into the water.

It was cold. Bolts of ice shot up from her ankles to her knees. She was a strong swimmer but her clothes and sneakers were weighing her down. Numbness was working its way up her body, starting with her toes, then her legs. She wanted to swim as far as she could and let herself be held by the ocean until she slipped out of its grip and just drowned. A watery, Shakespearean end to this psychosexual tragedy, a clichéd coda to the clichéd climax of her clichéd life.

Sarah had dog-paddled a little deeper into the water when the selfishness and absurdity of her suicide sank in. Who was she kidding? She didn't want to die. She loved her parents. Had she remembered to tell them that before she'd left the house? She wanted to know what grade she'd gotten on her politics paper. And the water was too damn cold. So she turned around and began to swim back to shore.

The current had carried her out much farther than she'd thought. It pulled her deeper, tugging her body with such force it felt personal. She realized her feet couldn't touch the bottom and a shock of fear ripped through her. Reaching with her toes, she couldn't even sense how far down the bottom might be. The fat man and his dogs were still bobbing in the water, tiny dots very far away now. Rain pelted the back of her head. She took off her sneakers and let them drop, hoping the lost weight would help her. She swam hard against the current, not seeming to move any closer to the shore. In the sky the clouds broke over the beach and the faintest rainbow leaked through the haze.

KURT HEARD THE rain slapping his helmet. The gray sky was thickening like a scab over the weak light of morning. He hoped he could make it home before it really started raining. He hoped the girl, Sarah, made it home okay. He'd left her sixty dollars, all the cash he had left in his wallet, and a note. *What did I tell you? The world isn't done with us yet. Fun night. Take care.*

What was he supposed to do? Hang around? She was smart and tough and clearly got off on little adventures like this. She'd be fine.

He needed gas but he was almost home and he needed a shower and his bed more. Nice rainy day to sleep and watch movies in bed. There was cold pizza left over in his fridge. He was looking forward to it. Basic needs, so easily met. Before him an almost empty highway and a peaceful day full of nothing. A song caromed around his head, an isolated line in pursuit of its full verse, *I can't keep track of each fallen robin*. How did the rest of it go? he wondered.

SARAH CLARK-DAVENPORT WAS willing to do the hard work of dying. She had not eaten much in weeks. She sipped water but did not drink it. The attrition of her cardiovascular muscle tissue was quickening. Her pulse was slackening. The air that flowed in and out of her body was slow and unwelcome.

Had she slept? She couldn't remember. She sat on the floor and gazed out the window. She had been in this spot for a long time, since before sunset. Now it was morning and she was still there. A robin landed on the windowsill. Sarah thought of Emily Dickinson. That bitch. She could never look at a robin and not think of Dickinson, and she hated her for that. She could not look at a robin without thinking of her sister, either: Mary, with her perennial gasps of awe at the sight of a simple bird.

"Please—" Sarah said to the robin, tears falling from her eyes without her permission. She lifted her hand to tap the glass.

NORA HAD JUST woken up from an afternoon nap. She'd left her window open and a cool breeze carried the scent of the sea into her room. How vulnerable it felt to sleep without a window screen. She brought her long white fingers to her fluttering heart. A line from Dickinson shot through her like a tranquilizer.

"Merry, and Nought, and gay, and numb—"

After the morning excursion to Delos, their tour guide had left the rest of the afternoon open for wandering, with a wine tasting and five-course meal scheduled for 8 p.m. What to do in the meantime? Nora had meditated already. She'd read her Buddhist self-help books and written in her journal. What she needed to do now and for the next four hours was to *embrace the moment*. Enjoy its spaciousness. It was so much harder than she felt it should be. Nora was used to time being broken into very specific fifty-minute blocks, each client a different shade of crazy coloring in the open spaces of her day. It was a problem of privilege, but a problem all the same, that relaxing into this vacation was so much bloody work for her.

She decided on coffee downstairs in the hotel café and then a walk through the village. She put on a white linen dress that showed off her lovely collarbone and a lavender silk scarf to cover it back up. For today it was enough that she was willing to walk and not run, to dress nicely and not hide in yoga pants.

In the lobby of the hotel sat the Italian widower from her tour group, drinking a cup of coffee and reading the local Mykonos newspaper. He folded it immediately when he saw Nora, a brightness in his eyes that Nora wanted to dismiss but couldn't. She ordered her coffee and took the seat next to him, as his gallant wave of hand bid her.

"I'm so impressed," Nora said, lifting his newspaper and refolding it more neatly. "Do all Europeans speak so many languages or just you? We Americans are so dumb in comparison. We only speak English and barely that."

"Oh, no. I look only at the pictures. It's all a-Greek to me." He smiled. He had several gold fillings in his molars that winked in the sunlight.

It took Nora a moment to get the joke, and the Italian widower waited for her, holding his breath until she did, then they laughed together hard and loud. Nora's scarf came unloosed from her neck and fell to the floor. He bent over to pick it up. He held it in his hand, not yet ready to return it.

. . .

BREAKFAST WAS OVER at Heart House. Two staff members, morbidly hungover, scraped spongy unfinished pancakes off plates, then stacked them in the dishwasher. Lauren herded the residents one by one into the living room, where they watched a sensationalist documentary on the possible alien origins of Stonehenge. They were supposed to be doing arts and crafts, but the missing-Karen controversy had screwed up the whole schedule.

"Here you go," Lauren said as she walked Sadie over to the window seat, surrendering at last to the chaos of the day. She laid some extra pillows on the bench for the woman, who looked both older and younger than she actually was. Lauren ran her fingers through Sadie's silvery hair, recently trimmed and seeming to sparkle in the morning light that streamed through the bay window. Lauren fluffed the pillows some more. "Nice and comfy," she said. It felt good to do this one thing right.

"Do you see him up there?" she asked Sadie, whose fingers were already pressed up against the glass.

"Hello, brother Bear," Sadie said to the sky.

TIANNA WAS USED to blaming her brothers for her troubles, but this time she couldn't. She and Miles and Avonte had not made it to the bonfire last night, but it wasn't their fault. It wasn't anyone's fault, really, that her grandmother's car had a busted alternator, and without a scapegoat to contain her disappointment, Tianna's world began to unravel.

"Why can't you get it fixed?" Tianna had wailed, her face dripping with tears and snot as she beseeched her grandmother, a woman she had until now assumed was all-powerful because she was fifty-six. This fiction was just beginning to dismantle itself and Tianna could not handle it.

"We can't just sit here," Tianna cried.

"I can't afford to pay attention," Maeve answered, "let alone what they charge at that crooked auto shop. They're swindlers! All of them!"

Tianna suggested asking Dorothy, Maryann, Beryl, Lucy—every name her grandmother had ever mentioned in her long tirades against the women in her social circle.

"It's none of their business what's going on under the hood of my car!" Maeve crushed a cigarette into a pristine glass ashtray.

"What about the bus?"

To this Maeve rolled her eyes and waved her hand in a way that let Tianna know the whole idea of going out was hopeless. Her mother was useless, her father nonexistent, her mother's boyfriends, Dennis especially, a burden, her teachers disgruntled, indifferent, and mean. Maeve was a decent woman—she never treated Miles or Avonte differently even though they were not her blood, a kindness not extended by Miles's grandmother whenever the three children stayed with her. Maeve's house was clean and well stocked with both real food and junk food. But last night her grandmother, the one official grown-up who cared enough to try, at least a little, proved to be as impotent as the rest of the adults in her life.

"We're on our own," Tianna told Miles. He was falling asleep on the pullout couch, his eyelids fluttering as he clutched Maeve's tablet in his arms like a teddy bear, the animated *Selfless Knight* playing too loudly on the screen.

Tianna could not go to school Monday and say she had done nothing on Last Day, so she would take matters into her own hands. She woke Miles early the next morning with the promise of breakfast ice cream ("Grandma told me we could have it. No, we don't have to wake her up and ask first. . . ."), then led her brother into the kitchen. She had already set up an offering—a big saucepot, a box of matches, yesterday's crumpled newspaper, the backpack Dennis's weird friend had given her, and a big mixing bowl of water.

"I need your help carrying this to the backyard," she told Miles.

Miles was sleepy and agreeable. He took the empty pot, paper, and matches while Tianna transported the backpack and bowl of water, careful not to spill it.

They went through nearly the whole box of matches before they were able to make one ignite. Minutes later they had a roaring fire going in the pot that they fed with ripped-up newspaper.

"Okay, go get your doll," Tianna told Miles.

"He's not a doll. He's Viscount Darkdoom."

"Whatever. It's time to burn him."

"I don't want to anymore."

"You have to—" she began, when a leaf of burning newspaper floated up out of the fire and collided with the dry, stiff bedsheets that Maeve had left too long on the clothesline.

"Oh shit," Miles said.

"Get the bowl!" Tianna cried, then pushed him out of the way as she scrambled to get it herself. She tripped on her way to the now-ignited sheet and spilled the water into the grass. The fire leapt from sheet to towel, working its way through Maeve's clean laundry. Tianna tried the garden hose but the spigot was so rusty she couldn't turn the knob.

"Mom's going to kill us," Miles said, reading his sister's mind. The children watched, stunned, while flames leapt up and up, as though yearning to grab the low branches of a tree.

TERRENCE LOOKED AT the white feathery remnants of the previous night's fire and heard her voice. He knew exactly what she would say: that his need to ejaculate onto recently vacated areas was a function of male privilege. It was the same cowardly assertion of dominance that had fueled the Columbian conquest of the indigenous lands now known patriarchically as the Americas. Marking his territory like a tyrant. Co-opting spaces as his own genetic field through a passive-aggressive violation of an empty—read vaginal, read feminine—space.

But it wasn't! It really, really wasn't, Terrence argued with her in his head. He was all for nonbinary gender egalitarianism. Like one hundred percent. This had nothing to do with that. It was just an itch, and when he saw the clean living room rug after everyone had gone upstairs to bed, or right now, this empty campsite—he had to scratch it, or it would nag at him until he couldn't calm down or concentrate on anything else. It relaxed him and it was so quick, averaging three minutes. It was a function of his OCD. Not his fault.

Oh yeah, and rape culture is not anyone's fault? Next you'll tell me mental illness is an excuse for racism and genocide? Her imaginary censure aroused him even more. Why did he love her so much? She was a forty-seven-year-old woman with flagrant displays of body hair, a lesbian happily married to a transgender man. She was a teacher at his goddamn school. Dr. Vasquez-McQueen could not be more out of his league; he had never wanted anything more.

Terrence kicked some dirt over the pearlescent dribble of his semen and buttoned his pants. He took a deep, relaxing breath. He looked toward the path where the others had set out on their morning hike. If he ran, he could catch up to them.

ARI AND ALISON Moss were fast asleep, their bodies pressed close as spoons, their minds awash in delta waves, pitching them toward the next round of dreams.

IN A QUEEN-SIZED bed on the fourth floor of Morning Pines, Myra and Marlene were, too.

JOSH LIKED TO leave the cage open, kindling the hope that his rabbit might hop into bed with him at night and snuggle. Just because it had never happened didn't mean it never would, Josh had told his mother, who smiled and let it be.

But when Josh woke up that morning, Arturo the Fifth was not in his bed or his cage. He looked in all of Arturo's favorite spots, under his bed, at the bottom of his closet, until at last he found the rabbit in the laundry basket in the bathroom, surrounded by seven newborn bunnies. Josh brought his mother in to confirm.

"Yep, seven of them. Arturo's a girl!" She waved the smoke twirling out of her cigarette away from the little nest in her dirty laundry basket, away from her son, and thought about what to do. The house was a mess and now the laundry stank like a barn on a day when the Laundromat would be closed. Her car needed gas and she was waiting for a check to clear before using her debit card, which was so maxed out she feared sparks might fly from the ATM if she inserted it. Josh looked at her with wonder and fear, with perfect trust. It was the same face he had shown her in his first minutes of life, as if he had known her from long ago, before either one of them had been born, when a perfect version of everyone still existed.

His mother ran the bathroom tap to extinguish her cigarette. "Go outside and pick some grass and weeds and stuff." She filled a hot water bottle and wrapped it in the now-ruined T-shirt from the top of the laundry basket. She put the water bottle in a shoebox and let Josh arrange the greenery on top of it, including several dandelions he had picked along with the grass, which his mother assured him was a nice touch.

"What are you doing?" Josh asked, as his mother probed each baby rabbit with her fingers.

"Making sure their hearts are strong and their bellies are full."

"Are they?"

"Uh-huh. Their mommy must have just fed them before we woke up."

"They're kinda ugly."

"Most things are in the beginning."

. . .

RINGO HAD JUST woken up from his nap on the floor of his workspace and immediately took the next customer in line, a stately old drag queen named Taboo.

"Do you mind if I just do an apple?" Ringo asked her. "My brain is fried. I can't think of another flower."

"Honey, you do whatever you want," Taboo said.

Jake had passed out leaning over the toilet, a safe enough position as he could not aspirate on his vomit, Janine decided, after checking on him one last time. She'd woken up from her own disco nap with a strong feeling of *fuck it*. For over two decades she'd been watching the boys make their art. All her boyfriends, even before Jake, had been tattoo artists. She'd lived her entire adult life like a stupid fucking groupie, and not even for a rich rock band. Not even for a broke punk band. But for tattoo artists. What was the point? "Fuck it," she said, and called the next customer into Jake's chair.

This was a big no-no. She was not licensed. She hadn't even been to school—Jake had discouraged her, for selfish and sexist reasons he didn't bother to deny. And Janine, if she was being honest, had allowed his barking to stop her, secretly glad of it, so that she didn't have to face the fear of actually trying. What if she wasn't as good as Jake? What if she was much better? How would it change their perfectly dysfunctional codependency?

With that she began inking the letters REDEMPTION on a man's biceps.

Tom was inscribing a double helix on the thigh of a woman a little older than he was. Maybe she was the one he would go home with. He'd been waiting all night and all morning for the signal, that it was time to stop. He wiped away her blood and looked into her eyes.

"You're pretty hot for your age," he said.

"Stop talking," the woman replied, shifting a little closer to him in the chair, "and this day might work out beautifully for both of us."

Tom mimed the zipping of his lips, pretended to lock them, then tossed the key behind his shoulder. The woman laughed without making a sound.

In the early light of May 28, the buzzing of needles continued, but all conversation stopped. A calm energy had taken over, quiet and diffused with light. Ringo's breathing began to synchronize with his customer's, as did Tom's and Janine's, until all of them, even Jake asleep on the floor, were inhaling, exhaling, together, without knowing.

IF WE ARE going to die, Bear and Svec decided, we die at home. They were in perfect harmony on this. Even if there is no one left there to mourn us. Home was where they belonged. And so with no assistance from Mission Control, Bear and Svec began the first steps of protocol for an emergency exit. They had calculated a landing in Kazakhstan during daylight hours, hoping a crew would be there to help them out. Now the only thing left was wonder, and it was terrible.

The rage of the past century had finally been released. The stuff of dystopian novels and movies, one nuclear bomb launching after another until everything was fried. Gone. "War. Big. Bigger than before. Biggest in all time," Svec said.

"Maybe." But maybe a few survivors? Bear wondered. He wanted to water the plants, to quickly design and rig a system to keep the mice appropriately fed for as long as possible, just in case.

"Comrade, no one is coming back here."

"Eventually . . ."

"Look." Svec took Bear by the hand and sailed him into the Cupola. The once blue gem was a whorling, frothy brown. The distinction between land and sea was so blurred it was hard to discern by sight exactly where on Earth they were looking.

"If we survive, if we find others who survive, coming back to station will not be priority for many, many years. In that time, station's orbit will decay. She will fall back to Earth with Yui inside her. All this will be destroyed."

"We have to hold on to some hope, Svec. I can't just nosedive into an empty pool so fast. We don't know what is going on right now. That is the truth. We do not know."

"You're right. But what can be done about it?"

PULLING THEMSELVES INTO the Soyuz, the two men shared a common nightmare—the very real possibility that no ground team would be there to pull them out after landing. There might not be a living soul for hundreds of miles. After six months in microgravity, they would have the leg power of arthritic, bedridden eighty-year-olds. Both men agreed that they were equipped to survive this. What they would not admit to each other: they might be the last humans alive.

"God bless Yui," Svec said.

"What?"

Svec heaved himself close to Bear, until he was close enough to hold him in his arms. "Night before Yui died, he held me like this." Svec thrust his hand behind Bear's skull and held it. "He kissed me. After, he went to bed and died. Was kiss of death. Goodbye. Can you see?"

Bear smelled vodka on Svec's breath and it enraged him. "Let's get this show on the road," he said. Svec was still holding Bear in an embrace. Bear tried to pry himself away but Svec held on. He pulled Bear's head closer and kissed him on the mouth. Then he slapped Bear's face three times, kissed him again on both cheeks, and let go.

Strapped into their seats, they hurtled toward Earth at five hundred miles per hour. "*Zhatka, zhatka, ya zhdu tebya,*" Svec whispered. A prayer, Bear guessed, wishing that he too had a prescribed set of words he could recite. It seemed comforting, even if it was imaginary, to incant the hopes of another time, something older if not bigger than himself. Bear had learned a prayer or two in his life, but nothing that had stuck. A few sentences, a few words even, would suffice. He settled instead for a list:

Rain, falling in sheets, falling in drops, collecting in gutters, streaming down drainpipes, slamming against the windshield of a car, swished away by wipers, returning a half second later like a report of gunfire, then swish, ratatatat, swish; bathtubs his girls used to splash in until their fingertips wrinkled and their teeth chattered; the obnoxious plop of a leaky faucet; a still pond troubled by a frog plunking below the surface; the spray of a car driving through a large puddle; the rhythmic gurgle and swoosh of a washing machine alternating the direction of its toss; the sound of his childhood dog lapping water from her bowl; the sound of gulping several long sips in a row on a hot day, ice tinkling against the glass.

THEY WERE DYING. They could feel it as surely as the sweat on their skin, as the ship rumbling all around them. Dreaming the same dream, dying the same death. *If nothing else,* Svec thought, *I am grateful to you, comrade, to hold the other half of this fear. If nothing else,* Bear thought, *we are home, we are—*

AS THEY BREACHED the atmosphere over Central Africa, the ship's parachutes opened. A silvery-brown matter sloshes out of the seats that once held them.

A POD OF eleven dolphins swim in the Bay of Bengal. Six juveniles, not all of them related, a mother and her newborn calf, two adult females, and a badly injured male who'd escaped a shameful battle with a male from another pod. The wounded dolphin keeps sinking too deep to catch his breath. The adult females take turns pushing him up to the surface for air. The nursing mother communicates to the group to swim slower, and they do. Darting through the warmer, shallow waters near the coast, they feast on a school of mackerel. One of the youngsters, a female with a uniquely low whistle, decides it is time to jump. Her body shatters the tensile skin of the water as she leaps into the air. A spray like a thousand diamonds rolls off her back. An act of joy and an invitation to play, there is no other reason for it. Her schoolmates follow her in scattered succession, jumping in and out of the water. The sun burns low in the sky, golden and overripe as a peach. Three of them are midair, the other eight underwater, when all of them melt from the inside out, leaving slimy, limp tendrils of their old form in the wake.

THERE ARE DEEP rich pools of sludge where the Amazon rain forest once breathed. The greenery now wafts a scent never smelled before, the reek of all life and all manner of death combined, like burnt hair, low tide, afterbirth, and sick. That river, now nameless, pushes its snake-like pattern into the earth, slowed down by the sedimentary weight of all its dead.

A TINY DUTCH garden enclosed by a stone wall steams like a hot bowl of brown stew. Stone-carved angels kneel in the dry granite fountain at the garden's center, the shadows of them stretching over the viscous roux, against the wall in dark, elongated repose.

THE SITES OF three different genocide campaigns on three different continents congeal into an even bigger pool of the dead.

A FLOATING RADIOACTIVE island made of fishing nets and plastic bags, almost a mile in diameter, rides the waves as ever off the coast of Fukushima.

· · ·

THE GOLD DOME of a mosque in Brunei glitters in the setting sun, its white stone still pristine at the top, as though purified by the approaching sky, its foundation laced with the brown accretion of matter lapping like a tide on its shore.

A U.S. NAVY aircraft carrier, named for a president credited with once forestalling the end of the world, floats across the roiling brown sea. Steam rolls off the surface of the ocean, all the life released now in a surge of heat. Enough heat to melt the thick plastic of the computers inside the ship, which slowly, then quickly begins to sink.

TREES BUCKLE AND collapse like grieving women, reduced now to a hot brown sap. Sunlight stabs the atrium of a cave, piercing the waves that splash against its glittering minerals, the remnants of stars.

Rays of light gleam against the brown water, where blooming clouds of dead fish, dead flora, dead plankton, and things even smaller rise and fall in eddies of brown foam.

The sea grows hot with death, the energy released boils even the most frigid water, until the oceans are seething with brown foam, and the steam rolls off the surface in clouds so thick they block out the sky.

Hills are blistered and brown. Grasses melt into slime, along with the millions of insects tunneling beneath them: the trillions of microbes, cell by cell, reduce and recombine into brown sludge. The sludge oozes everywhere. Dripping down fjords in Norway, smearing the faces of Mount Rushmore, bleeding beneath the fast-melting snows of Kilimanjaro. What were herds of antelope, oryx, buffalo, are now dark smears on the plains. The brown ooze of human communities dries up in the hot sun, leaving stains on the cement of the cities they built.

For a while the lights stay on. In Tokyo, London, Times Square, screens still flash images of beautiful women twirling their skirts, lying on the beach, rubbing lotion into their skin. Generators continue to burn unmanned for several hours until the systems governing the power plants across the globe start beeping and shut down. Pumps that keep running water in its place shut down, too, flooding the streets of the dead.

AIRPLANES, WHOSE PILOTS have liquefied to puddles in their cockpits, whose passengers are now seeping into the upholstery of their seats, fall by the thousands out of the sky. Trains skid off their tracks, knifing long wounds into the earth that soon will be sealed with the liniment of sludge. Across the globe, highways are littered with smashed cars, embolisms of gleaming metal on corridors east and west, north and south. Oil fields burn black smoke. Gas plants explode. Nuclear reactors, scrupulously programmed, remain intact for a while longer, until they, too, combust.

TIME PASSES. ATOMS of carbon dance in perfect terror. Ocean waves beat the shore.

AND HIGH ABOVE it all, a message in a bottle. Before launch, Bear and Svec had sent a small craft through the airlock, hurtling via timed thrusters they had programmed manually to travel as far from the earth as its fuel would take it, then sailing forever after on its own trajectory into deep space. Among the data installed, all their findings from decades of research, all the records of their time on the ISS and their observations of their home below, and three objects they hoped one day, if never fully understood, would be loved as relics from another world: Svec's son's handwritten list of astronauts, Bear's harmonica, Yui's favorite Val Corwin book.

.　　.　　.

ALL WAS WATER and waste, heat and odor. Cell membranes puckered and shrank, nuclei collapsed, all the constituent parts of life recombined into one plasmic ooze.

What was lost? Mitochondria, proteins, reproductive organs, bones, gymnosperms, voices, music, faces, hunger, dreams, flowers, fields, ferns, snakes, crabs, snails, algae, bacteria, stories, traffic, apologies, wolves, holidays, rage, anthills, rhizomes, gratitude, pain . . .

What remained? Clouds. Great big clouds. Shadows. And wind. And beauty remained. It had existed before, and always would, whether or not it could be borne.

IT WAS OVER almost as soon as it began. The sun continued to rise and set, moving across the galaxy, a distinct but ordinary flame in the deep. Planets continued orbiting in their ellipses. And it would be like this for a very, very long time, before the first thing happened, then another, a cause, and then its effect, and then the new story that would begin.

ACKNOWLEDGMENTS

This book was not easily born. Cindy Spiegel was a wise, patient, and trustworthy editor. I won't embarrass you with the superlative ("the wisest . . .") though I know this is true. I am so fortunate to work with you twice. Thank you, Cindy. This story is immeasurably better because of you.

Big thanks to Jim Rutman, whose extemporaneous emails are more lucid and thoughtful than my best rewritten prose. You were a wonderful support, truly going above and beyond, long before there was anything substantial to support. It's an honor to work with you.

A whole team of talented people at Penguin Random House have again worked to make the difficult progression from draft to book appear easy: Mengfei Chen, Kelly Chian, and copy editor Deborah Dwyer did with grace and skill.

I would not have put up with this book beyond its very ugly first draft if not for the intelligent and kind appraisal of Ariel Colletti, who gave the first read. Thank you forever.

Stephen Taylor, you are the smartest, most well-rounded and well-read person I know. I wanted above all to write something you would like. I'm glad I got to meet you again.

Paul Citroni, Elyse Citroni, and Kayley LeFrancois, I am so lucky to call you family.

I wrote a good chunk of this book in a postpartum fugue state. There were times I didn't think I'd survive, let alone make art again, once I became a solo mother. Marika Lindholm, you were a guide and an inspiration; your generosity kept me going, along with our ESME.com dream team Cheryl Dumesnil, Katie Shonk, and Heidi Kronenberg.

For love, support, good advice, and the occasional invaluable hour of childcare (in order of appearance on my phone contact list): Adam Gardener, Cassie Bachovchin, Cathy Casey, Chelsee Shiels, Debra Crist, Joan Pelletier, Kathleen Cunningham, Dave Andalman, Dawn Mordowski, Lauren DeLeon, Donika Kelly PhD, Emily Einhorn, Enoka Strait, Melissa Febos, Halley Feiffer, Jumana Grassi, Katie Freeman, Lauren Gello, Michelle Gomez, Beckie Hickok, Kenny Hillman-Love, Jenny Hobbs, Lynne Jay, John Cusack, Gabrielle Kerson, Greg Koehler, Megan Krebs, Leina Boncar, Linda Gnat-Mullin, Christine Love-Hillman, Lynn Buckley, Amy Meyer, Molly Oswacks, Jamie Panagoplos, Diantha Parker, Patti McDannell, Sharon Pinsker, Kate Rath, Robert Atchinson, Lucy Rorech, Onnesha Roychoudhouri, Amy Stewart, Brian Avers, Emily Stone, Joanne Swanson, Victoria Morey, Teddy Wayne, Mark Wright, Pam, Michael & Cece, Midday, my family, and Z.

ABOUT THE AUTHOR

DOMENICA RUTA grew up in a working-class, unforgiving town north of Boston. Her mother, Kathi, was a notorious drug addict and sometime dealer whose life swung between welfare and riches, and whose highbrow taste was at odds with her hardscrabble life. Ruta is a graduate of Oberlin College and holds an MFA from the Michener Center for Writers at the University of Texas at Austin. Her stories have appeared in the *Boston Review*, the *Indiana Review*, and *Epoch*, and she has been awarded residencies at Yaddo, MacDowell Colony, Blue Mountain Center, Jentel, and Hedgebrook. The author of *The New York Times* bestselling memoir *With or Without You*, a darkly hilarious mother-daughter story and chronicle of a misfit nineties youth, Ruta lives in New York City.

domenicaruta.com
Twitter: @DomenicaMary

ABOUT THE TYPE

This book was set in Electra, a typeface designed for Linotype by W. A. Dwiggins, the renowned type designer (1880–1956). Electra is a fluid typeface, avoiding the contrasts of thick and thin strokes that are prevalent in most modern typefaces.